Brady read worry and fear in Susan's expression as they stood outside the café with their heads bent together.

He touched her cheek lightly, wanting to reassure her. "We'll be okay. Every day that passes is a day closer to finding the truth. We're making progress."

Susan tapped her foot against the sidewalk. "I'm glad you feel confident about this. I feel like we're walking into a trap. The police are looking for us. Special Forces military men are looking for us. Justin's killer is still at large." She let the rest of her breath out in a whoosh and held her head in her hands.

Brady ached to draw her into his arms, to offer some comfort. More than emotional comfort, he was aware of his body hardening at the image of her pressed against him.

He'd made love with her less than twelve hours ago, and he was ready for more.

Dear Reader,

I believe that lost love can be reclaimed. In this book, Brady Truman believes he's done the right thing in giving Susan the chance to live her life without him. His job is too dangerous and takes him away from home too often. When a terrible injury ends his career, Brady has plenty of time for regrets. His biggest regret is letting go of Susan, and when she needs him, in typical Truman brother style, Brady goes to her aid.

Susan has tried to move on with her life, but Brady isn't an easy man to forget. He shows up again when she most needs someone in her corner. Time has given them a new perspective on what's important. They've never really gotten over each other and they're forced to confront those lingering feelings. Forgiving and forgetting is a tall order, especially when it comes to matters of the heart. But happiness is never out of reach, not when love is still in play.

Happy reading!

C.J. Miller

SHIELDING
THE SUSPECT

—

C.J. Miller

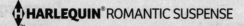
HARLEQUIN® ROMANTIC SUSPENSE

Recycling programs
for this product may
not exist in your area.

ISBN-13: 978-0-373-27840-4

SHIELDING THE SUSPECT

Copyright © 2013 by C.J. Miller

Printed in U.S.A.

HARLEQUIN®
www.Harlequin.com

Books by C.J. Miller

Harlequin Romantic Suspense

Hiding His Witness #1722
Shielding the Suspect #1770

C.J. MILLER

is a third-generation Harlequin reader and the first in her family to write professionally. She lives in Maryland with her husband and young son. She enjoys spending time with family, meeting friends for coffee, reading and traveling to warm beaches around the world. C.J. believes in first loves, second chances and happily-ever-after.

C.J. loves to hear from readers and can be contacted through her website at www.cj-miller.com.

To Jacob, my real-life love at first sight.

Prologue

Brady Truman's life wasn't as he'd planned. It was far, far worse. He shifted some of his weight to his bum knee, stifling a wince as pain shot up and down his leg. He gritted his teeth and took another step. More pain. It had been this way for two months. Two months of therapy, rehabilitation, surgeries and medical procedures as the doctors saved his leg from amputation and tried to restore function. Brady didn't want to walk with a cane for the rest of his life.

Then again, he didn't want a lot of things and choices had been taken away when an enemy had shot him.

He didn't want to live with the disfiguring scars on his leg and the weakness in his knee. The surgeons had done everything they could. They said he was lucky that they had been able to save his leg.

Lucky. Sure. It was the last word he'd use to describe his current state.

The physical rehab was difficult, but he hated the psychotherapy more. Too much digging around his psyche about events that didn't matter and trying to make a mountain out of a bump in the road. Brady avoided bumps. He didn't stop and scrutinize them.

Adjusting to life outside the military would be difficult. He'd seen friends try it and fail, returning to the military because they needed the structure and discipline.

For Brady, returning to the military wasn't an option. He couldn't return to his former position with the Special Forces. His injury guaranteed he would never be stealthy and athletic enough and he couldn't expect his team to trust him again after his colossal screw-up. A pararescueman needed to be strong, nimble and responsive. Brady didn't credit himself with any of those traits. Not anymore. Brady let out a grunt of pain when his knee collided with the side of the hospital bed.

His balance was off, like everything in his life.

A tap at the door. He'd gotten accustomed to doctors, nurses and specialists coming and going, and he didn't know why they bothered knocking. Brady had no illusions of privacy in the hospital.

"Come in," he said, hiding signs of his discomfort and displeasure. It was one thing to harbor resentment and anger. It was another to act like a pansy and complain about his circumstances. Bad enough he was feeling weak, but worse to have others think it.

Brady didn't want any more drugs forced on him and the more perfect a patient he was, the sooner he could be discharged. He wanted to go home. Staying in this hospital was making him crazy. He hated being caged in with nothing to do except exercise his leg and think. Too often his thoughts turned to the past and the mistakes that had led him to this point.

It wasn't a doctor or nurse who entered the room. Instead, a familiar and unwanted face from the past.

"Justin," Brady said, unpleasantly surprised to see his old pal from the air force walk into his room. The circumstances kept getting worse.

He and Justin had hung out occasionally with a mutual friend back when they'd both been enlisted, but they hadn't spoken in more than a year and Brady was fine with that. He had nothing to say to the man who had betrayed him. They'd formed a competitive relationship from their early days in the military, but Justin's relationship with Susan had taken things from competitive to combative.

"Brady Truman, I never thought I'd see the day you had to walk with a cane."

Brady didn't smile or take the bait and reply with a smart retort. He should tell Justin to get out of his room, but he didn't want to give the man the satisfaction of knowing his words had cut deep.

"It won't be for long," Brady said. He'd been walking around his room for close to twenty minutes, near his upper threshold for endurance. He wasn't admitting his leg was ready to collapse and he needed to sit. Not in front of Justin Ambrose.

"I heard you spoke to Susan the other day," Justin said.

Brady had spoken to Susan, but she'd done most of the talking. She had been waiting in his room when he'd returned from his session with the therapist. At the thought of Susan, the memory of making love with her lodged in his mind, making it difficult to focus on the conversation. She was a true beauty with long hair and expressive brown eyes, a narrow waist he could wrap his hands around and soft, delicate skin. At least his injuries hadn't killed his libido. Whether they were bad for each other or not, Brady would never stop wanting Susan.

His brief discussion with Susan wasn't Justin's business. "Yes. She came to the hospital."

No point in denying it and no point in delving into details. If Susan wanted Justin to know something about their conversation, she would tell him.

"Susan and I are engaged. Did she tell you that?" Justin asked.

She hadn't. But Brady had known. His brother Reilly had mentioned it to him. Reilly and Susan worked together at the police station, Reilly as a detective and Susan as a sketch artist. It was a job she'd taken to supplement her income from selling her artwork.

"I'm aware of your engagement." Their engagement. Susan belonged to another man. Though he'd heard it before, the words hit him with blunted pain.

Justin bared his teeth and Brady took a sliver of delight in knowing his caginess was getting to the other man. "If you are aware of it, then stay away from her and don't jeopardize what we have. You walked away from her. Don't think you'll win her back with some poor, hurt veteran routine."

Brady took exception to almost everything Justin had said. He wanted Susan to be happy and he would never put her in a place to make a difficult decision, like asking her to choose between him and Justin. After the way Brady had treated her, she'd probably choose Justin anyway. She deserved what Justin was offering. A house. A family. A stable life. A boring life perhaps, but a stable one.

Things Brady couldn't offer anyone. Couldn't offer before and certainly couldn't offer now. His knee throbbed and he forced more weight onto his good leg and the cane.

"You're engaged. She made her choice." Leave it at that.

"Yes, she did. She chose me," Justin said, his expression radiating superiority.

Justin was former air force and he had friends and family who were still active duty. He could provide Susan the type of life she deserved, but he was also under his father's thumb. Brady couldn't help wondering what Lieutenant General Tim Ambrose thought of Susan. Brady had gotten the impression Justin's father wanted his son to pick a Stepford wife who would blend in with the Ambrose family's social circle. Brady couldn't picture Susan as servile, submissive or thrilled to take a role in the political games that were played by military men at Lieutenant General Ambrose's level.

"I'm happy for her," Brady said. For her. Not for Justin. He couldn't have cared less about Justin's happiness. Bitterness seeped into his chest, taking some of the heat off his stinging leg. Though Brady wasn't good enough for Susan, it wasn't easy to watch another man with the woman he desired. Hell, two years ago, he would have gone crazy with jealousy to think about Susan with another man. He'd had to let her go. For her sake. He was a disaster for her.

"If you're happy for her, then stay away. We don't need you nosing around," Justin said.

Justin hadn't changed. Despite his lofty façade, he was still plagued with self-doubt and the constant need for reassurance, just as he had been in the military. Brady wasn't in the mood to stroke his fragile ego.

Brady's thigh muscles shook with fatigue. He dug deep for the energy to remain standing. "If Susan is satisfied with you, you have nothing to worry about." Justin needed to leave so Brady could rest.

Justin glared at him. "Don't mess with me. My family is powerful and you'll regret it."

Brady didn't care about power or worry about Justin's threat. The Truman family was loyal and resourceful. Brady's mother was former CIA, his dad a former Navy SEAL, his brother Reilly was a detective and his oldest brother, Harris, an FBI agent. Over the course of their careers, they had made contacts and alliances with people in influential positions. Even Brady had a few connections he could reach out to if a situation became too dicey. But none of those connections could help him walk again or erase what had happened in the past and win over Susan.

Is that what he wanted? To win over Susan? He didn't want to watch Susan marry Justin, but like everything else, Brady couldn't do anything to change it.

Brady's knee gave out and his other leg couldn't catch his balance despite the cane. He fell, his cane skidding out from under him, his head slamming into the rail on the hospital bed.

Justin's laughter faded as two nurses raced in, shooed him from the room and assisted Brady.

Brady's leg hurt only second to his pride.

Chapter 1

Six months later

Brady shifted in his easy chair and stretched his legs in front of him, flexing his foot and rubbing at the pain that shot from his heel to his thigh. His right leg ached when he sat for too long. Sadly, most of what he did involved sitting, as well as thinking and occasionally taking the edge off with a cold beer.

He had nowhere to go and nothing to do except twice weekly rehabilitation appointments. One of those appointments was with the shrink from the hospital. He dreaded those visits.

It was late and most televisions stations were showing infomercials. He reached for the remote to change the channel, but stopped when a knock sounded at the door. Who was visiting this late?

He planned to ignore it and hope whoever it was

went away. Instead, keys in the lock jingled and then his brother Harris's voice called, "Brady?" as the door swung open.

Brady didn't want to deal with a family visit right now. "What are you doing here?" he asked, knowing he sounded surly. But that was how he felt. Surly and angry. He didn't like people dropping by unannounced. Lately, he didn't like seeing people at all.

"Oh, my sincerest apologies. Am I interrupting your doing-nothing time?" Harris asked dryly.

"What do you want?" Brady asked. He wasn't in the mood for a lecture.

"Since you aren't returning your phone calls or emails, you left me the option of finding time away from an undercover operation so I could talk to you about something important."

Guilt mushroomed through him. Brady should have returned his family's phone calls, but he wasn't ready. He didn't want them—or anyone—to see him this way. Now he'd forced Harris temporarily off an undercover mission. He'd add that to his list of screw-ups. He shut off the television. "You're here. Say what you need to say." Whatever it was, Brady wasn't going to like it.

"Reilly is in trouble."

Brady hadn't expected that and he rose to his feet. The words lit a fire under him and for the first time in months, Brady had good motivation to get off his butt. "What trouble?"

"Reilly was the first responder on a murder scene and he's been accused of tampering with evidence," Harris said. "He's on administrative leave pending an investigation into the matter."

Reilly, the middle Truman brother, was a celebrated

detective, his recent promotion a reward for the tough cases he'd solved. He would never compromise the integrity of an investigation by hiding or manufacturing evidence. "That's ridiculous. Why would he tamper with evidence? What idiot would believe something like that?" Brady asked.

"The mayor believes it."

"The mayor?" Brady didn't like the pompous windbag who served as mayor of Denver, but since when did the mayor insert himself into police business?

"Since the mayor is in tight with Lieutenant General Ambrose, and it's his son who is the murder victim—"

Brady started. "Lieutenant General Ambrose? Justin's father? Justin's dead?" Confusion streamed through him. What about Susan? How was she dealing with her fiancé's death?

"That's right, Justin Ambrose. Your favorite person," Harris said. "The mayor wants the guilty party found and he's decided the guilty persons are Susan and Reilly."

Brady's blood pressure soared and disbelief tumbled through him. Susan killing someone was more ludicrous than Reilly tampering with evidence. "The police will find the real culprit and then the mayor will look like the idiot he is and eat crow."

Harris snorted. "I'd agree if the lead investigator on the case wasn't a 'yes man' jockeying for a promotion and too lazy to do actual police work."

"It can't be that bad," Brady said.

Harris held out a folder. "It is. Look at the file."

Brady had respect for his brother's colleagues and had liked the ones he'd met, but every job had its share of incompetents. He opened the file and scanned Harris's notes. It was bad. "What can I do?"

Harris sniffed and then wrinkled his nose. "The first thing you can do is call Mom so she can stop worrying about you. Then you need to take a shower, grab a shave, change into clean clothes and rejoin the rest of the world. This place is a dump. Take some pride in yourself."

His brother's comments were justified. Brady felt and looked like crap. He hadn't had a reason to care. Until now.

"And once I re-civilize myself?" Brady asked, letting his voice drip with sarcasm.

Harris nodded at the folder he'd handed Brady. "Read that cover to cover. I've kept notes on the case, nothing you can't read in the news. Justin's yacht was found covered in his blood and Susan was the last person seen with him. She was at the scene with blood on her hands and clothes."

"What? She was where with what?" Incredulity and concern tore through him.

"Susan was on the boat. Justin's body hasn't been found. The ME states with the amount of blood at the scene, Justin couldn't have survived. The police are looking for a body."

Brady closed the file. "She didn't kill anyone." He didn't need to read reports about the case to know he was correct about that. "Was she with Justin when he died? How did she keep herself from being hurt?"

Harris blew out his breath. "Susan doesn't remember where she was and she can't explain what happened or why. She has no signs of a head injury or concussion, and the lab didn't find anything in her system that suggests she was drugged or sedated. She has no alibi for the night in question. I don't believe she killed him, but I can't offer any evidence or theory to the contrary. She hasn't been charged because Justin's body hasn't been found."

When Susan was under stress, she shut down. She'd dealt with terrible things from her childhood, like having an abusive alcoholic for a father and an imbalanced mother, by ignoring them and pretending as if nothing was wrong. As an adult, Susan's coping methods were better. She'd pour her emotions into her artwork, work through the problem and eventually talk about it, but her initial reaction was silence. The one sure way Brady had to get her talking was to get her into bed and let her direct the post-coital conversation. Whether it was the intimacy of the act or that she was relaxed and contented, Susan was most open with him during those times. But her old defense mechanism could be triggered if the situation was desperate enough.

No way would she hop into bed with him now. Not only had he lost his chance with Susan, she was grieving for her fiancé. "Stress-induced amnesia?" Brady asked, wanting Harris's opinion.

"Could be. My best guess is that her inability to remember is psychological," Harris said.

"What makes the police think Reilly is tied up in this? Because he was first on the scene? Wasn't his partner there?" Brady asked, worry for his brother mingling with concern for Susan. Brady wanted to go to her, to see if she was okay, to talk to her and comfort her. Even as the thought crossed his mind, he squashed it. He was the last man she'd want to see or speak to. His presence would only make it worse for her.

"Reilly was first on the scene and when he realized it was Susan involved, he called for another team to investigate. He waited with Susan on the dock, while his partner waited at the marina for backup to arrive. He and Susan's friendship survived your relationship and she still does freelance sketch work for the department, so they've kept in touch."

Brady had met Susan through Reilly at a party. The image of Susan the first time he'd seen her snapped to mind. Her beautiful, shy smile had caught his attention. He'd approached her and found she was easy to talk with and eager to see the best in people and situations. Her positive attitude had been refreshing.

Harris continued, breaking through Brady's thoughts. "Once it got out that Reilly was first on the scene, Lieutenant General Ambrose talked to the media and his pal, the mayor, and connected them through you and painted the picture like something unseemly had occurred. The media loves tidbits about Reilly. He's a pseudo-celebrity after the cases he's solved for the city."

Not shocking. The media twisting a story into a lurid and seedy tale was common and nauseating. Brady was surprised anyone reacted to the sensationalism and irrationality of the story. The public could be riled into a frenzy with the right words, the right pictures and the right people pushing their buttons. Why didn't anyone stop to think about the idea of a detective—a decorated detective—leaving Susan, the alleged killer, at the scene of the crime with blood on her hands? If Reilly had wanted to cover up anything, he would have dealt with that first. The accusations were ridiculous.

How could he help? Susan wouldn't want to see him and Reilly was capable of defending himself. Sleuthing wasn't his area of expertise. However, if they needed someone to bungle the investigation at a critical moment, Brady had some experience with that. "I'm not a detective and I'm impaired at the moment. What do you want me to do?" Brady rubbed his knee.

Harris snorted. "Cut the crap and quit acting like a sissy stewing in your own tears. Your knee is fine. Get off your lazy rear end and talk to Susan. Work with her to find out what happened the night Justin was killed. Her memories might come back, but the stress she's under could be concealing something important."

Susan wouldn't withhold information if she had it. "Why can't you talk to Susan?" Harris was the one trained in FBI interview and profiling tactics.

"Two reasons. My career gives me a few more boundaries. I'm working an operation at the moment and I can't bail out or juggle both. Too much is at stake. Second reason, and more importantly, you know Susan better than I do. You can help her remember."

It had taken Brady time to earn Susan's trust and when they'd broken up, he was sure that trust had been demolished. "What makes you think Susan will talk to me about the murder?" Brady hadn't told his family the details of why their relationship had ended or about her visit to the hospital when he'd been a world-class jerk to her.

"You're a Truman. Your brother needs you. You'll do whatever is necessary to help Reilly."

Harris was right. The Trumans stood by each other. It was how they'd been raised. Integrity, honor and loyalty defined their family. This situation had to be killing Reilly and putting a strain on his marriage to Haley. They were a strong family and Brady felt like the weak link. Could he be useful in his current state? What if he made it worse for Susan and Reilly?

"Anything else?" Brady asked, shoving aside his self-pity. The idea of his brother suffering and having done nothing wrong had spurred him to act.

Harris hesitated. "There is one more thing. Reilly is worried about Susan. We don't know why she wasn't also a victim and why she didn't sustain physical injuries the night Justin died. Since the police have decided to focus on Susan as a suspect, they're not interested in providing her with police protection. Reilly believes there's more going on and Susan's not out of danger yet. While you're helping her sort this out, you need to look out for her."

Spending time with Susan had convoluted mess written all over it. He wasn't the soldier he'd been before his accident. His body was damaged and weakened, his confidence shaken. Was he capable of protecting her from a killer? What if she was attacked? Would he respond and protect her or hesitate and get her killed?

Then again, what choice did he have? His brothers needed him. So did Susan. Despite the ugly history, he would talk to her and do what he could to help.

The constant gnawing dread never let up. Susan Prescott clocked out of work, sliding her employee badge through the gallery's timekeeping system. It had been another horrendous day. She was leaving via the side entrance, hoping the reporters waiting to speak with her would remain in the front. She altered her route every day to avoid a confrontation.

Susan didn't have answers to the questions they asked. Why had she killed Justin? Where had she put the body? Why wouldn't she give closure to his family?

How did someone answer those questions? They were meant to bait her into saying something she'd regret. She didn't know anything about Justin's murder. She hadn't been involved. At least, she didn't think she had. Frustration worked at her. Why couldn't she remember?

Susan pushed open the side door. Reporters and cameramen snapped to attention and began shouting at her. A jolt of anxiety ripped through her. Susan focused on her car parked a few yards away, blinking back the tears that sprung to her eyes, a combination of sadness, humiliation and grief. Anything she said would make it worse, but she wanted to shout the only answer she knew, which was she didn't know anything.

A hand grasped her elbow and Susan pulled her arm free, spinning and coming face-to-face with Brady Truman. The last man she'd have expected outside the gallery. He looked disheveled and tired, not that she was in any position to judge. She was sure she looked worse. The aggravating thing about Brady was that even exhausted and unkempt, his charisma and good looks were undeniable. Every part of him tempted her.

It wasn't the time to fixate on Brady's tremendous appeal. Extending one muscular arm in front of them, he led her through the crowd, forming a path to her car. He took her keys from her hand, unlocked the doors and helped her into the passenger side. He climbed in the driver's seat, fastened his seat belt, held down the horn in warning to the media to move and drove them away from the gallery and the crowd.

Susan shook off her shock and confusion. "What are you doing here? You told me to leave you alone." She had tried to talk to him in the hospital. He hadn't been interested in hearing what she had to say.

"I need to talk to you."

Being this close to Brady, her heart raced and her skin tingled. He still had that effect on her. "About what?" The answer snapped to mind as the words left her mouth. "Look, if this is about Reilly, I'm sorry. I know he was placed on admin leave because he was at the scene. He's my friend, and he and Haley have been wonderful to me. I never meant for that—"

Brady shook his head. "I'm not here to blame you. I'm here to talk. I know you, Susan. I know you're a good, honest person. I want you to tell me what happened with Justin the night he died."

Susan stared at him. She would have told him if she could. "I don't know what happened to Justin. I didn't kill him."

"I know that."

Susan stared at Brady for a long moment. "You don't think I killed him?" Most everyone else did. Why not Brady?

"Things ended badly between us. That doesn't mean I think you killed the next guy you dated," Brady said.

A show of support from one of the last places she'd expected it. "Thank you for believing me, but I don't see what I can do to help Reilly."

Brady pulled her car to the side of the road and parked. He faced her. "Susan, come on. It's me. I know how your mind works. This isn't the first time you've been through something terrible and blocked it out.

When you get upset, you shut down. I know what this must be like for you."

Susan rubbed the heels of her hands into her eyes. "You know what this is like? Sorry, no, you don't." Justin was dead and everyone blamed her. Brady didn't understand what that felt like.

"Susan, I know you better than almost anyone."

Susan had trusted Brady once and confided in him her deepest thoughts. He had been her go-to person. He had been the man she had wanted to spend her life with. That was the past and she'd put it behind her. "You don't know me anymore. Things have changed."

"Things have changed. People don't change. Not that much."

"Brady, I'm in the middle of a disaster. I can't deal with you or with whatever the reason is that you're here." Her words were similar to the ones he had spoken to her six months before, when he was a recovering patient in the hospital. They had wounded her fiercely. She hoped her words didn't have the same effect on him.

"I can help you," Brady said. His voice was low and soft.

Right. Help her how? Did he realize how bad her life had become? If he wanted her to help clear Reilly's name, she didn't think she could. "If anyone would listen to me, I would tell them that Reilly showed up at the scene and didn't have a thing to do with Justin's death. The police don't want to hear my side of the story." Susan had worked for the police as a freelance sketch artist for the past five years and it hurt that people who she'd considered friends had turned their backs on her.

"I know." Compassion laced his voice.

"I'm followed everywhere by the media."

"I know."

"The mayor, Justin's family and the police think I'm responsible for Justin's death."

"I know," he said.

His simple, two word answers were annoying her. "Then you know everything I do, so why are you here?"

"I'm here to help you. To protect you," Brady said.

A nice sentiment, but not one she'd buy. "You can't protect me. No one can. I got myself into this and I'll get myself out of it."

"Don't be stubborn, Susan. You don't have to do this alone."

She had never been able to count on anyone to stick around for her. How could she put her trust in Brady now? He'd left her once before. "Of course I do. I'm alone now. I've been alone all my life. I don't want your help."

Susan turned away from Brady, hating the pity she read on his face. Not everyone was lucky enough to be born into a family like the Trumans. For better or worse, some people had to muddle through life on their own.

Susan pulled another blanket over her. The draftiness of the old farmhouse didn't usually bother her, but the past several nights, nothing had made her feel warm. Justin was dead. The guilt was crushing her and breaking her down. At different times over the past few days, she'd felt someone watching her. The police? Justin's family? The media? She'd never actually seen anyone, yet the uneasy sensation persisted. Her world had been turned upside down and shaken, and now everything felt wrong and uncertain. Maybe she was losing her grip on her sanity.

She couldn't remember what had happened the night Justin had died. She'd tried. Had she blocked out his murder because it was too traumatic to remember? Had she played a role in his death? They'd ended their relationship, but Susan hadn't been angry with Justin when she'd met him on the boat. She hadn't wanted to hurt him. She was the one who had told him it was over. She'd realized she wasn't in love with Justin and Justin deserved better. Was it possible she had killed him, disposed of the body and didn't remember it? The police and media seemed to believe so.

Had it been a robbery gone bad? She absently touched her necklace, a gift from Reilly's wife, Haley, that she cherished. Nothing had been taken from the boat except her camera, and she wasn't certain it had been stolen. Normally, she was exceedingly careful with her expensive camera and equipment. Where had she left it?

The confusion surrounding that night made it difficult to say that she hadn't misplaced the camera, lost it or taken it somewhere and forgotten it. The more she tried to remember, the more frustrated she became. Her sleep-deprived mind was only half functioning. If she were rested and relaxed, could she break through the mental walls blocking her memories?

To add to her stress, Brady's appearance a few days ago had shaken her. She had been too flustered and emotionally wrung to deal with him. Why was he offering to help now after making it clear six months ago he didn't want her in his life?

Going over the incident outside the gallery, she was bothered by how rude and hostile she had been to him. Brady had walked out of her life over a year ago and she wanted to get over him.

She'd met Brady at a barbecue at a police colleague's home. Reilly had brought his younger brother, the Special Forces pararescueman who was on leave from the air force. The attraction and chemistry had been instant and hot. Susan had never experienced a connection that strong with a stranger.

Brady had strolled over to her and introduced himself. Susan preferred to be the listener in conversations, but Brady had drawn her out. He had asked her questions about her work and her hobbies. She'd loved telling him about her artwork, her sketches, her paintings and the photographs she took. His focused interest in her had made it easy to talk to him. He'd made her feel as if everything she said to him was incredibly riveting.

By the time the party was breaking up, Susan and Brady had been talking for four hours. They'd spoken on the phone every day after that, had their first date a week later and remained together through Brady's deployments over the next several years. His returns home had been wonderful and exciting.

She'd never seen the breakup coming.

Susan had told herself and her friends she was over him.

Then, six months ago, Reilly had told her that Brady had been injured in combat, and the fear that had struck her had left her physically shaken. Reilly hadn't known much about his brother's condition, only that he was en route to the nearest hospital for surgery. Brady had returned to America after a few days to recuperate and by that time, Susan had been engulfed with worry. She'd had to see him. She couldn't stop herself. Susan had to know he was okay.

He hadn't seemed okay. She had sensed a heavy, underlying resentment and anger in him. Though she could chalk some of that up to his negative feelings for her, more had been at play. Brady hadn't been willing to confide in her. She'd wanted to help him, but he wouldn't let her in. He had dismissed her, turning her worry for him to frustration with herself. What had she expected Brady to say to her? That he was sorry? To offer some explanation for why he'd broken up with her?

That his rejection had hurt was telling. She wasn't over Brady. She couldn't write him out of her life. Her unresolved feelings for Brady doubled her guilt over Justin. Why wasn't she grieving for Justin as deeply as she'd grieved when she'd lost Brady?

Susan turned off the television. She wasn't paying attention to it anyway. Though sleep had eluded her many nights, she was exhausted and her eyes were heavy with fatigue. If she were lucky, she would fall into dreamless sleep.

Susan awoke to the sound of Brady's voice. Was she dreaming? Sweat covered her skin and her sheets were knotted around her body. Why was it so hot? What was that sound? She fought with the blankets to get some air.

A shadow appeared and grabbed her by the shoulders. Susan screamed and coughed, her voice choked by the heavy air. Her eyes were burning and adrenaline spiked in her veins.

"Susan, it's Brady. Your house is on fire. We have to get out." He tore the rest of the blankets away from her body.

Brady? What was he doing in her room?

She wore only a blue nightshirt, her legs bare. She needed clothes. Brady didn't give her time to think or react. He dragged her to the ground, and the floor was hot under her hands and knees. She followed him at a crawl out of her room and into the hallway.

The front door at the bottom of the stairs was open. They crouched low as they thundered down the stairs. Brady stayed next to her, keeping one guiding hand on her back. Smoke warred with the oxygen in the air. Susan coughed, cupping her sleeve over her mouth, trying to draw fresh air. None existed. Brady's gaze met hers, and alarm flickered in his eyes while the flames crackled and hissed around them.

"Keep going," Brady shouted over the roar of the fire.

The heat from the fire was unbearable and her lungs heaved. Fresh air. They had to get outside. The house groaned and screeched under the assault from the fire. Dizziness assailed her and she grabbed at Brady to steady herself. He slid his hands around her and under her knees and carried her from the house.

The cold night air refreshed her, a dramatic change from the heat inside. Brady set her on the ground.

"Are you okay?" he asked. Susan stared at her home, now consumed in flames. Was she okay? No. She wasn't. This incident alone was bad. On top of everything else, it was cataclysmic.

Confusion and sadness weighed heavy on her heart. How had this happened? She hadn't lit a fire in the hearth that night. Hadn't cooked dinner after work. Didn't fix herself a cup of tea to relax. How had this fire, which was now consuming her home, her artwork and her possessions, started?

Questions flashed in rapid succession and she spoke the two that repeated most often. "What happened? Why are you here?" She'd made it clear outside the gallery she wouldn't—couldn't—see him. It hurt too much.

Then again, him saving her life put a fresh, bewildering twist on her feelings. Gratitude, desire and security mixed with guilt in a heady cocktail, jumbling her emotions.

Brady rubbed at his knee, pain written on his face. His injury! She'd been worried about herself and her house. What about Brady? He'd risked his life for her.

"Are you hurt? Is your knee okay?" she asked before he could answer her first questions.

He looked at her unblinking, emotionless. "I don't know what happened. I saw the flames, called 911 and rushed inside. I didn't hear your smoke detectors going off."

Had they malfunctioned? Or was something more sinister afoot? Susan had never been the paranoid type, but events over the past week had put her on high alert. "Why are you here?" she asked again.

Brady shifted on his legs and stood, shaking out his right leg. "I explained the other day why I've been hanging around. Reilly's gotten caught up in this and I need the truth. He's worried about you, and given the current state of his career, he can't look out for you. He wants me to."

Susan's jaw slackened. Her friendship with Reilly didn't include talking about Brady often. He was a subject they both avoided. Reilly knew she wouldn't be comfortable with Brady involved in her life. "I asked you to leave me alone and you were spying on me?"

He blew out his breath. "No, Susan, come on. I was making sure you were safe."

Had he been the person she'd sensed watching her? She shivered, feeling a combination of cold and uneasy. "Did you look in my windows?"

Brady's eyes narrowed in indignation. "No, dang, Susan, I'm not a creepy pervert. I was making sure you got home from work safely and no one was harassing you."

"I'm trying to handle things." She shivered again and rubbed her arms. Brady removed his jacket and slipped it over her body. It smelled like a combination of smoke and Brady. The scent of him was both comforting and arousing.

Brady glanced at her burning house. "I'm seeing a number of threats coming in your direction and while I know you're independent and can handle yourself, I don't know if you realize who you're up against."

Brady wanted to help her. Protect her. Had Brady figured out something she hadn't? Susan had tried to sort out how her life had spun out of control. She had tried to remember what had happened the night Justin had died. She had come up empty on answers in both cases.

Every time Justin's name came to mind, which was at least a hundred times a day, guilt and hurt slammed her in the gut. That she wasn't emotionally shattered by his death only compounded the guilt. She missed him and she was sorry for his family and what they were going through, but she wasn't experiencing the gut-twisting, heart-wrenching heartbreak of lost love. She had been on his boat before he'd died and she couldn't recall anything to help the police. Had she been involved? She wasn't a temperamental woman, but the circumstances made her question everything.

Justin had been a good man. He'd deserved better than a violent death. "I don't know who I'm up against because I don't know anyone who would do this to me."

"Justin's murderer."

Susan tried to wrap her mind around Brady's words. "If the person who killed Justin wanted me dead, they could have killed me that night, too."

Brady's face took on a serious expression. "My theory is that you were a good scapegoat for his murder and now that enough time has passed to leave the investigative trail cold, you're a loose end that needs to be tied off."

Chapter 2

Brady's words slammed into her like a hammer. Someone wanted her dead? "Who would kill Justin and try to hurt me?" Susan asked.

"That's the big question," Brady said.

Susan rubbed at her temples where a headache of massive proportions was brewing. "This doesn't make any sense. I don't have enemies."

Brady inclined his head. "You don't exactly have any friends in your corner right now either. Well, except my brothers and me."

If she allowed Brady in her life, would he explain why he had walked out of it to begin with and give her closure?

No, that wasn't like Brady. Discussing emotions wasn't on the agenda. As much as she had wanted to be part of his world, as intimate as her relationship had been with Brady, she had never reached the status of being family to him. She remained outside his inner circle, an inner circle he didn't allow anyone inside except his parents and his brothers. Bitterness oozed from her chest and she worked to hide it. She had tried. She'd put her best into her relationship with Brady, and despite their chemistry and the effort she'd made, it had still failed.

If nothing else, his reappearance in her life had given her something to think about aside from the fire and Justin's death. Though she hated to admit it, she felt safer with Brady around. He had a way of taking control of a situation and putting her at ease.

But how much could she rely on him? Was he sticking around this time, or would he bail if it got too complicated? History could repeat itself.

The cold had begun to cut through his jacket and her nightshirt. She shivered and rubbed her legs. Approaching sirens sounded in the distance.

"Come with me," Brady said. "I have a blanket in my truck."

He helped her to her feet and limped to his truck, one arm supporting her. Brady hadn't answered her question about his injury. He was in pain, but he hid it well. Brady dug a blanket from the back of his truck, wrapped it around her legs and told her to wait in the cab. The truck sheltered her from the wind and biting cold, but not from the view of her home.

Her house was still in flames, her possessions destroyed. All she had left were the pajamas she was wearing and the necklace she'd gotten from Haley, one of the few people who'd stood beside her since Justin's death. Susan watched helplessly as the fire trucks arrived and firefighters hooked up their hoses, pouring water onto the farmhouse. Despite their efforts, it was too late to do any good. The farmhouse was old, the wiring outdated, and the fire had been merciless.

No one had been hurt, and she was glad of that, but everything that mattered to her had been taken in an instant.

The ambulance arrived and the paramedic assessed them both, first treating Brady, who had an injury on his arm. An EMT procured a pair of sweatpants, a sweatshirt and a pair of shoes from a neighbor for Susan to wear over her nightshirt.

Hadn't she suffered her share of heartbreak in the past week? What did she have left? Her eyes drifted to Brady. Once the most important man in her life, she couldn't trust him. He'd hurt her once. He'd do it again.

Two police officers walked toward her and dread coiled in Susan's stomach. She had no reason to fear these officers and yet, her experiences with the police in the last week had been less than stellar. Borderline catastrophic.

When they approached, Brady broke away from the paramedic and came closer, positioning himself at her side. "Thank you for the speedy response time," Brady said to the officers.

Susan glanced at him. Nothing on his face gave away sarcasm. Why was he playing nice? Reilly was a detective, one of the best. Did Brady know these officers through his brother?

"We need some information from you," one of the officers said, directing the statement at Susan.

When she'd been brought in for questioning after Justin's murder, she'd known to ask for a lawyer. Did she need one now? "Do I need an attorney?" Asking the question made her feel guilty though she'd done nothing wrong.

The two officers exchanged looks.

"We're not holding you under suspicion of starting the fire. If our investigation leads in that direction, we will need you available for questions," the other officer said.

"If you're uncomfortable saying anything now, we can go to the station later with your lawyer," Brady said.

Brady was behaving as if they were friends. They weren't friends. They were barely civil to each other, tonight being the exception. "I can talk now," she said.

Susan was relieved that the officers needed only her basic information and promised to call when the fire investigator had finished examining the scene.

When the officers walked away, Brady knelt in front of her and looked her dead in the eyes. "What were you doing right before the fire?"

Did he think she had something to do with the fire? The idea infuriated her. "I was sleeping. And before that, I was watching TV."

Behind Brady, a movement in the trees bordering her property caught her attention. She paused, squinted, trying to see who—or what—was there. Was it another nosy neighbor, her imagination on overdrive or someone with malicious intentions? She hadn't called the police to report her unease and sense of being watched. They wouldn't have believed her and she didn't want to add fuel to their case against her by appearing insane. As far as the authorities were concerned, she was a criminal and every moment she had outside jail was a gift.

Another movement in the trees. "Brady." His name left her mouth in a whisper.

"What's the matter?" he asked, leaning close.

Their gazes locked and for a moment, Susan lost herself in his dark eyes. Brady had the same dark eyes as his brother Reilly, but at close range, she could see flecks of light brown the color of wheat in them. She let him draw her close, even when every other thought screamed warnings to stay away.

Though she felt silly for speaking the words, it felt important to tell someone. "I thought I saw someone in the trees."

Brady didn't question her. He didn't tell her she was seeing things because she was tired. "I'll look. Stay here." He stalked in that direction to check it out, his limp drawing her attention. He disappeared into the dark and worry fogged her brain. If Brady was still recovering from his injury, could he protect himself? She had never before questioned his abilities. Before he'd been wounded, Brady had been a force to be reckoned with. She believed him strong and capable. If nothing else, sheer will drove him.

She waited for Brady to return. When he reappeared, his limp was less noticeable. Was it an injury that came and went? Was that a good sign for his recovery?

"Did you see anyone?" she asked. Please let Brady have seen something that would help.

He stilled. "No. I didn't." He spoke the words quietly.

She took a deep breath against the battering disappointment. If anyone had been there, Brady would have found him or her. Had she imagined the shadow?

Lately, she'd felt on display every time she left the house. Neighbors and friends had turned on her, blaming her for Justin's death, whispering behind her back. Those who knew her mother and her father whispered about history repeating itself. Their stares had made her paranoid. "I thought someone was there. I swear someone was watching me."

"Maybe it was a neighbor, coming to see if you were okay."

"Right," she said, anger lacing the word. She'd lived in Denver all her life, and in this neighborhood for the past ten years. Everyone knew her by name, knew who she was. Some had purchased her artwork and had it hanging in their homes. Friendships and relationships had splintered the moment Justin was murdered and the police had made it clear she was their top suspect. Few people wanted to be seen with her and those who did were punished. Like Reilly.

Susan coughed, the cold of the night sharp against her lungs and disappointment heavy on her shoulders. She felt trapped and without options. Her life was falling apart and at the moment, Brady's help was the only lifeline dangling within reach.

Brady studied Susan's face. Exhaustion framed her eyes. She hadn't been sleeping well. The urge to pull her into his arms was overwhelming. He wanted to do something, anything to make her feel better. Though he wasn't here to comfort her, gentleness and kindness could help. He could relax her and earn her trust. He'd coax the missing information out of her.

He'd meant to help her as a friend. But when it came to being close to her, touching her, those boundaries were unclear and his body had its own ideas. Making love with Susan had always put them both at ease. Kissing her had been a lengthy and intensely pleasurable activity. She liked having her feet rubbed and her calves massaged at the end of a difficult day and he'd been happy to oblige her. Taking care of her had been important to him.

Brady quashed those thoughts. That was the past. The landscape of the present was much different.

Susan's fiancé hadn't been dead a week. She was heartbroken and grieving. She didn't want Brady in her life. She certainly wouldn't want him in her bed. If she knew what he was thinking, she would shut him out completely.

Her current frame of mind wasn't conducive to learning what he needed to about Justin's murder. Brady would have to win back her trust. Maybe they would never stand on the same ground they once had, but he'd settle for getting close enough to help his brother.

"Do you have a place to stay?" Brady asked her.

Susan rubbed her forehead. "I can call my mother."

That wouldn't be easy on her. Susan didn't have a good relationship with her mother and if anything, her mother would add stress. "I don't know what's going on yet, but from what I can see, this investigation is being bungled. Badly. The police suspect you. They're not looking out for you. I can. I will. Stay with me. I'll keep you safe," Brady said.

Wariness flickered across Susan's face. "That isn't a good idea."

It was a great idea. He could keep her close, protect her and work on establishing a friendship with her.

"I'm planning to watch over you and keep you safe. I can continue to follow you around, or you can make it easy on me and stay close."

"Easier on you?" Susan asked.

Brady shrugged. "It will be harder on my leg if I have to follow you around all the time with you working to dodge me."

Indecision and a hint of compassion flickered across her face. "Staying together will create more problems than it solves."

For her or for him? He could control himself. Brady knew Susan well enough to read her emotions. She needed someone to look out for her. She was run-down and exhausted. A gentle push and she'd agree. "You need a place to stay. You need someone to watch your back. I can offer both, no strings attached." Why had he felt the need to add the last phrase? Of course he wouldn't expect any attachment from her. He'd had his chance for her love and friendship and had blown it. Twice. Once when he'd broken up with her and again when she'd visited him in the hospital. Now, she was hurting, her heart broken over another man and she needed time to heal.

Susan folded her arms over her chest. "I don't have much choice at the moment, do I?"

He didn't mince words. "No, you don't." Given Justin's murder, Reilly's suspicions and the events of the evening, Susan needed someone to protect her. Brady would be that man. His knee stung as if to remind him he was working with a deficiency.

He hated that he was weak and questions about his abilities flickered through his thoughts. She'd agreed to stay with him, but if tested, would his injury get in the way and prevent him from protecting her? Would he fail again at his duty, leaving Susan for dead and Reilly paying the price for a crime he didn't commit?

Ten minutes later, Susan was buckling her seat belt in Brady's truck. The same pickup truck he had driven when they'd dated. She ran her fingers over the dash, memories invading her senses. Before she could tumble into reminiscing about the past, a loud voice screamed in her mind to stay somewhere else. Anywhere else. Staying with Brady was a mistake. The last time she'd spent the night at his place, they'd been lovers.

The last day they'd been together before Brady ended their relationship, they'd spent at the park. The weather had been unseasonably warm and Susan had her new camera and lenses. Brady had played in a pickup football game with a few friends he'd run into. He hadn't wanted to leave her especially when he had limited free time, but she'd enjoyed sitting on the sidelines and taking pictures. Justin had been playing in the game that day, as well. It was the first time she had met him.

She'd sensed the tension between Justin and Brady right away and had chalked it up to good-natured competition on the football field. It was only later, after her relationship with Brady was over and she'd been dating Justin, that Justin had explained he'd known Brady from their time in the military. They'd been in basic training together though their careers had taken different paths. Much to his father's disappointment, Justin had left the air force after a couple of years, preferring work as an accountant, and Brady had remained in the service.

Susan had loved watching Brady play football. Her camera captured him in action as he ran down the field, the look on his face when he caught the ball and his intensity immediately before a big play. She'd planned to take a few of the best shots and arrange them in a photo frame as a gift for his mother. With the holidays coming up, she and Brady had been talking about their plans and Susan had been hoping for an invitation to his parents' house for Christmas.

Susan had never gotten the opportunity to edit and print the photos for Brady's mother. Without Brady in her life, it had been one of the loneliest Christmases she could recall.

Brady had meant more to her than she had to him. She had been tied in from her soul. Brady had his own way of connecting and yet keeping her at arm's length. The only way she knew how to move on was to forget what she could and leave the past behind.

They'd been on unequal emotional footing. If she was going to survive this, she had to be as cold and detached as he was. She was too tired to think of alternative places to stay, but tomorrow, when she was fresh, she would relocate. "Thank you again for helping me. I'll find another place tomorrow."

"You can stay as long as you need to, darlin'. I'm not rushing you out. I want to keep you safe."

Darlin'. A casual endearment he'd used a thousand times in the past. The urge to lean closer and rest her head on his shoulder nearly overpowered her. She could let Brady take the reins and make decisions and figure out what had happened to Justin. But that wouldn't be safe for her heart. It wouldn't end well. It couldn't. She would too easily give him her trust and her heart, and he would leave her again with more questions and more anger.

Susan closed her eyes and sealed off her heart from the barrage of memories and emotions that swirled inside her. Worrying about Brady should fall dead last on her list. She was emotionally debilitated by the events of the week. With a little sleep and time to think, she'd stop picturing Brady taking control, stop imagining Brady as her lover and shut down those worthless feelings for good.

"I have some charcoal and paper if you need it."

Her eyes popped open at the sound of Brady's voice. The melodic quality spoke to her, made her feel hot and tingly. Why hadn't she put those sensuous feelings to rest long ago? He'd walked away from her. She'd reached out to him in the hospital when he might have needed a friend, and he'd rejected her. No explanations, no apologies. Her suspicions rose. "Why do you have charcoal?"

"You made it look easy when you drew. You swore it was therapeutic. When the shrink at the hospital insisted I give a new hobby a shot, I tried drawing."

Brady had tried drawing with charcoal? He'd never expressed interest in art before. "I'm surprised you gave it a chance. Did you like it?"

"I couldn't draw anything. I tried. You create beautiful pictures and make it look effortless. Most of my attempts looked like scribbles and smudges a blindfolded preschooler would draw."

Despite the heaviness of her heart, she laughed. It was a laugh she needed and some of the tension released in her chest. "You need time to work with them," she said. "Art doesn't come quickly to everyone. Maybe you'd do better with a different medium. Like photography." She touched the owl necklace at her neck, combination jewelry and storage device where she kept pictures she cherished. Though photography had been a hobby since her teens, she'd gotten more serious with it when she'd been dating Brady. He'd been an amazing subject. "We offer introductory classes at the gallery."

"I don't think I was cut out for artwork," Brady said. "A hobby that frustrates me isn't what the shrink has in mind."

It was the second time he'd mentioned the therapist and it startled her. Brady was normally closed off about anything that affected him emotionally. She'd suspected his physical injuries had a deeper impact on him. To what degree was he coping? Losing his position with the pararescuemen had to have devastated him. His career had meant a great deal to him. He'd put it before everything else. Including her.

"Why the mighty frown?" he asked.

Susan needed to better censor her facial expressions. Especially around Brady. A natural observer, he watched the world around him and was excellent at deciphering thoughts and feelings from a look, a movement or a hand motion. Despite his outgoing and high-energy nature, when he wanted to relax, he could sit for hours and observe. They had done that together some days. She with her sketch pad in her lap, using what she saw for inspiration and Brady with his arm around her. She slammed closed the door on those memories. They were too painful to revisit now.

"Just thinking." She had enough problems in her life. She didn't need to give specifics.

"We'll work this out."

He sounded sure of himself and that was classic Brady. Determined when he set his mind to it. But if solving the case were that easy, the police would have done so by now. Granted, from the beginning the lead investigator had seemed bent on blaming her.

"The police haven't come up with anything and all that's keeping me out of jail is that Justin's body hasn't been found." Sadness bit into her. Justin deserved a proper burial to bring closure to his family and the people who'd loved him.

A muscle flexed in Brady's jaw. "The killer probably disposed of the body in the water. It would be difficult to carry it down the pier without being seen."

"The police divers haven't found anything yet. They're waiting for a body to wash up on shore," Susan said. The image of Justin's body floating in the water made her sick.

"The detective in charge of the case is eager to wrap up the investigation and please the mayor and Justin's father. He's looking for a promotion. He's taking the most likely suspect and the most likely scenario and swallowing it as fact," Brady said.

Susan had gotten the same impression from the police, that they either hadn't found other suspects or hadn't considered them. "I don't know what other options they have."

"They can do better. Since it's unlikely they will, it's up to us. You were at the scene. You know what happened. You can remember."

She whirled on him. "I can't, Brady. If you think

I'm lying about remembering, you can let me out of the truck now. If I knew what happened, I would tell you. For that matter, I would have told the police. That night is a black box. I feel terrible about it. I feel terrible knowing Justin died and I was in the room. I didn't do anything to stop it. I haven't been useful in helping the police find his killer. I haven't remembered anything important. I don't know what happened that night."

Susan let out her breath in a rush. His questions called to mind her doubts about her involvement. She couldn't imagine a scenario where she would physically assault Justin, but the few scraps of evidence pointed to her. Which is why she hadn't told the police that she had broken up with Justin. It would only make her look guiltier. She'd realized she'd never been in love with him, and pretending and lying to herself was a mistake. Starting a relationship with Justin when her heart was broken over Brady hadn't worked. Susan should have ended the relationship before it escalated into a marriage proposal. Her track record with men was pathetic.

First Brady, then Justin. When it came to love, she made terrible decisions. "I don't know what happened," she repeated.

"Whoa, whoa," Brady said, holding up his palm. "I wasn't accusing you. I know you can't remember. Harris thinks given the right conditions and enough time you might. I wasn't implying you were lying."

Susan ran a hand through her hair. "I've tried a thousand times to remember what happened. I've gone over and over that night and tried to figure out where it went wrong." She had been on the boat at Justin's invitation. She'd regretted visiting the boat and wondered if under different circumstances Justin would still be alive. What if she hadn't ended their engagement, and instead they had been out that night at a movie? What if they had decided to stay in and have dinner at her place?

"Maybe the problem is that you're trying too hard. Putting too much pressure on yourself," Brady said.

Relaxing wouldn't come easily. Brady had an infuriating way of simplifying matters. "Maybe I should take a few days at the spa and see if anything comes to mind." Her fingernails bit into her hand. "Oh, wait. Everywhere I go, people look at me as if I'm a pariah, so that wouldn't be fun. I don't have any money or any clothes and they frown on that at the spa."

Her voice was reaching near shrieking. The shaking in her hands gave away how upset she was getting. She went quiet and took several long, deep breaths. Since Justin had died, she'd been teetering on the edge of losing her composure a dozen times a day.

"Feel better?" Brady asked.

"No," she said, snapping at him.

"Why didn't you call me when you knew you were in trouble?" Brady asked.

The question was ridiculous. Brady didn't want her in his life. He only wanted her around now to help Reilly. "And say what?"

"That you needed help. I would have come."

When Brady had rejected her again at the hospital, she'd written him out of her life permanently. She'd worked up a lot of courage to visit him. He'd shot down her attempts at civility and friendship.

"I don't think of you as part of my life anymore." As a friend. Or as anyone she could count on.

Brady didn't respond. She could read his reaction. He was hurt. "Brady—" She hadn't been trying to throw verbal daggers at him.

He shook his head. "You're right. I don't deserve your friendship."

He turned his truck off the road onto a dirt path.

Susan didn't have the emotional energy to talk about their crippled relationship. "Where are we going?" she asked, not recognizing the location.

"My place. I moved."

Trees lined both sides of the winding dirt path. No streets signs were posted along the road. The divots in the road made the truck bounce and Brady navigated to avoid downed tree branches. It was not a welcoming place; in fact, it was borderline foreboding. Why had Brady chosen to live here?

The truck's headlights illuminated a small cabin at the end of the dirt road. No other lights brightened the area.

"This is where you live?" she asked. She didn't see neighbors or other cars.

"For now."

"Alone?" she asked.

"My landlord has a place farther down the road."

Susan squinted into the dark. What road? Choosing to live here was a deliberate way of separating himself from the world.

She didn't comment further. As isolated as it was, it was a step up from the trailer park where her mother lived. At least here, she'd be with someone who could protect her if Justin's murderer made another attempt on her life.

They climbed out of the car and Brady circled to

her side. The man had presence, and Susan was aware of how close he stood even though she couldn't see him in the dark. He radiated dominance and strength.

Brady set his hand on her lower back and she shivered. Touching was not a good idea, but Susan couldn't see where they were and allowed the contact.

Brady escorted her to the front door, opened it and turned on a light. She was greeted by a tiny, dark space, with mismatched furniture, clothing and other items in general disarray. This wasn't like him. Military life, with its rules and organization, had suited him.

What had happened to him? What had happened to her? They had once been happy, in love and with high hopes for the future. Brady had once shown up at the police station to surprise her, tracking her down through Reilly and Haley. Susan had been working with victims on a particularly tough case and he'd been patient and supportive, bringing carryout Chinese food for everyone involved in the case and waiting for her to finish her sketches of the suspects. The case had been a disturbing one and she had been grateful to have Brady with her that night.

He had been her best friend and he'd walked out of her life. The memory of the past and the events of the night came booming down on her. A sob caught in her throat.

"Hey, darlin', everything is fine." Brady came behind her and placed his hands on her shoulders.

He read her emotions even when she tried to suppress them. They'd had a finger-snap close connection from the moment they'd met. Brady could be across a crowded room and with one look, know what she was thinking. That connection had been too much too fast and had burned out. Nothing that hot and intense could burn indefinitely.

Brady's fingers rubbed her shoulders, unknotting the tension that had been building since she had woken up on Justin's boat with his blood on her hands. Brady's comforting gesture sent pulses of heat over her skin, across her body, pooling in her chest. Her body remembered, and reacted to, his touch. To this day, making love with Brady had been the most amazing intimate experience of her life. The closeness and tenderness she'd shared with him couldn't be replicated with someone else. She knew. She'd tried, pretended and failed.

Guilt assailed her for having those thoughts. Shouldn't she be focused on her grief for Justin, not her anger and unresolved feelings for Brady? Though her romantic feelings for Justin had been gone for some time, he'd been an important part of her life. He deserved respect and remembrance.

The urge to turn and bury her face against Brady was overwhelming. When he took her in his arms, he made her feel better. Treasured. Loved. Even if it was a charade, it was one he played well. She had believed it and believed him. To reach out and try to reclaim that small bit of happiness was tempting. To press against him, to kiss him, to run her hands over his strong body. The way they'd moved together, made love together and danced together had been in complete harmony. Was it wrong to want a few minutes of relief from the constant ache in her chest?

She battled her wild emotions, beating them back with a vengeance. It would be wrong to give in to her urges. Susan couldn't protect her heart if she let Brady hold her. Fool her twice, shame on her. Susan shrugged away his hands. She wouldn't let herself fall for this again. Her life was chaotic enough.

"You can't say everything will be fine. You don't know how bad it is. I don't understand why this is happening to me and you can't possibly explain it."

Brady turned her to face him, but didn't let his hands linger on her. "That's true. I don't have any idea what you've been through since Justin died." Was it her imagination or did his voice catch over Justin's name?

His eyes drilled into hers. "You and Reilly are good people who got caught in something bad. I think Justin might have had a side he kept secret from you."

Justin and Brady didn't get along and they never had. They tolerated each other and they'd been cordial. Even so, accusing Justin of being two-faced struck her as wrong. She wanted to remember the good things about Justin, not harp on his negative traits.

"Justin was a good man. What do you think Justin hid from me?" She'd force Brady to back up his words.

"I'm sure he didn't tell you everything about his life."

"Perhaps, but he didn't go out of his way to hide anything either," Susan said.

"He told you why he left the military?" Brady asked in a tone that peeved her.

Justin had talked about his time in the military. "He didn't like it. It wasn't for him," Susan said. "Not everyone enjoys risking their life for the adrenaline high." She didn't add that Justin's father being a high-ranking officer in the air force had set expectations on Justin that had been difficult for him to achieve.

"Okay," Brady said, his expression blank.

Anger incensed her. What was he not telling her? "'Okay?' What does 'okay' mean?"

Brady crossed his arms over his chest. "It means I don't think he told you everything."

"If you know something, tell me." A demand. She was in no mood to coax the information from him.

Brady ran a hand through his hair and waited a few moments before answering. "Justin didn't voluntarily leave the air force. He was kicked out. His dad pulled strings to keep him from being dishonorably discharged and preventing his offenses from being made public. It was more than him not liking the lifestyle. It was him not liking to follow rules."

Susan narrowed her eyes. "His offenses? And what rules?"

"Word got around base that Justin and a few others had trouble keeping their hands out of the company till. They were accepting kickbacks from vendors who supplied the base's convenience stores with food and drinks."

Justin had never mentioned anything about it to her. "I can't believe he would do that. Especially with who his father is."

Brady snorted. "I think his father is why he did it. Justin didn't like that his father was in charge of enforcing the rules. Tim Ambrose doesn't let anyone forget he's in charge and he likes to be in control. Justin bucked the system when he could."

Susan had met Justin's father several times and she'd gotten the impression he wasn't happy with her as his son's choice for a girlfriend. She'd assumed it was a hang-up about her past, maybe her humble upbringing or her mother's problems with the law. Perhaps he hadn't liked that he couldn't control Justin's decisions in regards to her. "Justin didn't strike me as a rule-breaker." If Brady was right, she had been in the dark about that part of Justin's life. It wasn't an "if" Brady was telling the truth. Trumans didn't lie, even when the truth hurt. Susan couldn't help but wonder what else she was in the dark about when it came to Justin. Something that would make him enemies? Something that would get him killed?

"I must sound like a fool for not knowing these things about Justin."

"Not a fool, just a woman who sees the best in people. Don't waste energy worrying about it. We'll figure this out together."

Susan closed her eyes. When he said together, she saw them as a team. With Brady, no such concept of team or partner existed. He ran the show and brought people along for the ride. In most circumstances, she didn't mind. Life with Brady was exciting and ever-changing. In this case, Susan wanted control. She wanted to do everything possible to clear her name. "If the police don't know about Justin's checkered past in the air force, maybe I should tell them. Maybe it will help them connect Justin to someone bad he was involved with in the present."

Brady shook his head. "Bringing a theory like that to the police without evidence won't help. Justin's father is involved in the case and calling the shots, at least from behind the scenes. He won't allow Justin's name to be dragged through the mud by allowing the past to enter the equation."

What about her good name? Everything she could think to do wasn't working. "When I've had some sleep, I'll feel better," Susan said. She'd been telling herself things like that for the past week. Every time she thought them, they were a lie. Nothing made her feel better or eased the guilt she carried.

"I'll throw clean sheets on my bed for you. I'll sleep on the couch."

She couldn't expect him to do that. He'd done enough and she didn't want to feel indebted to him. "I don't mind sleeping on the couch."

He waved his hand dismissively. "Half the time I sleep on the couch anyway. Don't give it another thought."

He put fresh sheets on the bed and tidied his room, tossing laundry in the hamper. He put a pair of clothes for her on the end of the bed. "These might be too big, but they're clean. I'll put out a towel for you in the bathroom."

Formal. Like they were strangers. She'd spent the night with Brady many times before and this felt bizarre.

Brady went to his safe next to his dresser and opened it, pulling out his gun. He checked it for bullets. "Holler if you need anything," he said over his shoulder.

He closed the safe and left the bedroom, shutting the door behind him.

She'd never seen him remove his gun from the safe before tonight. He was taking the threat to her life seriously.

Susan pushed aside her worries about staying at Brady's and her anxiety about Brady needing to use the gun. It was late and she was tired. The day had been long and difficult. A quick shower to scrub the smoke and fire stink off her and then sleep would feel great. She wouldn't think about what waited for her tomorrow. She would take one day at a time. Same as she had when her father had been murdered.

Exhaustion tugged at her and she hurried through a shower. If she weren't covered in smoke and grime, she might have skipped it altogether. She dressed in Brady's clothes and crawled into bed, closing her eyes, knowing Brady would find his way, unwanted, into her dreams.

Brady shifted on the couch and reached under it to check his gun. He wanted it in arm's reach. Not since his work as a pararescueman had he needed to sleep with a gun beside him. Then, he'd had his team around providing backup.

Alone with Susan, he was her sole protector. Was he up to the task? His skills were out of practice and he wasn't nimble on his feet. When he'd been with the pararescuemen, he'd worked with in-depth intel, extensive resources and top-of-the-line equipment. In protecting Susan, he had none of that. He didn't even know whom he was protecting her from.

Doubts ran through him, but the events of the last week didn't leave him much choice. He needed to look out for Susan. Brady wasn't naïve enough to believe whoever was stalking Susan would give up.

Someone believed Susan knew something about Justin's murder and they didn't want it revealed. If they believed it, then Harris might be right and Susan held the key to solving Justin's murder. Had she been drugged? Or was she blocking the trauma of the memory?

Brady's knee ached and he reached to massage it.

He'd pressed his body hard going into the fire to help Susan. Now that his adrenaline was slowing, he was paying for it. Unable to get comfortable on the couch, he sat up and grabbed the file Harris has given him on Justin's murder.

Brady had read it a dozen times and thought it over twice that often. He'd made his own notes in the margins, most of which consisted of questions without answers.

His attention swerved to a noise at the front door. Was someone testing the front lock, trying to open the door? Harris stopping by again uninvited? Brady's landlord made an appearance only when it was a matter of life and death. Connor was also former Special Forces and more of a recluse than Brady was. He hated trespassers.

Brady wasn't taking chances. He retrieved his gun from under the couch and checked again that it was loaded. He wouldn't open fire until he saw who was foolish enough to break into his home.

Scratching at the door. A screwdriver trying to pry it open? He didn't have a window facing the front and the door didn't have a peephole. He could swing the door open and surprise whoever was there, but he'd prefer to know who was on the other side. What if more than one person was looking for Susan? How quickly could Brady take them out and prevent them from getting to her?

Doubts flooded his mind. His Special Forces training had taught him that success in an operation was ninety percent mental. Brady had failed in a big way once, letting down his team and himself when the stakes were life and death. Brady pictured himself freezing, gun in hand, letting an enemy get the advantage. He shook off the memory. Could he succeed now when the stakes were as high?

Wood breaking sounded loud against the silence of the room. The door gave way under the weight of a man dressed in black. The man swung a gun around the room, sweeping for occupants.

Brady ducked behind the couch and strained to listen. Was anyone else attempting to get inside the house? His landlord, a paranoid SOB, had built one doorway entry into the house, but the cabin had several windows in the other rooms. Brady listened for the sound of breaking glass.

The floor creaked as the intruder moved around the room. Brady waited, following his movements. The intruder tracked closer to the bedroom, much too close to Susan for Brady's comfort. He needed to get between Susan and the attacker.

"Drop your weapon and I won't kill you," Brady said. His knee might be damaged, but his aim was impeccable.

"I could say the same to you," the man said, pivoting in Brady's direction.

Brady prayed Susan stayed asleep or at least remained in his bedroom, where she was safer. "Last chance," Brady said.

"Don't get involved in this. I don't want you. I want her."

The sound of breaking glass echoed through the room, followed by Susan's scream. Someone was in Susan's room!

Brady moved his position and aimed. What if Susan came out of her room and he hit her? What if the bullet ricocheted? Anxiety tightened his throat and Brady pressed down on his shoulders and steadied his hands.

A red beam traced across the room from the attacker's gun, a bullet sure to follow in its path. The attacker squeezed off a shot. Brady heard it whiz by his ear. If he'd been a second later in shifting, he'd have been hit. Brady fired his weapon. His aim was true; the attacker dropped to the ground, injured or dead.

"Susan!" Brady screamed, barging into her room.

Susan, her back to the large dresser across from the bed, was staring in horror at Brady's landlord. Connor was pressed against the wall to the left of the door, gun in hand. Another masked man was dead on the floor. Connor made an appalling sight, his hair long, a full beard covering his face, his clothes wrinkled and worn. The first time Brady had met him, if he hadn't known who Connor was, he would have been nervous around him. Connor carried an agitated energy, as if he was ready to spring at any moment.

"Are you okay?" Brady asked Susan.

"What is going on? Who is this? What's happening?" Her voice shook and her hands trembled.

"This is my landlord, Connor. Someone else broke into the cabin. I took care of it." Brady swung his attention to Connor. "Anyone else outside?" he asked.

Connor shook his head. "Heard them approach. Loud engine. Should have announced their presence with fireworks. Would have been quieter. Followed this guy inside. Just sorry I didn't get him before he got through the window."

Brady hadn't heard anyone, but that was part of what made Connor spooky. He had an eerie ability to sense trouble. Or had Brady screwed up again? Should he have heard the attackers' approach before they'd reached the front door? That would have been his first mistake. His second was letting the man get a shot off before stopping him.

Brady had lost his touch. His reactions were slow. Was it more than his physical response failing him? Was he destined to forever make critical mistakes in protecting the people he'd sworn to keep safe?

"Susan's ex was involved in something and now Susan's attracted attention from the wrong people," Brady said.

"They're trained. Sloppy and loud, but trained," Connor said, echoing Brady's thoughts about the attackers.

"Thanks for coming out to help," Brady said. Connor hated to leave his place. At least, that's what Brady assumed. He'd never seen the man leave the property. When it came to Connor, Brady didn't ask questions and respected his desire for privacy.

"Told you when you moved in, I had your back," Connor said. He nodded toward the broken glass. "I'll get something to cover that and get it fixed tomorrow. I'll do a perimeter check tonight. Stupid fools to come on this property." With that, he strode out the bedroom door.

"We need to call the police," Brady said.

"No! Not again," Susan said. "Do you know how this will look? The police think I belong in jail. What will they think when I'm involved in a fire and a killing in the same night? They'll think I killed him. Them."

Panic and anxiety twisted her voice to a higher octave. Brady reasoned with her. "First, the gunshot residue will be on my hands, not yours. Someone entered my home. I defended us. We've done nothing wrong." That his shot had hit its mark would be telling to anyone with common sense. An untrained woman with a gun would have had shots that went wild.

"What about the man who Connor killed?" Susan asked.

"Connor will talk to the police about that," Brady said.

Susan nodded slowly, her eyes skating to the broken window and the man on the floor. "They just burst through the window."

"We're lucky Connor was around."

Susan folded her arms over her chest appearing calmer. "I know we were. I didn't know at first what was going on. He's intense."

"Connor is an interesting man with an interesting story," Brady said. He wouldn't share what little he knew with her or anyone. Connor was a private and territorial man who patrolled his grounds like a gray wolf. Brady had been grateful to be allowed to stay at this cabin.

"I don't want anything more interesting to happen. I want dull. I want boredom and sleep." Susan's voice sounded close to breaking into tears.

She was scared and hurting and Brady wanted to stop it. Until he got to the bottom of Justin's murder, Susan would suffer. It was a consequence he couldn't live with.

Chapter 3

Two men had wanted to kill her. Susan wrapped her arms around her waist, feeling as if she was coming apart. Brady and his landlord had each killed someone to protect her.

A small sliver of hope had existed that the fire at her home had been an accident. But an attempted attack in Brady's cabin underscored that someone wanted her dead.

Would this incident persuade the police they had the wrong suspect in Justin's murder? Would they look at the men who had been killed and move them to the suspect list? Were they friends of Justin's? People she knew?

Brady turned on the lights. Connor was outside checking the perimeter for more assailants. What if this wasn't over? How much more could she take? Worry and sickness swamped her and she collapsed on the bed, afraid her legs wouldn't hold her.

Brady knelt over the body and glanced at her. "I'm going to take off his mask." He spoke slowly, offering a warning.

She nodded, but didn't move from her place on the bed. She didn't trust her legs to support her and she didn't want to look at the man dead on the floor.

Brady peeled away the attacker's mask. "I don't recognize him."

Would she? Was he the man who had killed Justin and framed her for the murder? If she saw his face, would it trigger her memories from that night?

"Susan, if you can, look at this guy. You might know him."

"I can't," she said, her empty stomach roiling. If she had anything in it, she'd have been sick.

"I'll help you." Brady's voice was tender and he crossed the room to her. "Take my arm. Don't lean against me. I have blood on my clothes and I don't want to get any on you."

A dead man's blood on her would give the police another piece of evidence to use against her. At least, for this murder, she had been alert. She could report what had happened and she had two witnesses to support her story. She grasped Brady's arm and crossed to where the body lay.

She stared at the man's face. Surprise rippled through her. She didn't recognize him. A stranger had attempted to kill her. This man might have killed Justin. What reason did he have to do so? "I don't know him."

"Look again. Be sure, Susan. This wasn't a random attack."

The pressure at her temples was nearly unbearable.

The edges of her vision danced. She concentrated on the attacker's face, imagining what he might look like with a smile or when speaking.

"I don't know him." Could someone have hired this man to kill her and Justin? It didn't make sense. If she didn't know him, did that mean she hadn't played a role in Justin's death? She wanted to believe it was true.

"I don't know who he was," Susan said. She grappled for answers. "Maybe he's on drugs." Weren't people on drugs irrationally violent when they needed a fix?

Brady didn't answer and she looked at him. He was watching her with indecision in his eyes.

"Brady?"

"I don't want to frighten you any more than you are."

Fear spread to every inch of her body. "You need to tell me what you think. I can't be more scared than I am." Terror was making her quake and turning her insides into slush.

Brady looked at the body and then at her. He let out his breath in a whoosh.

"Brady. Tell me."

Brady took her arm and they moved a few steps from the body. "His gun isn't what I'd expect from a street thug. His movements were trained and precise. I think he's military, former military maybe, possibly Special Forces based on his equipment. He was sloppy getting inside the cabin, but this could have been a last-minute operation after they bungled the fire at your house."

Susan was glad Brady's bed was behind her. Her legs gave out and she collapsed onto it. She was in grave danger and she had no one to turn to for help. What chance did she stand against Special Forces operatives? She couldn't expect Brady to keep her safe indefinitely.

Could she count on the police? She didn't think so. They hadn't assigned her protection or been worried about where she'd stay after the fire. They were bent on holding her as the prime suspect in Justin's murder.

"I don't make enemies, especially not powerful ones who'd want to send military operatives after me. The last person I had an ordeal with was you. And you aren't behind this." Her messy history with Brady had been painful, but it hadn't ended in a way that made her fear him. At least, not fear that he would do bodily harm to her. Her heart? Her heart was another matter.

What reason did someone have to hurt her? "Besides you, I don't know any Special Forces operatives." The pained look on his face made her wish she could retract the words. Brady was *former* Special Forces, a sore point for him.

Brady unmasked the second man in the living room. Susan didn't recognize him either.

"I need to call the police," Brady said.

"Okay," she agreed, knowing he was right. She was aware he was speaking into the phone, but she was unable to focus on his words. She was rooted to the chair. What could she do? Run away? If the men who had killed Justin and tried to kill her were dead, was she safe? Or were more men coming? Where could she hide? She'd been tracked to Brady's almost immediately. What had Justin been mixed up in?

Brady ended his call and watched her, worry clear on his face.

"What do we do now? If these men killed Justin, could it be over?" she asked.

Brady sat on the floor next to the easy chair, his gun in hand. Why was he holding his gun? "We don't know if these men killed Justin or why they were after you or even if they were working alone. Until we know the whole story, I don't know if you're safe."

Susan glanced at his gun again. "Is that why you haven't put your gun down?"

"That's correct. Connor's tough, but I won't take chances."

How was Brady holding it together? He had shot and killed someone. She would be near catatonic if she was in his position.

"How are you feeling?"

His brows furrowed. "I'm fine. Why?"

"You killed someone."

"Wasn't the first time."

He spoke the words so carelessly she tripped over the implication. He had been in the military. He had been involved in active combat. Of course he had killed before, but she had never thought about him shooting someone. "Doesn't it affect you?"

"I was raised to protect myself and the people around me. If that means I have to use lethal force to do so, I don't feel guilty about that. I warned him. He went after you and you were unarmed. I didn't have a choice."

Susan's heart tightened and her guilt intensified. "I did this. I'm responsible." Justin was dead and she hadn't been useful in providing information about the night he had died. Reilly had helped her and had been a friend. In exchange, he had been benched at his job pending an investigation. Brady had killed someone to protect her, someone who had broken into his cabin to get to her. Every man who was close to her landed in trouble.

Brady took her hand in his. "Look at me."

She met his gaze and blinked back the tears that threatened to spill. Her pulse beat erratically.

"You did not do this. The man I killed is responsible for his death. He broke into an armed man's home and threatened his girlfriend." Brady cleared his throat. "His ex-girlfriend. When he made those decisions, he risked his life. For that matter, coming onto Connor's property unannounced is a terrible idea."

Brady was offering some explanations, but none of them made sense to her. She didn't know these men or why they'd wanted to kill her. She didn't know why Justin had died. She and Brady waited in silence. As she heard the police sirens blast through the stillness of the night, anxiety cascaded through her. This wasn't over and it wouldn't be until they knew what had happened to Justin.

Brady's irritation with the police had reached new heights. The detectives at the scene hadn't arrested them, though the police and emergency response personnel had whispered about Susan and made their suspicions about her clear. They wanted Justin's murder pinned on her shoulders.

Brady had repeated to the detectives that he had fired the gun and killed the intruder. Connor had done the same. Their hands were swabbed for GSR. Still, gossip ran wild. The events of the past week were not painting Susan in a good light. More irritatingly, the police didn't appear to take the threat against Susan seriously. Brady told the cops about the fire at her home and how she had needed a place to stay, hence her being at his house.

One of the detectives on the scene seemed annoyed that Brady was pressing the issue of Susan's safety. "Look, Mr. Truman, we don't have the resources to monitor someone around the clock. I'll put in a request to have some uniforms in a marked police car drive by the house every few hours to keep an eye on the area. It's the best I can offer."

Irritation spun through Brady. "Whoever wants to kill Susan is determined. Only driving by every few hours gives the criminals another chance at her life."

The detective sighed heavily. "Maybe you killed the men looking for Ms. Prescott and she has nothing further to worry about. Unless you're keeping information from me, it doesn't sound like she has enemies to be concerned about."

"The fact that men *were* looking for her warrants an investigation. These were trained professionals, not common criminals. Susan was targeted. I want to be sure that she is safe, and the police should, too," Brady said. Brady didn't believe the two men he and Connor had killed were the entirety of the danger. Susan didn't recognize the men, leading Brady to consider they were murderers for hire or part of a larger conspiracy. Justin's death had released an avalanche of problems. At present, it was Susan who was in the path of destruction.

The detective screwed up her lips and lifted her brow. "One thing both incidents have in common is you. Maybe she would be better off away from you."

Brady didn't dignify the detective's comments with a response. Until the police department got its act together and realized Susan was a victim in this, Brady would protect her.

Brady's cell phone rang and he didn't recognize the number. The detective he'd been speaking with had already stepped away to talk to her partner. Brady wrote her off as useless in this matter. Brady answered the phone. "Brady Truman."

"Truman, it's Tim Ambrose."

Justin's father. The three-star lieutenant general. Brady respected the rank, if not the man himself. Though Ambrose couldn't see him, Brady straightened. "Hello, sir."

"I've heard from some of my contacts you're having a rough time."

Brady couldn't be sure exactly what Ambrose was referring to, but based on the timing, he guessed it wasn't his knee and physical rehabilitation that concerned the older man. More likely, Ambrose had caught wind of his involvement in protecting Susan. News traveled fast in the small circle of the air force, and bad news spread even faster. "It's been unpleasant. How can I help you?"

"I'm glad you asked. I want my son's killer brought to justice and I don't think your involvement with her helps that effort."

Brady hesitated. Ambrose was referring to Susan as Justin's killer.

"I want that, too." Finding the killer would stop the suspicion surrounding Susan and Reilly.

"Why are you helping her evade justice?" Ambrose asked, the anger in his voice thinly veiled.

The hackles rose on Brady's neck. "I'm not help-ing anyone evade justice. I'm helping an old friend to stay safe." How much did the lieutenant general know about the case? Did he know about the fire at Susan's home? The recent attack at Brady's?

"I'm not a man to tiptoe around a problem. Let me say it to you plain. If you help Susan Prescott worm out of responsibility for my son's murder, you won't like the consequences. I'll open your military record. I will have someone investigate inconsistencies and put a different slant on your work. Under a microscope, I'll bet we'll find offenses that will lead to a court martial. If that fails, when Susan is charged with Justin's mur-der, you'll be named as an accomplice to the crime."

A threat. An outright threat. Tim Ambrose had the power and the connections to carry through every warning he'd given. Brady's military record would be tarnished, his family name disgraced and he'd be brought to trial for a crime he had nothing to do with. Why was Ambrose convinced Susan was responsible?

Brady mustered the last threads of respect he had for the position to cover the anger in his voice. "Sir, I want justice for your son." He strove for neutrality.

"Then put some distance between you and Susan. Get out of the way."

"I can only do what I think is right." Not making a verbal commitment one way or another to the lieuten-ant general. Brady had no intention of walking away from Susan. He hadn't learned what he needed to in order to clear Reilly or Susan, and the people who had tried to kill her wouldn't give up until they were successful.

The men who had entered his home to kill Susan

weren't run-of-the-mill criminals. Brady recognized the signs of a trained and vicious tactical killer. Multiple weapons. Knife. Gun. Wire. A trained killer didn't give up, not when they wanted to hit their payday.

"I don't care for acts of disobedience," Tim Ambrose said.

Anger riled him. Brady wasn't in the military anymore and this wasn't an overseas military appointment. Brady wasn't being disobedient. "I'll get to the bottom of this. You'll be the first to know when I find evidence against Justin's killer."

"I don't need evidence. I know Susan Prescott is responsible," Ambrose said.

"We'll let the police do their job," Brady said. As he spoke the words, he pictured Ambrose making his next call to the mayor. Would Brady's refusal to walk away from Susan add to the pressure the mayor would apply to the police to arrest her?

"Yes, we will. You know I play golf with the mayor. He's interested in seeing this case resolved and I'd like to keep the collateral damage to a minimum. Your brother is a police detective, am I right?"

Hot rage exploded across Brady's chest. To threaten him was one thing. To go after his family was another, far more serious offense. "You know he is."

"It's my understanding he's currently under disciplinary action for his involvement in the case and it would be terrible if his career was damaged because of his relationship with my son's murderer," Ambrose said, again refusing to call Susan by her name.

Brady's teeth were grating so hard, he couldn't speak.

"You might want to keep that in mind when you're

making decisions. Do you understand? Truman? Truman—"

Brady disconnected the call. He wasn't interested in listening to more threats. He had the feeling he'd thrown down the gauntlet with Justin's father with his response and non-response. Brady would need to be very careful where he stepped. Tim Ambrose would make good on his promises and had reminded Brady that he had more to lose.

Susan was sitting on the porch of the cabin, her knees curled into her chest, watching the scene around her, police collecting evidence and the coroner bagging the bodies. The sun had begun to rise, rays of light breaking through the trees surrounding the cabin.

Brady sat next to her. "How are you managing?"

She shrugged. "I'm sorry I pulled you into this."

She hadn't pulled him in. He'd wanted to help her. He'd insisted. "It's good I was here. Connor, too. You and Justin must have pissed off the wrong people."

Susan faced him, her eyes glimmering with unshed tears. "It must be impossible to believe, but I don't think I've angered anyone. I can't think of anything Justin or I have done to cause this backlash." She pressed her lips together. "You had to kill someone because of me."

Brady inwardly cringed. He had shot the man in his home, but his reaction hadn't been quick and decisive. Would she feel safe if he admitted he'd hesitated? What was happening to him? Lives were at stake. Disgust at his behavior roiled through him.

He'd been trained to respond to threats without emotion. When emotion entered the equation, mistakes followed. After his failure with the Special Forces, he'd thought he'd learned that lesson. He'd known the objective of his mission and he'd known the enemy. He'd faltered, questioned his reaction and doubted his judgment. Because of it, good men had been put in danger. Could he continue to keep Susan safe knowing he was dragging around the psychological scars of his mistakes?

"I'm glad you weren't hurt," Brady said. Not an answer to her statement, but the truth. "When the police clear out, I'll ask Connor to keep an eye on you. I have a few errands to run."

Susan rubbed her forehead. "What can I do to help?"

"You can rest. Try to get some sleep. You won't remember anything about Justin's murder if you're exhausted and stressed."

Susan leaned her head on his shoulder. "I'll try. I want to help. I want to remember."

Brady banded his arms around her. His every muscle was attuned to her, his thoughts focused solely on her and protecting her. Could he keep her safe? They had a lot on the line and Justin's father had raised the stakes. The faster she remembered, the better it would be for her and his family.

Susan tried to sleep, but couldn't slow her thoughts enough to relax. Staying in Brady's cabin made it difficult to think about anything except the men who had broken in and her jumbled history with Brady. She had a million reasons to want him out of her life and one big reason to be grateful he was in it: he'd saved her. He'd come to her aid when no one else had. He was standing by her side as her world crumbled and helping her pick up the pieces. That counted for something. It did. But did it count enough for her to let him into her life in a real, permanent way?

No. The answer came swift and sure. She'd made the choice once before to allow him in and he'd hurt her. In her foolishness, she had visited him in the hospital seeking friendship. He'd tossed her out. She'd keep clear and firm boundaries with Brady. It was better for both of them.

Giving up on sleep, Susan threw back the covers and grabbed the sketch pad and pencils Brady had left on his dresser for her to use.

She began sketching without anything particular in mind. Maybe it would help her to clear her thoughts and open her memory. If Justin's killer believed she knew something important enough that she needed to die, she had the slim, fleeting hope she could bring him to justice.

Her hand paused over the paper. She'd been drawing Justin's boat on her pad.

Justin had loved his boat. If she returned to the scene, would anything from that night come back to her? Would being at the marina jog her memory? The idea of returning to the boat made her stomach queasy. But she had to do something aside from sit and wait for something else bad to happen. No one could remember for her.

Justin deserved justice and Reilly deserved to be found innocent of the ridiculous accusations that he had covered up the murder.

Susan touched her owl necklace, glad it had been saved from the fire. Since Haley had given it to her, she'd worn it constantly. On the USB drive inside the necklace were the only pictures she had left. An odd sensation skittered over Susan's nerves. Pictures. She had pictures of Justin's yacht. Could looking at them jog her memory?

Brady had left to run errands and his landlord was sitting on the porch. Eerily, he wasn't moving or pacing. He sat still, watching the road.

Susan looked for Brady's laptop and found it on the kitchen table. She powered it on, unplugged the USB from the necklace and inserted it into the computer.

A few moments later, she was paging through her pictures. A picnic she and Justin had attended earlier that year. A shot of Justin and his father, one of the few where they looked relaxed and happy. A picture of Justin on his boat. Susan held her finger over Justin's image and focused on the boat. Could she recall anything about that night?

No nagging sensation spurred a memory and no sudden recollection flooded to mind. It looked like the yacht before it had been covered in Justin's blood. Susan shivered and flipped to the next picture. Justin was sitting at the small table in the galley. Behind him were the cabinets and one of the yacht's hidden safes was open.

She and Justin had stored their passports and money inside it when they took the boat out on the water. She squinted at the picture, noticing something else inside the safe. Books? When did Justin put books inside the safe? Opening the picture in the computer's photo-editing software, she blew up the image and zoomed in on the safe.

Something was inside other than their wallets and passports. What was it? Had the police emptied the safe when they were searching the boat? Could she get a list of the boat's confiscated contents? Was she being silly, grabbing on to an irrelevant detail to have something to think about and feel as if she was helping solve his murder?

It was probably nothing, but she couldn't stop thinking about it. Could she contact the detective in charge of the case? Would he share any information with her?

Susan paced around the cabin considering her options. She needed to talk to someone who understood what she was going through, and only one person came to mind. She dialed her mother's number and regretted making the call the moment her mother answered.

"Hey, Mom," Susan said, bracing herself for the worst.

Her mother sounded tired and surprised to hear from her. "Susie, I've been worried about you."

Worried, but not concerned enough to stop by to see her. Or call. In the years since her father had died, her mother had become paralyzed by the inability to make decisions or take any action. She feared the world would scrutinize and attack her every move. "I guess you've heard I've landed in some trouble," Susan said.

Her mother made a sound of acknowledgment. "Do you think it's a good idea to talk to me? The police will twist this conversation like I helped you."

Worried about herself or worried about her daughter? "Mom, stop. The police are not dragging you into this. The charges against you for dad's murder were dropped. It was self-defense. The prosecutor even said so and apologized. It was years ago and it's over. The people who worked the case have moved on." How many times had she spoken those words to her mother over the years?

"It took them long enough to realize I was protecting myself," her mother said, bitterness heavy in her voice, which too many cigarettes had left roughened.

Her mother had spent three months in jail while the police conducted their investigation into Susan's father's death. It had forever changed her mother's life—and Susan's. "I'm not calling to involve you in my problems. I just want to talk to someone who might understand."

Her mother let out a sharp bark of rancorous laughter. "I understand all right. I understand you're being railroaded and the cops and the media won't give you a moment's peace until they have someone's head on a platter. They won't care if you're the guilty party or just someone who can take the blame. You'd be smart to disappear and put this behind you."

Suspicions and accusations based on her own experiences. Susan's heart beat faster. In the years since her mother was cleared of her father's death, Susan had fought not to let her mother's paranoia alter her thinking. "I can't run away and hide because I'll look guilty. But I can't stand how people have decided I'm guilty without evidence and before a trial. Justin's father believes I'm guilty. My neighbors think I'm guilty. Friends think I'm guilty."

"Are you?"

The question, coming from her mother's lips, hurt more than anything. "No, Mom. I didn't kill Justin." Though she couldn't be certain, she didn't believe she'd killed him.

Her mother coughed. "You have it in you. You're from the same stock as me, Susie. If he beat you, if he hurt you, you need to tell the truth about what happened."

On a soul-deep level, Susan feared her inability to remember the murder was tied to her involvement and that somehow, she had played a role in Justin's death. Shaking loose that thought, she concentrated on facts. The men who had come to Brady's were strangers. If they had killed Justin, she couldn't have been involved with them. "I didn't kill him, Mom, and I don't know how to make anyone believe me."

"People will think what they want about you. The more you claim innocence, the worse it will be. You've got to hold your head high and don't let their words tear you down."

Better advice than she had hoped for from her mother. "I'm staying with Brady."

"The Truman boy? Why? I thought he left you."

Again, Susan had underestimated the power and sharpness of her mother's words. Her mother wasn't saying anything untrue. It was more Susan's wish that her mother would have more faith in her daughter and soften life's blows with gentler words. "He wants to help me." Brady had gone to great lengths to protect her. She didn't want to misread his intentions, but he was proving to be her greatest ally.

Her mother harrumphed. "I wouldn't trust it. He has an agenda like everyone else. He'll sell you out if it will help him."

"He can't sell me out because I didn't do anything wrong." Convincing someone of Susan's guilt didn't net him anything. He had as much to gain in clearing her name and subsequently Reilly's, as she did.

Her mother laughed. "Guilt is a matter of degree. You've done something wrong. We all have. It's whether it can be twisted and used against you in court. Maybe you led the murderer to Justin. Maybe you did something to get a killer's attention. How can you be sure you're innocent?"

She had broken up with Justin. Could the police use that for motive? Had she done something that could be misconstrued as evidence against her? "Brady and I want to find Justin's killer."

Her mother was silent for a long moment. "Don't go chasing problems. You might find something that will only serve to hurt you."

Was her mother right? Was she better to lay low and wait for the police to find the killer? Or would inaction land her in the guilty seat, paying for a crime she didn't commit?

Brady stopped by Susan's house, or what remained of it, and climbed out of the car. Crime-scene tape surrounded the house, though Brady guessed it was more to prevent curious neighbors from getting too close and hurting themselves than to keep the scene pristine for an investigation. In the light of the morning, the house looked worse than it had the night before. Part of the house remained standing, but the interior was a charred mess. Though the fire was extinguished, the heavy scent of burned wood filled the air.

Brady knocked on the doors of the neighbors around Susan's house. No one had seen anything the night of the fire. No strange cars on the street, except his, no one fleeing the scene and no one lurking in the copse of trees around Susan's house.

Though she didn't have anything to help Brady figure out who had started the fire, Susan's next-door neighbor had a lot to say about Susan's personal life. "It's a shame she killed that nice man she was dating. I always thought there was something off about her."

"What do you mean?" Brady asked. He wasn't in the mood for gossip, but any thread of information might help.

The neighbor leaned in conspiratorially. "I heard her mother killed her father. Children learn what they live."

Brady hid his annoyance. Susan had told him about that dark part of her life, which up until this incident, had to be the most traumatic thing Susan had experienced. Susan and her mother had been abused by her alcoholic father for years. One day after a particularly bad and violent binge, Susan's mother had killed her husband. She'd had enough of the abuse and had fought back. She'd eventually been cleared of the charges, but not before Susan had been temporarily placed in foster care and both her and her mother scarred for life.

Susan had worked hard to separate herself from that childhood trauma and build something more for her life. "The police haven't arrested Susan in connection with any crime," Brady said.

The woman waved her hand dismissively. "It's only a matter of time."

Brady thanked her, even if her words vexed him. Susan didn't deserve to have ancient history follow her or to define the woman she'd become. Susan was a smart, well-educated, creative woman with a good heart who had gotten a raw deal. She was slow to trust and reserved at times, but that hadn't stopped Brady.

Susan's quiet nature had captivated him and the more he had learned about her, the more he'd wanted to know. Once she'd let him inside, he'd discovered a passionate and expressive woman—both in the bedroom and out. Shaking off the past, he refocused. His thoughts could linger there for hours and he wasn't here to reminisce. He was here to find some clue about what had happened and why.

He wasn't surprised her neighbors hadn't seen anything. The time of night hadn't helped visibility. He'd been looking at her house and hadn't seen anyone on the property. If Brady's theory was correct and the men trying to kill Susan were former Special Forces, they would know how to get in and out undetected and get the job done. But their methodology had been careless, both for the fire and the break-in at his cabin. Why not enter her home and kill her instead of hoping the fire would? Had the killers wanted the fire to look like an accident and changed their methods when Susan escaped and fled with him?

Who had Justin been tangled up with? Justin could still have been in contact with the guys he'd served with and they could be working their old fraud schemes. Maybe they had escalated to more dangerous games and that had led to Justin's murder. Brady had thought Justin would have been finished with illegal activities after he'd been caught and discharged from the air force, but perhaps the lure of quick money was too great. Maybe his accounting job didn't give him the excitement he craved. In any case, whoever was chasing Susan had proven to be persistent.

Was Brady capable of protecting her from mercenaries for hire with Special Forces training? He felt a twinge of pain in his knee as if it were reminding him of the injury, and frustration welled up inside him. He had been coping with a bum knee for months, coming to terms about what it meant for his career—an ending—and for his new life—nothing good.

Gone were runs in the early morning. Forget obstacle courses and physical training. Rock climbing with buddies. Hiking in the mountains. He couldn't count on his knee to hold up under any pressure. Walking long distances pained him at times. When they'd been dating, Susan had admitted she didn't like extreme sports, but she had gone rock climbing with him, tried paintball and traded in her skis for a snowboard on several occasions. Her willingness to try new things impressed him. Her camera had accompanied her and she had a knack for capturing the emotion and excitement of the moment. Her pictures were all he had left of those days.

Brady could forget about playing sports. He wasn't the man he'd once been and his deficiencies affected every aspect of his life. He'd failed in the service and he'd almost failed again last night when he'd hesitated to pull the trigger. Brady second-guessed every decision he made. He didn't trust his instincts and that self-doubt slowed him down, creating a vicious cycle of self-recrimination that put the people who'd depended on him in danger. Susan wasn't as safe with him as she once had been. That knowledge twisted in his gut.

Susan was sleeping when Brady arrived home. He used the quiet to search the internet for articles about Justin Ambrose's murder. The more information he could gather, the better chance he had at figuring out what had happened. He had compiled his notes in the folder Harris had given him, keeping a log of facts and ignoring commentary from judgmental reporters.

Susan came out of his room, appearing tired. Had she slept well in his bed? His clothes hung loosely on her frame in a way that made him think about stripping them off her body. Razor-sharp desire pierced him and he considered pulling her back into his bedroom and laying her on the bed. Making love to her and sleeping beside her would give them both the release and relaxation they needed.

Except she was heartbroken over Justin. With Justin between them, Brady needed to keep his hands and his thoughts to himself. She needed comfort and compassion, not lust and sex.

"I thought I heard you," Susan said.

"Was I making too much noise? I didn't mean to wake you." She needed the rest.

"I wasn't sleeping. I was waiting for you. I have something important to tell you." She pressed her lips together and clasped her hands.

Waiting for him? He was reading between the lines, but he heard something in her voice akin to desire. Or was it just that she wanted to talk about the night Justin had died and he was letting his imagination run away with him? "All right, go ahead." He hedged his anxiety, trying to keep the pressure on her light.

"I was looking at the pictures on my USB drive." She pointed to the necklace she wore. "I have a picture of Justin on the boat with the contents of his safe in the background. There's stuff in the safe I've never seen before."

Brady had noticed the necklace and wondered if it was a gift from Justin. She wore it constantly. He waited for further explanation. Many people with boats had on-board safes. "And?"

"Maybe it's important. I want to go to the yacht and look around. It might jog my memory. If I can get into the safe, maybe I can find out if Justin had something important inside."

Brady was willing to do whatever would help, but he wanted their decisions to be well thought out, with all the angles considered. He had to keep her out of harm's way. "The police could have confiscated the contents."

"I'll call the detective working the case and ask if they searched both safes. They already processed the scene, but only Justin and I knew the combination and no one asked me for it. There's a good chance whatever is in the safe is still there."

The police had Susan in their sights as the top suspect. If the safe contained a lead, could they trust the detective to follow up on it or would he bury it? "We should see what's in it first before we involve the police. If it will help your case, we'll call the detective and tell him about it."

"This could help," Susan said.

The rising excitement on her face and in her voice was the most promising sign he'd seen in her. He hated to put a damper on it. "We could get in trouble for being on Justin's boat. It's a crime scene and we don't have clearance," Brady said.

"It's not a crime scene anymore. The police have done their work and cleaned up. I had a key before my house burned. Justin gave me an open invitation to use his boat."

What if someone at the marina recognized them and called the police? What if returning to the scene brought a fresh wave of police attention and charges down on Susan? "Who is in charge of Justin's estate?" Brady asked.

"His father, I'm guessing," Susan said.

Brady hid his revulsion. A confrontation with Lieutenant General Tim Ambrose was the last thing that would help them. "What are the chances he'll be on the yacht?" Brady asked.

"Unlikely. Justin has the marina slip through the end of the year at least. His father has his own boat docked elsewhere. He doesn't have a reason to be on Justin's boat."

"If you're caught, that won't help your defense," Brady said. "You don't have the legal right to break into Justin's boat and it will look like you returned to the scene to either hide something or plant evidence. Give me the combination and let me go alone." He could handle the task without putting Susan in any unnecessary risk.

"I want to help. You've done enough for me. The key Justin gave me was lost in the fire, so it's not breaking in, I just don't have access to it at the moment. The police have it out for me and I won't take any chances. I'll wait until it's dark, sneak onto the boat, look around and get out without anyone seeing me. With any luck, I'll remember something important," Susan said.

If visiting the boat jogged her memory, they had everything to gain. But what if it caused more trauma? She would go to the yacht regardless of what was safe. All he could do was try to protect her. "I won't let you do this unless you bring me with you. If you say 'no,' I'll find a way to stop you from going alone," Brady said.

"I'm not asking you to help me."

"Understood. We'll look around and if we can't find anything, we hightail it out and won't go back."

Susan nodded. "Agreed. I need to call my boss and tell him I can't make it into work tonight. I need the money, but I need to get onto that boat more."

Brady gestured to the phone on the wall. "Feel free."

Susan dialed a number on the phone and Brady stepped away to give her privacy.

Susan dialed her boss at the art gallery. To this point, he'd been understanding about Justin and the situation. She'd worked at the gallery for almost a decade and this incident was the first where she'd missed some of her shifts.

After he came to the phone, Susan made her request brief. "I need off tonight. Something important came up. I can switch shifts with someone if you want."

A pregnant pause from Pete. "Listen, Susan, I hate to do this, and I most especially hate to do this over the phone, but it might be a better idea if you didn't come in at all."

Tension coiled in her stomach. "What do you mean 'at all'?"

Pete sighed. "I mean our customers are getting nervous with you around. I'm losing sales. I think it's better for us to part ways."

Her stomach dropped. Pete was firing her? "I've worked for you for ten years."

Pete sighed. "I know. I'll arrange your severance package and—"

"No! I don't want a severance package. I want you to believe I'm innocent. Everyone thinks I've done something horrible. You know me. You know I wouldn't kill someone."

"I think it's better for business—"

Anger welled up inside her and her throat tightened. Susan didn't make any effort to suppress it. What Pete was doing was wrong and she wouldn't make it easier for him by playing nice.

"You think it's better for yourself. I've been loyal and I haven't done anything wrong. I don't deserve this." She slammed down the phone, knowing she would break into tears if she stayed on the phone another moment.

Brady was watching her from the couch. He'd heard her conversation. In the small cabin, it would have been impossible to miss. "I'm sorry, Susan."

"I was fired," she said, hating the catch in her voice.

"I heard."

She took a few steps toward Brady and he stood and closed the distance between them. He slipped his arms around her shoulders, bringing her against him, and she let her arms go around his waist. The tightness of his stomach pressed into her breasts and the strength of his arms anchored her. Her life had been blown apart and whenever she thought she'd lost everything that mattered, something else dropped out from under her.

Except Brady. She'd thought he had been lost to her months before and now, here he was, with his arms around her, being the one rock-steady person in her life. Impulsively, she slid her hands under his shirt and pressed her hands into the firm muscles of his back.

He tensed as if unsure how to respond. She'd once loved the easiness of touching him. Brady was uninhibited and in many ways her opposite when it came to sexual relationships. His openness with her, the way he made sex both intimate and fun, had drawn out a side of her she hadn't known existed. She missed that.

Susan brought her hands around his waist and to his stomach, walking her fingers to his chest. She lifted the fabric of his shirt and brought her lips against his hot skin. He didn't ask what she was doing. He knew.

She knew what he liked. How he liked to be touched, kissed and caressed.

He responded to her, heat crackling between them. She lifted her face, offering her lips, and he captured them in a long, slow, sultry kiss. Their ugly past and current problems were momentarily blotted out. Why had they broken up when they were this good together? It was a question she had long held that he'd never answered or explained.

His mouth was expertly skilled, his hands the perfect amount of softness and roughness against her body. In these few moments, she felt the most together she had in weeks. Maybe months. It wouldn't hurt to forget her problems for an hour and see where this led.

Brady broke the kiss, taking a step away from her. His body was rigid, his shoulders stiffening. "I'm sorry."

An apology? They were the last words she'd expected and they frustrated her. She had started the kiss. Why had he ended it?

"I'm not."

"This isn't what you're looking for. I'm not what you need. Not in this way, not now."

Who was he to tell her what she needed? "At this moment, I'm looking for someone to make me feel good for a few minutes. Or, since it's you, I figure it might last a few hours. I want an escape from this." She gestured at her herself and her surroundings. "I'm not asking for a commitment. I'm not even asking you to explain anything about the past or work through our problems. I want a distraction." A hot, delicious distraction.

Brady opened his mouth to respond and then closed it. "You're grieving. You're hurting. I want to help. But this won't make you feel better. You'll be angry at yourself and at me later."

He was rejecting her? Humiliation and anger welled up inside her. "Fine, Brady. That's fine. But do me a favor and stop telling me what I need. I think I'm in a better position to decide that than you are. You should worry about what you need and figuring out your life. Because looking around, I think you've got some demons to chase away, too."

Brady's eyes flashed with anger. "What demons do I have, Susan? That I lost my job? That I don't have anything worthwhile to contribute to anymore? Correct me if I'm wrong, but you just lost your job, too. How do you feel?"

"I feel like I'll get through this and I'll find another job." Somehow. Some way. "And it's ridiculous to say you don't have anything to contribute. You have lots to contribute. You're helping me. You're protecting me. If I stop thinking positive, where does that leave me? Homeless, jobless and alone. Forget that. I don't accept that as my life."

Brady gestured to his knee. "I don't have the option of thinking positive and pretending everything will be okay. This will prevent me from taking care of you the best way I know how. This ruined my career. This—" He stopped and took a deep breath. "This may be the reason I'm not good enough to keep us from getting killed."

Chapter 4

Tension stretched between Brady and Susan on the drive to the marina. They hadn't spoken much since their argument earlier in the day.

Brady was the first to break the silence. "Do you remember what the weather was like the night Justin died?" Colorado winters could fluctuate from bitter cold with biting wind to surprisingly warm.

Susan steered her thoughts away from her fight with Brady. She was going to Justin's yacht to remember, and getting on that track was important. "It was warmer than usual, but breezy. I had taken off my sweater in the car after I left the gallery."

"Did you drive directly from the gallery to the yacht or did you make any stops?"

Brady wanted to walk her through that night. She'd been over it many times. She went along with his questions, hoping one would jar a memory loose or Brady could help her look at the night from another angle. "I stopped to pick up take-out Chinese food. I was hungry and Justin didn't always keep the boat stocked."

Ten minutes later, with Brady pressing her for every detail, Susan let her head fall against the headrest. "I remember a lot from earlier in the night. I had the receipt from the takeout restaurant in my handbag. The police took it as evidence. I imagine they found the cardboard containers and plasticware in the trash. Those memories are clear. And then, everything just stops."

"You can do this, Susan. Those memories are in your head. You can let them out."

Simple in theory, but proving impossible in application. "I'm trying, Brady. I really am. I've told you I'm trying to remember. We've been over this before." What if her memories returned from that night and she realized she'd done something awful to Justin? What other reason did she have to block them?

Brady was persistent. "Let's look at this from another perspective. Did Justin have enemies? Enemies vicious enough to kill him, frame you and then try to murder you?"

Susan swallowed hard. She had gone over and over Justin's life looking for elements out of place, anything that would have tipped her off to Justin being involved in something criminal. "Do you want me to admit the truth? That I might not have known Justin as well as I thought I did? He never mentioned his troubles in the military to me, so what else did he keep from me?" Brady's revelation about Justin's life in the air force had shaken her confidence in how well she'd known

Justin. She might not have been head-over-heels in love with him, but she'd trusted him.

Brady nodded once, as if satisfied by her admission. "Harris said you were tested for drugs after the murder."

Susan nodded. "Yes. The ME took my blood and urine to check for drugs and alcohol."

"What did they find?" Brady asked.

Disappointing results. "According to my court-appointed lawyer, nothing of note. I'd had a glass of wine that night, but it barely registered in my bloodstream."

Brady's lips twisted in thought. "Tell me more about Justin."

"You knew him. He was Justin. He was safe. Calm. Rational. He didn't get excited about things." Things. Or her. She and Justin had never gotten to that can't-live-without-you, obsessive, overly heated phase in their relationship. They'd never left a party early because they couldn't wait to be alone. They'd never spent an entire day in bed together, blowing off responsibilities because they were too involved with each other to care about anything else.

Nope, those experiences were exclusive to her relationship with Brady. She'd waited for them to happen with Justin and they never had. Susan had rationalized that she and Justin were different. They had been in a more mature place. Their relationship had staying power.

After a while, it had started to feel as if something was missing. As if they were both settling because they were a good match on paper.

"We were having problems," she said. Guilt gushed

through her. Should she talk about the negative parts of her relationship with Justin? It didn't feel right.

A long pause. Why had she said anything about her and Justin? Brady hadn't asked about their relationship. He had asked about Justin. If anything, her and Justin's fighting and problems gave her motivation to kill Justin. Her mother's words haunted her. The police could spin their issues into something sinister and claim she and Justin had had an argument that had turned violent. Like the circumstances between her mother and father. The parallels between the two stories were disturbing.

"What kind of problems?" Brady asked.

Her insides clenched. She would have rather talked about the problems in Justin's life, if she'd known what they were. If she had been a better friend to Justin, would he have confided in her if he'd been worried about something or someone? "We were arguing a lot. We weren't spending time together as often." When they had been together, they'd fought, sometimes about pointless things. "He wanted me to set a date for the wedding and I wasn't sure when I wanted to get married."

"You've always wanted to be married," Brady said, his voice carefully neutral.

Yes. She had wanted to get married. To Brady. When they were dating, she hadn't pretended otherwise. But life wasn't a game of musical bachelors. If one man didn't fit, she couldn't plug in another man and have the same desires and hopes for the future. It was a lesson she'd had to learn. A hard lesson.

"To the right man. Not just to anyone."

She could almost hear Brady grinding his teeth.

What had him on edge? Talking about Justin? A former lover's pointless jealousy? Was he remembering the time they'd fought about their future together? Susan had brought up the topic of marriage with Brady and he'd seemed distant. The more distant he'd become, the more marrying him had played on her mind. She'd mentioned it more often. Had that driven him away?

"Is that why you left? Did it bother you that I wanted you to propose?" No point in being coy about it. She'd made her intentions clear then; why not address it now?

Brady glanced at her before answering. "It bothered me, but it wasn't why I left. I knew as long as I was a parajumper, I couldn't be married."

"I would have waited," Susan said, the words springing to her lips before she could stop them. They left her vulnerable to another rejection.

"I'm sure you would have. That doesn't explain why you made Justin wait," Brady said, turning the conversation on a dime.

"I wasn't sure I wanted to marry him," Susan said.

"Then why did you say yes when he asked?"

Susan swallowed the knee-jerk reaction to defend herself and worked to keep her voice calm. "Justin provided stability. He wanted to have children. He had a house and a good job. He got busy around tax time, but for the most part, he came home for dinner." A checklist. He'd satisfied a checklist she had created.

"Sounds like everything you want." No sarcasm, only a touch of pity.

"It takes more than a list of qualities to make a relationship work." Again, a lesson she had learned the hard way. Her relationship with Brady had had some indefinable quality to it; the chemistry and the connection had been strong. She hadn't had those things with Justin.

Brady glanced at her and she read sympathy in his eyes. Or was it sadness for her? How did he feel about her dating someone else? She was sure he had dated other women since they'd broken up. How could a man like him not find willing, attractive women circling?

"Reilly told me when you got engaged," Brady said. "I was overseas at the time."

That news surprised her. When Brady had walked out on her, she'd assumed he'd want no part of her and his family would have sensed and respected that.

"Why would he tell you?"

Brady rolled his shoulders. "He knew I cared about you and would want to know. I thought about sending flowers to congratulate you, but decided it would send a mixed message."

Her heart beat stronger, faster. He'd known. Known and done nothing. Wasn't that a clear sign he was finished with their relationship?

"And what mixed message was that?"

"That congratulations was mixed with a desire to be part of your life again."

A few words could annihilate her. Was she that sensitive to him after so much time had passed? "Isn't that what you're doing now?" He'd rapidly become the leading man—the only man—in her life.

"No." The word was said with finality and a heavy thud.

Frustration and resentment leaked from every pore. Brady was like this, closed off, unavailable, and yet she'd started thinking he'd changed. A smidgen.

She didn't trust herself to speak without letting her

voice break. Susan grabbed the radio dial and turned it on. She changed from his preprogrammed station to a country music station.

She didn't want to talk anymore. If one more word passed her lips, the facade she'd built would crack and she would break down into tears.

Brady wanted Susan to move on with her life and have the things he couldn't give her. A home. A family. A husband who was with her day in and day out and who was worthy of a woman like her.

A few months after they'd ended their relationship, Reilly had told him Susan had moved on with Justin. Brady's reaction had been a cluster of emotions: happy she'd have the life she wanted, angry she'd found someone so quickly and sad that their relationship was over. For good. He'd suspected Justin had been interested in Susan for a long time. When Brady and Susan had been dating, Justin had flirted with her and paid extra attention to her. He hadn't waited long after Brady was gone before swooping in.

Brady had been the one to walk away from Susan, but she'd been the first to move on with her life.

Knowing her relationship with the man who'd taken his place wasn't as ideal as he'd believed wasn't any solace. Justin had brought Susan into this nightmare, the legal problems and danger.

What reason did someone have to kill an accountant? Perhaps Justin had been involved in tax fraud or was cooking the books for a criminal element. His lack of scruples while in the military suggested he'd be willing to break the law when it suited him. Could he have been involved with drugs?

"Was Justin a heavy drinker?" Brady asked.

Susan brought her hand to her mouth in thought and his attention was dragged to her lips. A mouth he had kissed before, a mouth that could deliver passion, heat and pleasure.

She let out a serrated breath. "He didn't drink often." Her voice sounded smaller, quieter than it had been a moment before.

She licked her lower lip and Brady marshaled his body's rising response and focused on the road ahead of him. "Was he using any other substances?"

"No. For crying out loud, Brady, do you think I would agree to marry someone with a drug problem? After what my parents went through?"

It wasn't a slight against her. Plenty of unsuspecting people became involved with someone and found out too late they were hiding a drug or alcohol problem.

"Just covering the bases, looking for possible reasons why someone would kill Justin. Did he carry a large amount of money with him? Wear an expensive watch?"

She folded her arms over her chest. "You know who his father is. His family has plenty of money and Justin had nice things. Justin had a small amount of cash on the boat that was untouched. None of the electronics were missing and I don't think he kept much of resalable value in his onboard safes. The only item that's missing is my camera, but I don't know if I lost it that night or it was taken."

Did Susan have an incriminating picture in her camera, a shot someone wanted to keep hidden? Brady hated upsetting and pressuring her for answers, but he wanted to get to the bottom of this. Brady's impatience was getting the best of him. He'd hoped to reignite her memories by walking through that night. When she'd gotten frustrated with his questions, he'd presented other theories, trying to find out if others could have been involved or if Susan had seen evidence of Justin's dark side.

Justin had one. He hid it well. But Brady's experiences with him in the military had told him something important about the man: he was willing to lie to get what he wanted and he had no qualms about wriggling out of responsibility for his actions. Justin hadn't been the ringleader of the air force kickback scheme and Brady figured Justin had matured and changed since then. A near miss with dire consequences should have changed Justin for the better. Brady was sorry to learn he'd been wrong. Susan was taking the brunt of whatever Justin had done or whomever he had pissed off.

Brady, on the other hand, was aware of his infractions, took responsibility for them, and felt bad for them. Breaking Susan's heart had been wrong, even if he'd thought he was doing it for the right reasons. He had loved her and his decisions had cost her trust. He didn't think he'd get a chance to win her back and if he was honest with himself, he didn't deserve one.

The upscale marina in Cherry Creek State Park was like a country club, with restaurants and weekend functions making it one of the best places to dock a boat in Denver that included a social life. Susan wore a baseball cap to cover her hair, but skipped the sunglasses, thinking they would attract attention at nighttime. Attention they were trying to avoid.

The sky was cloudy and a light rain was falling.

Anxiety thrummed in her veins. Brady, on the other hand, appeared unconcerned, his posture relaxed, as if he had all the time in the world to go anywhere and do anything. Despite his outward appearance, he was on high alert. He wasn't taking this lightly.

Brady slung his arm over her shoulder and lowered his mouth close to her ear. "Relax. You look ready to jump out of your skin. We need to blend."

Touching her set her more on edge. The electric press of his skin against hers excited her.

"I am as calm as I can be under the circumstances." She didn't have Brady's experience in covert operations. This was her first and she had much at stake. If she got onto the boat and couldn't remember anything, what could she do next? Where could she turn?

Brady's thumb rubbed her shoulder and she shrugged off his arm. That was enough touching. If he wanted her to focus and be calm, touching wasn't a good idea. It unhinged her, and until she was apathetic toward him, it was better he not. "Please keep your hands to yourself."

Brady remained close at her side. "We're pretending to be a couple."

She narrowed her eyes at him. "You said earlier that kissing wasn't a good idea."

"I'm not kissing you. I had my arm around you."

Like the contact was any less smoldering. "Is it different Brady? Really, is it?" Both made her feel like going up in flames.

"One involves my mouth and the other my arm. It's different."

Not to her. His ability to build barriers and shut her out was amazing. She wasn't to the point of believing he felt nothing when he was close to her, though he was better at ignoring it and controlling his reaction. They might not trust each other and they might have scores of problems between them, but the memories of their lust-fuelled relationship burned between them. "Just keep your hands—and your mouth—to yourself so I can concentrate on why we're here," Susan said.

"Lead the way," Brady said, sliding his hands into his pockets.

"His slip is on the third pier," Susan said, straightening her shoulders and taking a deep breath.

She lowered her head to the ground as two men walked by, talking loudly with beers in their hands. Susan didn't know them, but she wasn't taking chances of being recognized. Justin's murder had no doubt been the talk of the gossip mill at the marina.

When they arrived at the third pier, they stepped onto the dock, walking plank by plank. Susan's fear ratcheted up another few notches. Was Justin's body floating somewhere nearby? The police believed it would be found in the area. They had sent dive teams to search the water. His body might have been dumped in the surrounding park, where it would be waiting for a hiker to find. Morbid thoughts that haunted her. Justin deserved to be laid to rest and his family deserved closure.

Susan folded her arms over her chest, trying to focus on the task at hand. She wanted the truth, to bring Justin's killer to justice and to clear her name. "Brady, wait a minute." Spinning on her heel, he stopped short, but his body was inches from hers. He didn't step away and she held her ground on principle.

"Are you sure you want to do this?" she asked. If

he was arrested because of her, if he got into trouble because of her plan, she wouldn't forgive herself.

She could smell him, the light, soapy scent of his clothes and the masculine scent of his aftershave.

"I'm certain. We've come this far. Don't lose your courage now."

Courage was a big deal to Brady. He associated it with acting with honor. "I'm not 'losing my courage.' I don't want to drag you into my mess. Look what happened to the last two men who were around me. Reilly is in trouble. Justin is dead."

"Thanks for your concern, but I'll be fine," Brady said, sarcasm lacing his voice. He took her elbow and they continued.

When they reached Justin's boat, Brady stilled.

Her heart was pounding so hard, she felt dizzy. "What's the matter?" she asked, looking around, certain they'd been caught.

"He named his boat after you."

Susan frowned. *Sketchy Lady,* Justin's nod to her, and a name he'd found amusing. She was an artist and she liked to draw, take photographs and sketch.

"He thought it was funny."

"What do you think?" he asked.

Susan sighed. Justin had bought the boat before they'd been engaged. He'd said buying it was the fulfillment of a dream he'd had since he was a child.

"I think he was poking fun at my work and my art." It had seemed like a laugh at her expense, but Susan hadn't said anything, thinking she was being oversensitive.

Brady looked at her, his eyes traveling down her

body. His gaze raked over her, leaving her skin pricking with heat.

"What?" Susan asked, brushing at the drops of rain on her face.

"I'm questioning for the hundredth time what you saw in him."

She'd tried to make it work with someone who was wrong for her. Lots of people did it, hence the high divorce rate.

"You knew him. He was smart and focused and career-driven." Safe and unadventurous, Justin was the complete opposite of Brady. When she'd started dating Justin, she hadn't seen his stability and practicality as a problem. He could sometimes be obtuse about her feelings and it was something she'd hoped would change as they grew closer.

"I did know him. That's why I'm surprised you went for it," Brady said.

"Went for what? Dating him?"

Brady snorted. "He had his eye on you from the moment he met you. That you were mine only made you more appealing."

Annoyance tweaked her thoughts. "You're saying he was interested in me because I was dating you? Doesn't that seem a bit egotistical on your part?"

Brady folded his arms over his chest. "No. It's the truth. Justin was always in competition with someone. The moment he met you, he wanted you. He was waiting for me to be gone to pounce."

"That's not true. He was being a friend to me because he knew I was hurt when you left." Hurt and confused.

Brady tipped his head to the side as if to say, *Do you really believe that?*

"I know you two didn't get along. He was still a good person," Susan said.

She turned away from Brady, cutting off further conversation on the matter. They needed to hurry. Walking to the boat in silence, they boarded. Susan took a deep breath and tried to slow her racing heart. The last time she had been on this boat, she had woken up alone in the living room with blood on her hands. She had been confused and sick to her stomach and had called the police. Shoving aside those memories, she focused on what happened before waking up on the boat. What had occurred that had led to Justin's death?

Fear tightened in her stomach and her thoughts skidded to a stop. "What if I remember that I killed him?"

Brady shook his head. "You didn't kill him. It doesn't make sense. You haven't done anything wrong."

Her mother's words replayed through her mind. Susan had done something wrong, but was it enough for the police to twist it into murder? No one was blameless. "But if I remember something incriminating—"

"If you do—and I have no problems saying this because you won't—then we'll deal with it. We'll tell the police what happened and we'll get clear on why someone wants to hurt you. At least it will be out in the open and we can deal with facts, not missing information and guesswork," Brady said.

Thunder rumbled in the distance and the rain fell harder, plopping against the hull of the boat.

"Give me a couple of minutes to get this door open," Brady said.

Susan turned her back to him and watched the dock

while Brady picked the lock on the door. His Special Forces skills were useful time and again. She got a thrill at his physical prowess. He was quick and agile, smart and shrewd. His strength was only second to his honor. He would never become a man who beat a woman. He would never turn into her abusive father. Knowing that with every ounce of her being had made falling for him and giving him her trust easier. What did she feel about Brady now? He wasn't her boyfriend or her lover. He was acting as an ally, but his loyalties were first to his brother. If Reilly hadn't been involved, Susan felt sure Brady wouldn't be either.

Susan squinted into the dark, the light of nearby boats casting shadows. Some of the boats were dry-docked. Those would be vacant. Were she and Brady alone? Was someone watching them? Or was it her paranoia? Goose bumps rose on her arms.

"Okay, it's open," Brady muttered.

Susan turned away from the dock. Brady stepped inside the main cabin and shined his flashlight around the small space. "Nice place."

Susan followed him inside with dread heavy on her chest. Lights from the dock glared through the curtained windows. They couldn't risk turning on lights and drawing attention.

Susan waited near the door, watching the pier for movement. Water lapped against the boat, rocking it slowly.

"Tell me what you did when you first stepped onto the boat," Brady said.

Susan looked around. This was where she had woken. In this room. She suppressed her nerves and focused. "Justin and I talked about work. About life.

We ate. We opened a bottle of wine. We talked." The maroon upholstered couch faced the wet bar, the grey carpet in between. The television mounted against the wall. That morning, blood had been spattered on the screen. She shivered.

"What did you talk about? Be more specific," Brady said.

Susan closed her eyes and inhaled. The boat smelled differently, like cleaning products and heavy pine air freshener. The crime scene cleanup team had done their job.

Justin had begged her to meet him. She'd broken their engagement the night before he'd died. Guilt twisted hard at her chest. Susan hadn't told the police that. More questions would have come and it would have been difficult to explain why she had broken up with him. It could be twisted into a motive for murder.

Ending their relationship had been the only option for her. She wasn't happy and had felt their relationship had been rushed, but not in a finger-snap, instant attraction way. Nothing like the day she'd met Brady. Had seeing Brady in the hospital affected her decision? He'd crossed her mind over the months with a mix of hurt, anger and longing. She had never dealt fully with those emotions and she wondered if they had dealt with her, encouraging her to end her relationship with Justin and find peace about the past.

How could she be in a relationship with one man while she harbored unresolved feelings for another?

She wasn't on the boat to think about Brady. Justin needed her. He didn't have anyone else who could speak about what had happened. What had she and Justin talked about? The conversation had been stilted and

Justin had been angry with her. Scorn had underlined every word and he'd taken verbal jabs at her. She'd felt she'd deserved them for breaking up with him. He had been hurt and angry.

"We talked about what we did at work. Annoying stories about coworkers." Not a lie. Not the whole truth either. Could she confide the whole truth to Brady? In the past, she hadn't hesitated to tell him her most private thoughts and secrets.

Thinking about Justin sent sadness crashing down on her, dragging her further into her morose thoughts. How had everything turned so terrible in such a short time?

"Did he say anything about work that could help? Did he have an argument with a coworker or a disagreement with his boss?" Brady asked.

Justin hadn't mentioned a specific argument with a coworker. Justin frequently had disagreements with coworkers. If he'd had another, it would have been an ordinary event. Susan had gotten the sense that it annoyed his coworkers that he behaved with an air of entitlement because his father was a lieutenant general in the air force and he felt it brought prestige to the firm. "Minor arguments. What could an accountant do that would anger someone enough to kill him?"

"He works with money. Other people's money. Money is a motive for murder."

Susan had thought about that. The economy was volatile. People were in desperate straits. But Justin was a corporate accountant. From what he'd said about his job, he analyzed ledgers, prepared reports and looked for cost-saving measures. "Justin never talked about problems with any clients."

"Doesn't mean he didn't have them," Brady said.

Susan couldn't talk to Justin's boss or his coworkers. Like the police, they were holding her responsible for the murder. She'd have no pull with anyone in Justin's office.

"Did you feel sick at any point? Did you lie down and fall asleep?" Brady asked.

She had been tired, but she hadn't taken a nap and she hadn't planned to spend the night on the boat. "The last thing I remember is talking with Justin at dinner. I woke up and my face felt sticky. I looked at my hands and they were covered in blood." She had called out for Justin. She had looked around the boat. She had found her cell phone in her handbag on top of the bar and dialed 911.

"How did you feel when you woke up?" he asked.

"I had a headache and I was nauseated. I was scared and confused."

She looked around the room again, willing her brain to recall some important slice of information. Rain was splattering hard against the boat's roof. She wished it were quiet so she could think. Letting out a cry of frustration, Susan paced. "This isn't working."

"Try not to get upset. It won't make it easier," Brady said, his voice low and soothing. "Try to let the memories flow."

Susan didn't want to sit or touch anything in the room. It was clean, but in her mind, everything was covered in blood.

"Did Justin have a gun?" Brady said.

Susan shook her head. "I don't think he had a gun. I'll check the safes." She wondered about the books she had seen in the picture she'd taken. Would they be in either of the safes?

Susan led the way to the bedroom. The bedroom safe was open and empty. Susan moved to the galley, removing the front of a cabinet and setting it on the floor. She reached into the cabinet and slid the false backing to the right, revealing the safe. Crouching in the cabinet, she opened the safe's combination lock. To her surprise, the safe was filled. "Looks like they only found the one safe." Had they searched the boat if they hadn't looked in the galley cabinets? Or was searching the boat not important? How much forensic work and gathering of evidence had been done?

Dread curled in her stomach. The detective assigned to Justin's homicide was sure she was responsible for Justin's death. Had the police done enough investigative work or considered other suspects? Was she the easiest target for a busy detective's caseload? Or had the real killer framed her for the murder, wrapping up the case for the police in a neat package?

Inside the galley safe were bills in small denominations, paperwork on the boat, several keys on a canary keychain, copies of Justin's driver's license and passport, and three notebooks. She took the notebooks from the safe and opened the top one.

"Are those the books you saw in the picture? What are they?" Brady asked.

They looked like Justin's accounting ledgers, lists of bills and expenses, some for the boat, some for his house. In the back of one of the books was a notecard with names and passwords. "His accounting sheets for his bills and some logins and passwords." Nothing mind-blowing. Disappointment assailed her. She had been clinging to the hope they would find something more inside them. Some indication why anyone would want to murder Justin and something that would clear her name or jog her memory about that night. The thought was silly, of course. Justin hadn't prepared a list of suspects for her to find in the event of his death.

Brady knelt next to her. In the cramped quarters of the galley, Susan had nowhere to move to get away from him. Brady crowded her, as if sticking close on purpose and trying to provoke a response from her. Her body betrayed her, desire plucking at her body and she fought the urge to lean into him for support.

If she needed emotional support, Brady wasn't the right person to turn to. She'd better burn that into her memory. The moment she let herself rely on him, he'd back away. He'd done it when he'd broken up with her and he'd done it after the kiss they'd shared in his cabin.

Brady took the second notebook from her. He paused midway through, paged back and then forward again. "What are these?" he asked, pointing the beam of his flashlight onto two columns, one with the date and one with an amount of money.

The ledger showed over two dozen payments, starting in smaller amounts and rising to larger sums over a period of eighteen months. Brady pointed to the last date in the ledger. "If these are payments, one week before he died, he made another in the amount of eighty thousand dollars."

That couldn't be right. Justin was well off, but he didn't have tens of thousands of dollars to spare. "Maybe they aren't payments he made. Maybe they're money owed for accounting services. Or maybe he's tracking estimated taxes for a client."

"In a ledger he kept on his private boat?" Brady asked.

It did sound strange. Susan flipped to another page of the notebook, looking for an explanation, and found none. "Justin didn't have this kind of money. He made a good salary as an accountant and he had some family money, but he didn't rake in enough to dole it out by the thousands. He wouldn't have given away this money and I don't know where he could have gotten money like this."

Brady took out his phone and snapped a picture of the pages listing the dates and dollar amounts. "What's in the other notebook?"

The other notebook proved as ambiguous. Some names, or nicknames, along with dates and payments. Brady snapped more pictures of the pages.

"Did he say anything to you about these?" Brady asked.

She would have questioned it if he had. "He never mentioned huge sums of money being paid out or in, but if those are Justin's billable hours, I can see him keeping close track of them." Justin had been meticulous and detail-oriented. It was part of why he had been a successful accountant, despite his personality conflicts with his coworkers.

A creak sounded and Susan jumped, clutching Brady's arm. Brady turned off the flashlight and pushed her behind him.

Was someone on the boat with them? The boat swayed in the water and the rain had let up, the pounding on the roof noticeably lightening. Susan peered around Brady's shoulder, trying to see into the dark. She released his arm, realizing her nails had been digging into his coat. Silence. Had the noise been the boat rocking in the water?

Brady's hand brushed hers, stroking silently in a calming gesture. She got the message without needing the words. She needed to stay quiet. The second, more reassuring part of the message: Brady would keep her safe.

Chapter 5

Another sound echoed through cabin. The wind? The slight shifting of something on the boat?

The next sound was clearer. The crackling, flicking, unmistakable sound of fire. Brady pulled her to her feet and they stopped at the entryway to the galley. Smoke, thick and acrid, filled her nostrils. Justin's boat was on fire!

Blood roared in Susan's ears. How could she stop the fire? Justin had a fire extinguisher, but Susan wasn't certain she could find it in the dark. They needed to get off the boat and warn everyone along the pier to get to safety. How quickly could a fire spread from boat to boat?

"Susan, come on!" Brady's voice broke into her thoughts. How long had she been standing, staring, paralyzed by the sight of the fire?

Brady dragged her out of the room. Dodging the

flames, Susan and Brady raced onto the main deck. The fire was spreading, cracking and hissing into the night air. They couldn't reach the pier, flames blocking their way. Were those people on the pier? The people who had started the fire? In the dark and with the flames from the fire dancing around them, it was difficult for her to focus her eyes.

The next boat was too far away to jump.

"Get in the water!" Brady shouted.

The water? It was cold and dark. They couldn't see where they were swimming. What was in the water? How deep was it? Was it safe to jump? The thunder rolled in the distance.

A loud pop sounded and Brady's hands were on her waist, throwing her over the side of the boat. The water was shockingly cold and stung her hands and face on impact. Susan struggled to pull off her shoes and peel off her jacket, the weight threatening to keep her under. She'd been on her high school's swim team, but this was different from swimming in a pool. The depth. The cold. The dark.

She heard the sound of bubbles in the water next to her and then Brady's arms were around her. The water was horribly, numbingly cold compared to his body. Which way was the surface? Disoriented, Susan kicked her legs, trying to move in a direction. Her lungs burned and strained.

Brady's arm tightened around her, pulling her. Her face broke the surface and found air. She gasped for breath and heaved a moment later, water spilling from her stomach. She coughed and sputtered, not realizing she'd been gulping water.

"Stop kicking me, Susan," Brady said, stress tight in his voice. His head bobbed below the surface.

Susan grabbed him, drawing his head above the water. "What's the matter?" He didn't answer, his eyes closed, pain written in tension across his face.

She treaded water for both of them. "Brady, what's wrong? Did you hit your head? Are you hurt?" He was floating, but his legs weren't propelling him through the water.

"Someone is shooting at us. My arm was grazed," Brady said.

His blood wouldn't clot in the water. They needed to get to land. If he lost too much blood and passed out, she could swim with him, but dragging him over the sea wall to land would be difficult. If she cried out for help, it might alert the person who had started the fire and shot at them. Susan wrapped her arm around Brady, paddling with her free arm away from the pier and other boats and toward land. She wouldn't let him drown.

The cold was paralyzing and fear slashed through her. Waves splashed over her face, causing her to swallow and choke on water. They needed to reach the shore and get dry fast or hypothermia would set in. "Don't pass out. Stay with me," Susan said, her muscles burning with strain.

"It's okay. Let me swim." He ducked under her arm and kicked with his good leg and one of his arms, each movement precise and strong.

"We can do this," Susan said, holding back a scream when something brushed her leg. *Please don't let it be a water moccasin or a dead body.* She commanded herself to calm down. Kelp. It was kelp.

She focused her energy on swimming, as together they fought to shore, crawling up on the large rocks beneath the dock. Susan slipped, the uneven surface slick with algae. Her knee slammed into the stone and she winced, trying to climb in the dark. Brady's firm hand guided her shivering body.

"We're okay. We're almost out," Brady said. His words reassured her. They'd be okay. If they could get out of the cold, dark water.

If a bullet had grazed Brady, how badly was he bleeding? What about his knee? Her medical knowledge was next to nil. Could she care for him or should she get him to a hospital? What if he got an infection or needed stitches?

Male voices drifted from the dock above them. "Where did they go?"

"Fools jumped in the water."

Brady's hand reached to her calf, squeezing. She stilled, hoping the waves crashing against the rocks and the thunder rumbling in the distance hid the noise she and Brady were making. Their panting was loud, her heartbeat banging like a drum.

"They've got to come up for air. We'll get them when they do."

"Maybe they drowned."

The men were talking about her and Brady. Were they the men who'd set the fire? How many were looking for her and Brady?

"Did you need to torch the whole damn thing?"

"She went on that boat to get something. I had to get rid of her and whatever she was after. We don't know how much Justin told her."

What did they think Justin had told her?

"She knows something. She's been lying from the beginning. Do you think she killed him?"

"I don't know and I don't care. I'm not paid to ask questions. You'd better learn the same."

"I think she killed him," the man said.

Disbelief sliced through her. They believed she'd killed Justin. Since the fire at her home and the attack at Brady's, she'd assumed the same men were responsible for Justin's death and were using her as a scapegoat. But if they hadn't killed him, was she to blame? Her doubts and fears renewed in force. Why would she have killed Justin? She hadn't been angry with him and she stood to gain nothing.

Susan strained to hear more of the conversation above them. Feet pounded on the pier and shouts of concern drifted to them. Justin's boat was most of the way down the pier, a good sixty feet away.

"We should have killed her before we set fire to her place."

Terror surged inside her. How many people were involved in trying to kill her? At least two men had attacked her at Brady's and two more were on the pier having set fire to the yacht.

"We didn't have the order at that point to outright kill her. It had to look like an accident."

Order? Who had assigned them the task of killing her?

"She's out there."

"She's got more lives than a flaming cat and now she's got someone protecting her. He and his bat-crap crazy friend took out two of us. This is getting out of hand and we need to shut her up by whatever means necessary. We can't have her blabbing about what she knows."

"What is she waiting for? Why didn't she go to the police right away?"

"Maybe she doesn't have proof yet and we're not waiting until she finds some. She's got a loaded gun and we're not waiting for her to decide to pull the trigger and destroy us."

Susan pressed her mouth together to keep her teeth from chattering. They were responsible for the fire at her home and knew about the attack at Brady's place. Someone had hired a team of men to kill her.

Brady pointed to a higher rock. "Wait there," he whispered.

Susan was shivering so hard, it was difficult to move or feel her limbs. She did as Brady asked, concentrating on not losing her balance. Brady swam a few feet away, disappearing under the water. How much blood was he losing? Where did he think he was going? Not back to the boat.

An impossibly long time passed. When Brady broke the surface of the water a few feet away, she let out the breath she'd been holding. He disappeared again and was then under the dock, climbing the rocks to get to her.

Susan rubbed her arms. How long would they have to wait on the rocks? Until the men disappeared? They could freeze to death. Her fingers tingled painfully.

What about Brady's knee? Was he okay? If he was in pain, he wouldn't tell her. He would suffer through it.

Brady wrapped his arms around her, trying to share warmth. "I couldn't see the men talking. They either

joined the crowd on the pier or are waiting for us somewhere. They know we have to get out of the water."

They were fifty feet from the next closest pier. They
could swim for it or attempt to get out of the water here,
climbing up the rocks, over the sea wall and onto the
grass. They could be spotted. The dark provided some
cover. The numbness in her limbs told her she had to
get out of the water here and now.

"Let's run for it. Is your knee okay? What about
your arm?" she asked.

The sharp intake of his breath revealed he was of-
fended. "My knee's fine and my arm has a scratch.
What about you?"

She couldn't see in the dark and the cold was numb-
ing her body. Her toes and fingers prickled in pain. If
she had bruises or cuts, they weren't severe enough to
bother her. "I'm okay."

"Stay close. Keep alert. Are you ready to run?" he
asked.

"Yes, I can run," she said. What choice did they
have?

They crawled onto land, pulling themselves over the
sea wall, concrete digging into her hands and belly. At
least she had some feeling remaining in them. Scram-
bling to their feet, Brady's hand holding hers, they
raced in the direction of his truck. Brady released
her hand and stopped. Susan skidded to a halt and
whirled. Brady was rubbing his knee with his hands,
pain etched on his face. "Go, Susan."

Nope. Wouldn't happen. She wasn't leaving him.
"Come on, Brady. Put your arm around me if you need
to."

Brady swallowed hard and slipped his arm over

her shoulder. It had to kill him to rely on her. He was an independent and proud man. But, it had been hard on her to rely on him, too. They started again at a jog.

The wind was brutally cold against her body. Shouts from concerned boaters rose in the air, the fire roared and sirens screamed.

Susan stopped and looked over her shoulder at the *Sketchy Lady*. Flames were consuming it. Her throat closed and she forced herself to swallow.

Terrified thoughts struck her one after the other, knotting in her stomach. This was the second fire she had been involved in. Would witnesses place her at the scene? Someone was trying to kill her and wouldn't give up until they succeeded. The men trying to kill her believed she had killed Justin. Had she?

"Susan," Brady said, shaking her. She looked at him.

"We have to keep moving," Brady said.

Her feet felt like lead, but she could move on her cold legs. "I'm sorry. I'm in shock," Susan said.

"Come on," Brady said.

She and Brady battled across the grounds of the marina and didn't stop until they'd reached Brady's truck.

Susan was out of breath, panting, shaking, her hands and feet numb with cold. "We have to go back and explain what happened," she said, between gasps. "Someone on the scene will help us."

Brady opened the truck and they got inside. He started the engine and cranked the heater to high. It blew cold, and Susan scrubbed her arms and legs with her hands, trying to build warmth.

"We're not going back. Whoever set the fire is waiting to kill us. Let's not give them another shot at it. We don't know who we can trust. Take off your clothes," he said.

"What?" She tried to follow his words. The cold left her hazy and confused. His voice poured over her hot and thick.

Brady reached behind the seat and handed her a flannel blanket. "Take off your wet clothes and wrap yourself in this so you can get warm faster."

What he'd meant as a life-saving gesture turned into something primal and heady. "What about you?" she asked, peeling off her socks.

Brady pulled off his shirt. The heater in the car spat warmer air, puffing heat on their frigid extremities.

"I'll make do. You need to get as dry as possible."

Peeling off her pants and her shirt, Susan wrapped the blanket around her body. An invisible force drew her closer to him. She slid to the driver's side of the truck and wrapped as much of the blanket as she could around Brady. "We can share our heat." Her bare skin against his warmed her, heat blooming between them.

"Do you have any injuries?" he asked, the compassion in his voice melodic and comforting.

He was hurt, but he was worried about her. That was Brady. He didn't put himself first. With his eyes wandering over her, her entire body went up in flames. Did he know how he affected her?

"I'm not hurt," she said, wishing for more between them than his wet jeans and a soft flannel blanket. "Let me see your arm."

His arm was bleeding and Susan grabbed the shirt she'd removed. "Wrap this around your arm."

"It looks worse than it is."

Of course he would say that. Concern ballooned

through her. She tied her shirt around it, pulling it tight. "What about your knee? Do you need me to drive?"

"When I get warmer it will be fine." Brady patted his pants and swore. "I lost my gun in the water." He pulled a notebook from the waistband of his jeans. "If that gun washes up on shore, it will show as registered to me. It will place me at the scene."

Susan shuddered following his line of reasoning. "The police will use it to tie to you to the fire. Or make them think you were involved in Justin's murder."

Her eyes connected with Brady's and she read the determination in them. "We'll solve this before they do. Then they can't pin anything on us."

Brady unzipped his jeans and then paused.

"What's wrong?" Susan asked. "Besides everything?" Had he seen someone coming?

"I'll leave my jeans on."

Susan looked at him. "What? Are you serious? It's cold. You'll be warmer without them."

A brief moment of indecision and then Brady slid his pants down his legs. "You might as well know."

"Know wha…"

Her voice trailed away at the sight of Brady's leg. From the knee down, the skin was scarred and puckered. Even in the dark, she could see how painful the injury must be. When she'd visited him in the hospital, he hadn't shared the nature of his injuries. He hadn't let her see anything.

She reached her hand to touch him and he jerked away. "Don't."

She stilled her hand. "Is it painful?" Had their jump from the boat worsened his injury?

He swallowed hard. "From time to time."

Like now. What had happened to him? "If you want to talk about it—"

"I don't. Let it go."

Typical of Brady to shut her out. Susan had more questions on her tongue. She snapped her mouth shut.

"We need to find somewhere to lay low," Brady said. "Whoever started the fire will be looking for us." His voice was ominous. He pulled his phone from his jeans pocket and opened it. "Waterproof. Should still work." He swore under his breath. "I got a text from Connor. We can't return to the house. It's not safe. A couple more guys showed up tonight and were waiting for us."

Their problems multiplied. More people were being sucked into this disaster. How many men wanted her dead? "What about Connor? Is he in trouble?"

"Nope. He'll go underground. If anyone knows how to disappear, it's Connor."

Brady tossed his phone into the cup holder. He looked around and pulled out of the parking spot.

Susan couldn't scrub away the image of Justin's boat on fire. "We need to tell the police what happened."

"We're not telling anyone anything. Susan, think it through. Until we know who the men looking for you are and how big this is, we're not trusting anyone. The police made it clear earlier they weren't interested in protecting you. I don't know if they have the ability to protect you. If I'm right and these guys are ex-Special Forces, you're running from an elite breed of fighters. They've been conditioned to track and kill."

"You're Special Forces, too. You seem less worried about killing and more concerned with keeping me safe."

The look on his face spoke volumes. He wasn't Special Forces anymore and mentioning it was insensitive of her. It didn't change that he'd been trained and he'd been good at what he did.

"I was a pararescueman. My first priority was and is the safety of the person in danger."

At the moment, she was the person in danger. His commitment to keeping her safe was part of what he'd been trained to do, an instinctual response.

"We need to think about who we can go to for help," Brady said.

They couldn't reach out to Connor again. Did they have any other allies? "What about Reilly? We can trust him," Susan said.

"I'm trying to clear Reilly's name in this, not wrap him up tighter. Harris and I have been careful not to involve him for his safety. I haven't spoken to him and I won't speak to him and drag him into this. I don't want anyone else hurt."

A chill traced along her spine. Those who had tried to help her ended up in danger. Reilly and Haley could be in trouble. Susan's hand went to her necklace. Brady was right. They had to make careful decisions and keep their friends safe. Until they knew who was after her, they were on their own. She picked up the sopping notebook.

Brady steered his truck with one hand and rubbed his free hand over her shoulder, generating heat friction. "Maybe the book will be salvageable. If not, I sent Harris the pictures I took and I have them on my phone. Harris can blow them up to get more detail. Those will have to do."

Brady was always one step ahead. "What do we do now? Where do we go?" she asked.

"I'll think of somewhere. We need to hope we don't get pulled over, cause this—" he pointed to their mostly naked bodies "—does not look good."

But he did look good. Amazing in fact. Bulging shoulders and rippling biceps, flat abdominals and toned thighs. He might have lost some weight since his injury, but he looked great. While she was sure she resembled a drowned rat, he looked unabashedly masculine. The injury, aside from worrying her, did nothing to destroy his attractiveness. Battle wounds. Heroic. Sexy.

"First priorities first. We need somewhere safe to get dry and warm," he said.

Warm sounded good. The cold had leeched deep into her core. She didn't know if she'd ever feel warm again.

"Great, just what we need," Brady said.

"What's the matter?" Susan asked, directing the air vents at them.

"I knew getting to the truck was too easy. Someone is following us on a motorcycle."

Brady's truck accelerated and Susan turned in her seat. A single headlight was gaining on them. Nothing about this night had been easy, but they'd caught a break making it to the truck without being stopped or shot at again.

"He's getting closer," Susan said, unable to control the hysteria in her voice. Was it one of the Special Forces men following them?

"Just hang on," Brady said through clenched teeth.

Brady drove the truck to its limits. The dashboard

shook under the speed of the engine. As Brady approached a cluster of cars, he wove in and out of traffic, earning him honks of protest from other drivers.

"I don't see him," Susan said. The glare of headlights, the overhead streetlights and the rain made it difficult to see.

Brady didn't let up on the gas. He pushed the truck, steering between cars. He took a hard left and the truck spun, fishtailing wildly.

Susan held on to Brady. Brady was a good driver. The truck wouldn't flip. They'd stay safe. Brady kept the truck on the road and didn't hit anything—or anyone.

Brady adjusted his speed. Susan quashed the urge to tell him to hurry, the panic inside her chest urging them to be as far from the motorcyclist as possible.

"Any chance you saw who was on the motorcycle?" Brady asked.

It had been too dark, the glare of lights blinding. "I couldn't see much. He was wearing a helmet. Someone is trying to kill us. I almost got you killed. Again." Horror and regret slammed into her. She'd pulled Reilly into this mess and she might have ruined his career, marring an otherwise glowing service record. And now, she'd dragged Brady into a situation where his life was at risk.

She turned and relief washed over her. She didn't see the single headlight of the motorcycle tailing them.

Brady's hand clamped on her side, rock-steady, strong and supportive in the way she needed. "We're okay. I'm not that easy to kill. I've been trained to avoid it." He tossed her a small smile.

"I've tried to avoid it, as well. Although I lack the

official training." She moved closer to Brady. "Did you hear their conversation? They think I killed Justin. What do they think I know? What was Justin doing that has someone so eager to see me dead?"

"Whatever it is, they want their secret to stay buried with Justin."

"How did anyone know we'd be at the marina?" The sick feeling in her stomach wouldn't let go. "I don't understand this. Any of this."

Brady's hands tightened on the wheel. "Think hard about your relationship with Justin. Go over every moment that made you think twice, any time your gut told you something was wrong or any reference Justin made to the names we saw in those notebooks. Some involvement he had with the military or former military friends."

Susan was lost and couldn't offer a lead to help them. Since Justin had been killed, Susan had tried to make sense of it. Tried to guess who would want him dead and had tried to put together the pieces of that night. Where did she start?

The first time Susan had met Justin's father, she'd known he didn't approve of her. The look on his face and that he wouldn't shake her hand had made her feel small. She'd tried extra hard to make Justin's family like and accept her. As many times as she'd seen them, nothing had changed. No amount of thoughtful gifts, polite conversation or invitations to spend time with her had changed their opinions of her.

It was completely different from how it had been with Brady's family. His parents had hugged her the first time they'd met her. Brady had stood at her side with his arm around her. It hadn't been so much of an

"I don't care what you think" attitude, but more "I'm proud to call this woman my girlfriend." Susan's gifts were received with appreciation and her phone calls and emails returned.

In some ways, Justin's and Brady's families' vocations were similar: protect and defend others. But when she was with Justin, she felt as if Justin needed to protect and defend her. With Brady's, she'd never felt under attack. She'd felt welcomed with open arms.

"He had plenty of involvement with the military. Look at who his father is. And he had friends from the time he served. They wouldn't have confided anything in me. His family and friends never seemed thrilled I was dating him."

She couldn't ask Justin's coworkers for their thoughts. Since Justin had died, she wasn't the grieving fiancée. She was the prime suspect in his murder. Susan had trusted the police to do their job and question people in Justin's life who might have information to help. The detective and his team had certainly questioned her enough. Were the investigators on the case as corrupt as the men chasing her? She didn't know who could be trusted anymore.

Susan took their clothes and flattened them on the seat so they would dry faster. The cab had heated nicely, and snug against Brady's body, her core temperature rose. She tried to open the notebook, but the pages were too wet, sticking together and tearing with pressure. Maybe if it dried, they could salvage information from it.

Brady ran a hand through his hair. "We're talking in circles. Did anything trip your memory while we were on the boat? You have to give me something to go on here. Anything. A name. A reason."

Susan could sense Brady's frustration and it added to her own. "I want to find whoever is doing this. I'm trying. I am." She was letting Brady down. She was letting Justin down. She hated that. Justin had clearly gotten involved in a bad situation, but until she had evidence of his guilt, she wouldn't write him off as the police and general public had done to her. Susan let her head fall against the seat. "I have no idea why someone would want to kill me. I don't know why Justin was killed. I didn't know Justin like I should have. I don't know anything." It ached to admit. It made her feel stupid, as if she'd missed something she shouldn't have.

Silence from Brady. She could see the wheels turning in his head.

"Can you dial a number for me?" Brady asked.

She threw the brakes on her despairing thoughts. "Yes. Of course." She took his phone from the cup holder.

He rattled off a series of numbers and Susan dialed.

"Can you put it on speaker?" he asked.

"This can't be good," a voice on the other end answered. It took Susan a moment to place the tone and timbre. Harris, Brady's oldest brother.

"How'd you guess?" Brady asked.

"A lucky hunch based on strange text message pictures. Is Susan safe?"

Brady was close with his family and the Trumans stuck together. Did they blame her for getting Reilly into trouble at his work? They wanted Susan to help clear Reilly's good name, but what would they think of her if she couldn't? When Justin's body was found and she was arrested, she wouldn't have the power to help anyone. Why couldn't she remember the most important night of her life?

"She's with me now and you're on speaker," Brady said. "Say hi."

"Hey, Susan," Harris said without a hint of animosity. "Too bad you hooked back up with the troubled brother again. That can't lead anywhere good. Why don't you ditch him and come see me? I could use a night out with a decent woman."

Teasing, of course. The Truman brothers' good-natured ribbing was part of their relationship.

"If I didn't drag trouble everywhere I went, I'd consider it. What would your mom think of me if I got all three of her sons in trouble?" Susan asked.

"Our mom adores you. She wouldn't blame you for this," Brady said.

"Tell me what you need," Harris said. When he spoke this time, his voice was all business.

"I need you to look at the pictures I sent you and see if you can tie it to a business or a personal account," Brady said.

"Clue me in here," Harris said. "What are we looking for? Gambling? Drugs? Fraud? Money laundering?"

"Don't know. Justin had some questionable ledgers in his private safe. The ledgers have dates and dollars amounts, high amounts. The pictures I sent you might help."

"It sounds like he was either getting or giving payments to someone," Harris said. "I'll dig up what I can and look at finances as a possible problem. Maybe I can make sense of these."

"I was thinking along the same lines," Brady said.

Was Justin having money problems? From what Susan knew about Justin's finances, he was meticulous about paying bills and wouldn't have gone into debt without a good reason. Aside from a few large purchases, like the boat, he wasn't a big spender. If he needed help, he could have turned to his family. "I'd be surprised if Justin was receiving payments from someone," Susan said. "He never behaved like he had an excess of money."

"The guy had a yacht," Brady said. "The money had to come from somewhere and boat maintenance takes cash every month. His cash flow might be heavy in and heavy out."

Brady and Harris seemed quick to believe Justin was in financial trouble. Susan's thoughts veered. Could Justin have been stealing money from a client? Was he involved in money fraud?

"Maybe he was worried about money because he was making payments to someone. Was he being blackmailed? Did he have obligations to a family member? Someone with a drug or gambling problem?" Harris asked.

Justin had been an accountant at a top firm in Denver. He and Susan had never talked about the money they earned in detail, an omission Susan had found odd, but had chalked up to Justin being private about his finances. Many people were. He'd seemed content with her modest living. He'd never mentioned payments owed to anyone. "If he was making heavy payments or needed money, he didn't mention it to me," Susan said. She had been his fiancée. She had been the person in whom he should have confided about anything. If Justin had been in trouble and hadn't told her, perhaps their relationship had been in a worse place than she'd believed.

Brady and Harris volleyed around more ideas. The more they spoke, the more uncomfortable Susan became. Despite ending her relationship with Justin, Susan had cared for him. Digging up ugliness from his past didn't sit right with her.

"Let us know what you find," Brady said to Harris. "Oh, and one more small problem. To darken the water, this might involve former military. The guys who've come after us are skilled and trained. Let's keep any digging under the radar and not draw more attention our way."

Harris whistled. "Reilly's bored out of his mind at the present. Concerned and angry, but bored. I'll have him do some discreet digging, as well. He might have some ideas about who these guys are and why they're after Susan."

"Are you sure it's good idea to get Reilly involved?" Brady said. "We've been trying to keep him out of this."

Harris snorted. "Do you think he's sitting home on his laurels waiting for something bad to happen? We can keep him out of it the best we can, but you know he's working twice as hard to get into it. He wants to clear his name and Susan's."

"Tell him to be very discreet. We don't know the scope of this," Brady said. "And while you're at it, ask Haley and Reilly to go out to dinner for a few hours."

"Will do. Shouldn't be a problem."

Susan was never surprised at the lengths the Truman brothers would go for each other.

"I'll be in touch with a number where you can reach me," Brady said.

"What's wrong with your cell?" Harris asked.

"I don't trust it. I'm going to ditch it and pick up a throwaway."

"How deep in are you? Wait, don't answer that. I don't want to know. Call if you need anything else. You know how to get ahold of me privately and securely."

Brady disconnected the call. "We can't take chances someone will track us. Credit cards, ATM cards, they have to go. Justin's killer wants to find you. We have no way to know who we're up against and what resources they have to track you."

Susan swallowed hard. "I lost everything in the fire. They won't find me through any of my cards or devices. But how will we pay for things? Food? A place to stay?"

"We'll find a way," Brady said.

He sounded confident and sure. How could he be? The problems were compounding at an alarming rate. Susan was holding on to her sanity by a thread. She took several deep breaths. Brady would take care of her. He might not be in her life for the long haul, and she might never trust him with her heart again, but he wouldn't let her down in this. Because in this she was the mission.

Susan didn't press him for more details. Like with Harris, when it came to Brady, some information she was better off not knowing.

Chapter 6

The difficulties Brady had had in his life were rapidly achieving train-wreck status. Being discharged from the military and meandering without a career or clear direction was bad. Breaking into a dead guy's yacht with the prime murder suspect, losing his weapon at the scene and then going on the lam with said prime suspect was infinitely worse.

Reilly needed his help and Harris had made it sound simple. Talk to Susan. Help her remember what happened to Justin. Clear Susan and therefore, clear Reilly. Done and done. He'd made his choices and now that he'd seen the threats to her life firsthand, he was more committed than ever to helping. The deeper they got into this situation, the worse and more complex it became. It didn't stop him from wanting to help. It didn't scare him. Protecting people was what he was born to do. He hated that his injury had made it impossible for him to work as a pararescueman and he despised feeling weak. But now, for the first time in months, he didn't feel worthless. As much as she needed him, he needed her.

Brady was a man who stood by the people he cared for and he was a man who'd protect them with everything he had. If he walked away from Susan, she wouldn't just go to jail for Justin's murder. She'd also be easier prey for Justin's killer and the people hunting her—which he now knew were not one and the same—and Brady couldn't live with that outcome. A sliver of doubt worked into his thoughts, slamming against the measure of worth that he'd built and amplifying his fear of being weak.

"What's the plan now?" Susan asked.

He didn't have a specific plan, but he'd tell her what he could. "We're dealing with two separate groups. Someone who murdered Justin and someone who wants you dead. Doesn't change our plans. We still need to keep you safe. I'll do my best to make that happen."

"You're making it happen. I'm still alive. Without you, I don't think that would be the case."

Had she caught the insecurity in his voice? "We've had some close calls. In the water, you saved me," he said. His knee had frozen and he'd needed to rely on Susan. He'd been lucky when he had been able to swim on his own. How long would his luck hold?

"I'm not keeping score. We're in this together," Susan said, something she hadn't really felt before now.

But Brady was keeping score and he didn't like the odds stacks against him. "I'm weaker than I was."

Susan threw up her hands. "So what? Brady, enough

with the self-doubt. Even in the state you are now, you're still stronger than most men. Your brothers believe in you. I believe in you. The only person who's questioning your abilities is you. Do you know how lucky you are to have your family believe in you?"

Susan's insecurity was showing now. Her mother had never been the picture of support, and after her father's death, it had gotten worse. Susan worked hard to please the people around her. Too hard.

"I believe in you," he said. Would she take his words to heart or dismiss them? As easy as she was on others, she was hard on herself.

"Then stop focusing on the negative, and let's keep each other safe," she said.

Brady liked Susan's spunk. She called him out the same way his brothers did. He needed that: a strong voice to keep him from wallowing and keep him focused.

As they drove along the highway, Brady prioritized their needs. First up, dry clothes. Clothes required money. Brady had some cash in his wallet, but not enough for the supplies they needed.

Susan was putting on a brave front, but he sensed her losing control. Right below the surface, she was shaken and raw. He'd see what he could do to calm her down. Sleep would help. Talking it out. Drawing. Getting her somewhere safe.

Starting at Reilly's was the simplest solution. "We need to switch cars with Reilly."

"If you think that's a good idea," Susan said, sounding doubtful. "We're supposed to keep Reilly out of this."

"I can't think of another way to get supplies. We

need shoes and dry clothes. We have next to no money. We'll have to raid Reilly's place. It's the simplest solution."

"Reilly could get in a lot of trouble for helping us," Susan said.

"He won't know he's helping us. He can't be blamed if I take action without his knowledge."

Susan gave him a look. "That's a gray area. He'll put it together and then you've placed him in the impossible position of deciding if he should tell someone we stole his car."

"If he reports it stolen, Reilly won't tell them who he thinks is responsible. He doesn't have a reason to speculate about who stole it."

Reilly's home was in a quiet suburban neighborhood of modest-size houses. Brady parked a block away, and he and Susan entered Reilly's from the back, running through the backyards of the houses on Reilly's street. Actually, it was Reilly and Haley's home. His new sister-in-law would have to forgive the intrusion. The night wasn't what he'd expected. Trekking around in the dark in wet boxer shorts was a low point.

The warmth of the house stung his freezing skin. Brady rubbed his hands together. Brady hated to involve his brother deeper in this problem, but his truck could be recognized. The people looking for Susan were dead serious about finding her. He'd take Reilly or Haley's car for now, and look for something else to drive soon.

"Let's make this fast," Brady said, feeling guilty. He shifted his body to hide the worst of his leg injury from Susan's sight. Seeing it in the light made him feel more exposed. Since being injured, he'd worn long pants to keep it covered. The sight of it still surprised him at times. He could only guess how repulsed it made others. His eyes tracked to the bare skin revealed by the gap in the blanket Susan was wearing. Soft, touchable skin his fingers itched to stroke.

Susan adjusted the blanket around her body. "Do I have time to shower? It will help me feel warmer and the stink of lake sludge is making me nauseated." She shifted uncomfortably.

A hot shower together played on his mind. It would be faster and satisfy his carnal desire for her, but Susan had meant alone. He hadn't bridged the gap between them and he wouldn't set himself up to be rejected. "Make it fast. Very, very fast."

Susan scampered to the upstairs bathroom and Brady took over the bathroom on the main floor. A quick shower washed away lake algae and debris. He found a first-aid kit in the bathroom and treated his arm where the bullet had grazed him. It had started to clot, a good sign. As long as it didn't become infected, he'd be fine. He'd had worse injuries in the field and hadn't been deemed unfit for duty.

He dug through Reilly's closet for warm clothes and found a pair of pants to cover his leg injury. Brady felt better the moment it was covered. He didn't want Susan asking more questions. He didn't want to discuss his failings as a pararescueman or as a man. He borrowed a duffel bag and tossed in more essentials.

Brady's phone rang and he glanced at the display. Lieutenant General Tim Ambrose. Had Ambrose heard what had happened at the marina? It wouldn't surprise him if the lieutenant general had eyes and ears everywhere, especially when it concerned his son. Brady didn't answer the call. What was the point of fielding more threats? Brady wouldn't walk away from Susan, not when she needed him more than ever. Brady slipped his phone into his pocket and made a mental note to ditch it somewhere and get a throwaway prepaid that would make him and Susan more difficult to track.

Susan appeared in the doorway to the bedroom. "I feel guilty, like I'm stealing. Should I leave them a note?" She was shivering. From cold or fear? It hadn't escaped his awareness that she was understandably upset.

"No, no note. No way for anyone to track us. Reilly and Haley will understand."

Susan stepped into the room and Brady's libido switched from nil to rampant. The white towel wrapped around her body fell mid-thigh and her wet hair hung down her back. Bare shapely legs and smooth, toned arms. Brady forced his eyes to Reilly's clothes. This wasn't the time to pull her into his arms and allow lust to take over.

Susan entered the walk-in closet and skimmed through Haley's outfits, hangers sliding along the bar as she looked at each item. "Haley has some nice-looking clothes here. I feel bad taking something."

She smelled fresh, like soap and citrus. Brady didn't let that tempt him.

"Haley won't mind. She's been through rough times, too. Pick something warm. Preferably layers," Brady said. Not a clingy dress or a short skirt. He needed her covered, for her health and for his sanity.

"Keep your back turned. I'm trying something on."

Temptation was standing inches from him. Out of respect for her and deference to her emotional state,

Brady marshaled his desire. He wouldn't turn, he wouldn't look and he wouldn't let lust get the better of him. Listening to the swish of fabric, Brady stamped out the mental image of her naked.

"Do I look ridiculous? I feel strange. Haley wears her clothes tighter. And she's taller. Do I look like a dwarf?" Susan asked.

Brady turned and drank in the sight of her. The jeans conformed to her body, accentuating the leanness of her figure and the curves she had in the right places. The shirt Susan had chosen was a good fit. He stepped closer and took her elbow, pivoting her. "Looks great to me." He would have preferred thick ski pants. Or baggy sweat pants. An outfit that wouldn't call attention to her incredibly feminine figure.

Susan pulled her arm away, alarm in her eyes. "Come on, don't play around."

He'd been trying to steel himself against the surge of desire, to pretend like he felt nothing for her. She'd still recognized the emotion on his face or maybe it was his voice that had given him away. Playing around wasn't what he had in mind. Not exactly. Touching her had ignited thoughts of taking her into his arms and making love to her. Needing each other now didn't resolve the compounded emotional problems they had. He knew it. He didn't want to accept it. His brain toyed with the idea of testing the waters. He suspected the physical connection was still there.

He took her hand and spun her to face him, bringing her body to his. "Tell me what you're thinking. This was a rough night. If you want to talk about it, I can listen."

She pushed at his chest. "I'm fine. Really, I'm keeping it together."

"I can see that." Brady could also read the worry and fear on her face and sense the unsteady emotions simmering a few millimeters beneath her careful control. Her courage and tenacity was something he'd always admired about her.

Susan licked her lower lip and lifted her head. "I'm disappointed. I wasn't expecting anyone to be at the marina tonight. I thought I would get on the boat and remember everything. I thought we'd find something that would help us."

The visit to the boat hadn't been a loss. "We might have found something to help us. We'll have to see what plays out."

Susan frowned mightily. "More questions. That's all I have from tonight. And you acting like this confuses me." She stepped away from him, and he let his hands drop, giving her the space she wanted.

"I'm trying to be a friend." After his past behavior and what she'd been through, friendship was the most she'd want from him.

An injured shadow passed over her face. "Be a friend and keep to a safe distance. I've already been clobbered by you. Twice. I don't need to go another round."

"Twice?" After they'd broken up, he'd made it a clean break.

Hurt flickered across her face. "You broke up with me and then I came to you, wanting to be a friend, wanting to be there for you while you recovered in the hospital and you didn't want me."

It wasn't that he hadn't wanted her. A part of him

had always wanted her. He didn't want anyone to see him as weak and pathetic as he'd been. Especially not Susan. "You misunderstood my actions."

She folded her arms over her chest. "I misunderstood? Then explain it to me. Help me understand."

Were they fighting again? He sensed an argument hinged on his words. "I want you to be happy. I'm not the man who can make you happy. When you visited me in the hospital, I wasn't in a place to be a friend to you or anyone."

She gave him a look of complete incredulity. "You're right. I don't understand that."

How was he bungling this? Clearing the air would be good for both of them.

"You want a husband and a house and children and a white picket fence. I can't give you those things. When you came to see me in the hospital, I wasn't in a place to deal with us." To deal with her relationship with Justin. To deal with her seeing him broken and fragile. To address the wreckage that was their relationship. It hadn't seemed worth it to rehash that baggage. He'd had trouble living with himself and his injuries. To this day, he had trouble with it.

"You don't get to decide what I do and don't want. I'm thrilled to know dealing with me is such a burden. That my friendship is worthless to you."

That wasn't what he'd said and if that was what she'd heard, he hadn't meant it that way.

"You aren't a burden and your friendship isn't worthless." Nothing about her was worthless. She was loyal and courageous and she saw the best in people. A lesser woman wouldn't have tried to be a friend to him after he was injured.

She narrowed her eyes as if trying to decide if he was lying. "You're helping me because you think I can help Reilly. What if that turns out not to be true?"

Brady wouldn't consider it. He would find a way to clear Reilly's name. He might be useless in other areas of his life, but he knew Susan. He knew how to talk to her. He could get inside her thoughts and help her remember. They used to have great conversations post-coitus. Lying in his arms, she would talk about her artwork, her life and her hopes for the future. He had loved listening to her.

The idea of pulling her into bed and letting the afterglow of sex coax the memories from her lodged in his mind. "Don't doubt yourself. I'm not only helping you because my brother is involved. I'm helping you because…" He wasn't sure how to finish that sentence. Because he'd always felt a connection to Susan? Because he didn't want anything bad to happen to her? Because the thought of someone harming her enraged him like nothing else could? "Because it's the Truman way to help someone in need." To do whatever he could to keep her safe.

What would she say if he suggested getting into bed? When they'd kissed earlier, he'd sensed something inside her. Desperation, loneliness and fear. Not the platform from which he wanted to launch a successful sexual experience with her. Could he charm her to a place where she felt safe, comfortable and open to making love and talking with him? Would that dislodge her hidden memories? She'd be furious if she discovered his motive, or at least his partial motive. Guilt struck him for thinking about using sex to get inside her head, but it might be the only way to unlock those memories.

"Don't doubt myself? You should listen to your own advice," she said.

He flinched. She'd seen his weaknesses and his uncertainties about his abilities. Insecurity quashed his thoughts of sex with Susan. She wouldn't be interested. "We'll figure this out. You and I, when we put our minds to it, are one amazing team.

"If we were such a good team, why did you give up on us?" Susan asked, setting her hands on her hips.

Brady jammed a frustrated hand through his hair. He hated that an argument could erupt between them this quickly. He didn't have the answers and he didn't have the words to make it better.

"I didn't give up on us. I realized we couldn't make it long term. I was wasting your time."

Susan pinched her lips together and glared at him.

He closed the distance between them and set his hands on her shoulders. They had been a great team. They'd had good times together and had been inseparable when he was in Denver. When she was close to him, he had trouble recalling the reasons they'd broken up.

He wanted to erase the anger and sadness from her face. Anything was better than her anger. The urge to kiss her strengthened in his veins. If his lips touched hers, flames would ignite as strong as they once had. One kiss, one hot, deep, lingering kiss. He knew how she'd taste. He knew exactly how she'd move against him. Knowing that didn't diffuse the mystery or temper his desire. It made him hungrier.

Memories simmered in his blood. Making love

to her for the first time. Waking up with her tucked against him. Surprising her after work with flowers. Susan surprising him by meeting him at the airport when he'd returned from overseas.

On the heels of those happy memories, the most difficult one: the first time he'd realized Susan had wanted him to propose. He'd known he couldn't give her the life she wanted. He'd been scheduled to leave for another tour the next week. He hadn't known if he'd return. He hadn't known when he'd next see her. He couldn't make promises about the future. Those thoughts had worked at him until he'd come to one conclusion: no matter how much he loved her, he had to let her go. He'd been wrecked over the decision. He hadn't seen another way to make her happy.

But he wasn't in the military anymore. Could he give her the life she wanted? Was it possible, even with his injury, to be the man she needed?

Susan whipped her face away from him staring at the closet wall. "Wasting my time? Just when I think you can't hurt me, you find new and fresh ways."

It hadn't been his intention to hurt her during any moment of their relationship. "Susan, you have to understand."

She balled her fists at her sides. "Why do I have to understand? Why can't I write you off along with all the other jerks in the world?"

He didn't have a good answer. He had been a jerk to her. He had hurt her. He didn't have the right explanation and he hated that.

He didn't want to be just another jerk to her. She had enough of those in her life. He kissed the top of her head, trying to calm her. Being so close to her, the smell of her hair broke his control. He wanted more.

Brady brought his mouth to hers and captured her lips in a fierce and demanding kiss. After several seconds, her shoulders relaxed and she parted her lips, opening her mouth to his. He sank into the kiss, willing her to understand. He had always wanted what was best for her. He wanted her to be happy and he was man enough to admit he couldn't give her what she needed and what she deserved.

His hands tightened around her waist, holding her to him. In a flood, sensual memories pounded into him. His body remembered exactly how this had felt, and reacted by settling into a supreme sense of rightness.

A sigh escaped Susan's lips and Brady forked his fingers into the back of her hair. He needed something to do with his hands, something to keep them from reaching for the hem of her shirt and pulling it over her head. The intensity of this kiss could break the barriers to sex and Susan wasn't ready for that. She was grieving and scared and those weren't the conditions he wanted if he slept with her.

His body flared with heat and the logical half of his mind commanded him to slow down. She had been through a lot. Too much. This was blowing off steam. This was releasing some of the raw emotion pent up inside her. This was giving her something to think about, a distraction. A hot, steamy distraction.

For him, a test. An exploration. An explanation. Seeing how they—how she—reacted. This kiss could creep into regret territory if it went much further.

Though his hands and lips protested, Brady pulled away and retreated a step. Susan had the slightly dazed expression of a woman who had been thoroughly and completely kissed. She hadn't expected him to stop. For that matter, he hadn't expected to stop that abruptly.

Brady took a deep breath and cooled his thoughts and threw cold water on his libido.

She brought her fingers to her lips. He ran a hand over his unshaven face and noticed the pinked skin around her mouth. He reached his thumb to touch her face. "I'm sorry. I should have been gentler."

She turned her head away from his hand. "No, you were...fine."

Fine? "I never stopped wanting you."

"That's refreshing, Brady." Her anger cut into him. "But wanting someone and being reliable and loyal are different things. All I've gotten from this is that sex with you would be great, but unfulfilling on a whole other level."

The sex would be good, but she had it right that he couldn't fulfill her needs. Not before and not in his current state. Even so, it pained him to hear her say it aloud. "I'm trying to explain things and making it more confusing," he said.

"Yes, you are. I don't get why you kiss me and then pull away. What are you afraid will happen?"

"That we'll sleep together and it will be for the wrong reasons."

"Tell me the right reasons," Susan said.

Was this a test? "That we both want to sleep together. That's it's not because we're lonely or angry or confused." Or because under the right circumstances, she'd relax and maybe even remember something important.

Susan stared at him. "With so much history between us, I don't know if those conditions will ever align."

Then they wouldn't sleep together. He wanted to sleep with her and it was a bonus that he believed she'd let down her guard and relax so the memories would flow. That she'd captivated him and he'd kissed her spoke to their chemistry, but not good judgment. "We should get moving."

They couldn't stay with Reilly and they wanted to avoid involving other family or friends. Checking into a hotel or motel would put them on the radar and until Brady knew the full scope of whom he was dealing with and how far their resources stretched, he was erring on the side of caution. They'd have to get creative.

He and Susan were on their own. He'd rip a page from his Special Forces playbook and stay off the grid for a while, at least until they had a plan.

"Where is it safe to go? What about your arm? Did it stop bleeding? And your knee? How are you feeling?" Susan asked.

His arm was feeling better, and his knee, well, that never stopped aching. "Both are manageable."

Susan frowned. "Brady? Where can we go now?"

She wanted answers. He grappled for a plan while trying to sound confident. "Connor has a cabin in Winter Park." It wasn't a luxury cabin, but it would be equipped with the basics and allow them to stay safe while they looked over the items they'd taken from the boat and planned their next maneuver. "He has internet access in his cabin piggybacked to the network of a nearby resort. We can track what's developing in the news and do some research without being traced."

Connor's cabin was located outside Arapaho National Forest near several ski resorts and clusters of vacation houses. It was small and plain enough not to attract attention. Skiers staying in nearby cabins would spend most of their time on the slopes, and if he and Susan stayed inside the cabin, they could go unnoticed for a few days. Ideal in one way and devastating in another. Brady didn't trust their chemistry wouldn't burn through his self-control.

"What if Connor is already there?" Susan asked. "If we're followed again, we can't put him in danger."

Brady was confident his friend had gone farther underground than his cabin. "He won't be there. He has hidey-holes all over the country. This is one that I know about."

"Winter Park might be good," Susan said. The hesitancy in her voice gave away she was remembering the trip they'd taken to Winter Park when they were a couple. Dinners by firelight, snuggling in the morning and waking to the sound of birds and the wind in the trees. Heaven.

They were destined to trip over emotional minefields wherever they went.

Images of her in his arms snapped into his mind. She'd never been camping or fishing, and he'd been nervous about their first trip away in territory unfamiliar to her. After they'd spent a few hours in bed together, she'd been relaxed and willing to sit on the lake and fish.

A great weekend. A great memory. Not a great place to revisit. But it was safe, off the beaten path and it would take time for whoever was looking for them to find Connor's cabin. Like with most everything the man did, Connor would have seen that the records wouldn't be easily traceable.

"I want to involve as few people as possible. Connor's place will work for now," Brady said, shoving aside memories of Susan in his arms. This wasn't the right time or place to reminisce. They were lingering on treacherous emotional territory.

Susan brushed her hair over her shoulder. Her hand was shaking. "I guess that's the best option at the moment."

He'd made the right call stopping the kiss, but he wasn't sure if he'd made the right call in starting it. "I'll pack some food. See if you can find boots and a jacket."

Brady left Susan alone in the closet. He'd keep his distance, even if that became more difficult by the second. Brady grabbed a few more items and then returned to the kitchen to get some food. He threw his wet clothes into a plastic bag and made sure he hadn't left anything behind. Taking a few things and borrowing Reilly's home was one thing. Leaving evidence he'd been inside was another.

Ten minutes later, Susan appeared in the kitchen. She'd brushed her hair into a ponytail. "I hope they don't mind if we take their food." Susan pressed a hand over her stomach.

"They'll understand. They're stocked," Brady said. "We'll drive about ten miles from here away from Winter Park. We'll drop my truck and use Haley's car." The more false leads he could give the people looking for them, the better.

They loaded Haley's car and Susan drove it out of the garage. Brady got into his truck. They left it, with his cell phone inside, at a bus terminal parking lot, and then he and Susan switched places so he could drive to Connor's cabin.

Susan opened a box of cereal. She also had a slip of paper on her lap.

"What are you writing?" he asked.

"Keeping track of what we owe our friends."

That list would be extensive. Aside from the material things they took, Reilly's discretion would be priceless. "Reilly isn't a friend. He's family."

Susan shrugged. "He and Haley are friends to me. They're returning home to a storm of crap including having their house broken into and Haley's car having gone missing."

It wouldn't be the first time the Truman family was involved in a difficult, dangerous situation. His mother was former CIA and his father was an ex-Navy SEAL. It was in his and his brothers' blood to deal with complex, risky situations. "Reilly knows I'll do whatever it takes to keep you safe and clear his name. He'd be madder if I didn't use the resources at my disposal. And we didn't break in. They left the door open."

Family loyalty defined the Truman family. His family was strong and steady, each member devoting their lives to protecting others. The contrast between their lives and his made it worse for Brady. He hated that he was weak. He had failed in his duty to his country and he had let his team down. He couldn't disappoint Susan, as well.

"We need to get our hands on some cash," Brady said.

Susan's heart sank. Getting cash had an ominous sound to it. They couldn't walk into a bank or ATM and withdraw from their accounts. It was risky and the men looking for them could probably monitor their accounts for activity. "I'm not committing another crime. I don't care how deep we're into this, I'm not mugging an old woman, or breaking into a house, or holding up a bank."

Brady lifted his brows at her. "I'm not suggesting that. You know me better. I have a sack stash near the library."

"A what?" she asked.

"I have an emergency kit stashed away. When I was working overseas, it was a good idea to have reserves available in case I returned and needed to lay low for a while. I was occasionally assigned tasks that were sensitive in nature and I needed a way to stay out of the limelight."

She stared at him for a moment, processing what he was saying. "Reserves?"

"Yup."

"How many do you have?" she asked.

"Several here. Some in other key locations."

More questions came to mind. What work had he been doing with the air force that might require him to stay under the radar for periods of time?

"We need the money and we don't have alternatives. I don't know how we're being tracked, but we are," Brady said.

Was someone following them now? "How will we get to your stash? And are you serious?" Susan asked.

"I'm serious. It's in a covert location. I couldn't risk someone stumbling on it accidentally. Too many questions. Too many logistics."

Another glimpse into the work Brady had done

overseas. Dangerous work. Work that could require he disappear for a time. He'd been all in, hadn't he? Whenever he talked about his work, his pride was obvious, but he was light on details. "You've never mentioned this before."

Brady lifted his shoulder as if working out a cramp. "It wasn't important at the time. It's important now. I won't be using them for work anymore. I thought about retrieving them sooner, but my parents taught me to be prepared. Turns out that was good advice," Brady said.

"Nice thinking," Susan said. Reilly had told stories about the Truman family and how they prepared and planned for their safety. She had never pictured Brady doing something so…paranoid. Then again, she couldn't call it paranoid since it would help them.

They drove to the Denver City Park and parked the car. It backed to the Denver City Library.

"Keep your head down. At this hour, I can think of two types of people in the park. People looking for trouble and people causing trouble," Brady said, climbing out of the car.

Susan followed close. "If you're trying to blend, why don't you slow down and move at a leisurely pace?" His long stride made it difficult to keep up and not look as if she was running beside him.

The park wasn't crowded, although a couple was walking their dog and several other people moved through the park, heads down, hoods up. The lights from the overhead lamps cast shadows across the ground.

"Let's make this fast," Brady said. "The less people who see us, the better."

"Where is it?" she asked.

"Buried."

"How are you planning to get to it?" she asked. They didn't have any tools and they could be spotted. What if the police were making rounds through the park and questioned them? Could they tell the truth about what they were doing?

Obtaining the stash pack couldn't be simple. What if the ground was frozen? How had Brady marked the exact spot where he'd left it? What if someone else had found it? Worries torpedoed through her.

"I'm planning to dig it out," Brady said.

Brady stumbled and grabbed Susan's arm to catch himself. He winced and met her gaze. She read the tension in his jaw and the pain in his eyes. His knee again. She wouldn't say anything about it. Not now. The sensation when his eyes connected with hers spoke loudly enough.

She was there for him like he'd been for her.

The permanence of that statement was undecided, but for now, each other was all they had.

The library was in sight and Brady stopped. Susan clasped his arm. "Here?"

"I need to orient myself with the landmarks. This isn't easy in the dark," Brady said. He picked up a branch and a rock from the ground and counted the trees outside. He moved back and forth several times, his limp noticeable. "I got it."

He shuffled into a thin copse of trees. Avoiding low branches and pine needles, Brady stopped behind a large tree with a thick trunk. He knelt down, winced and began digging with the stick. The ground was cold and frozen and progress was slow. He shifted his weight several times and extended his injured leg.

Brady lost his balance and fell backward, knocking his head on the trunk of a nearby tree.

"Brady!" Susan knelt next to him, helping him to sit up. "Are you okay?"

Brady rubbed the back of his head. "My balance is off. I haven't eaten enough. Let's get this done and get out of here."

His clipped tone indicated he didn't want to discuss it further. He was in worse shape than he was letting on. Would he admit it if he needed to rest?

Susan pressed her lips together, wishing she could ask questions about his injury without making him more defensive. "Can I do anything to help?" To help him dig or to help with his knee? The additional question would hurt his pride.

"We need to chip away at the frozen dirt."

Susan glanced over her shoulder to check that no one was watching. The trees blocked most of the light from the street lamps, good for hiding, but bad for seeing what they were doing.

"I'll try using the rock," she said.

They scratched at the ground, working away the frozen chunks of earth. Susan looked around again, feeling someone watching them. She didn't see anyone. They were alone in the small forest. She shivered, expecting someone to jump out from the shadows.

They dug for more than an hour before a piece of string appeared. Brady reached into the hole and whipped the string left and right, breaking the dirt and drawing it up. More help from the stick and it was free.

He slid the package under his arm. "Let's get out of here." He struggled to his feet and kicked dirt into the hole.

Did he have everything they needed? He didn't check the contents. Would he be able to walk to the car or was his knee too stiff? She slipped his hand over her shoulder, pretending she wanted the warmth. He could lean on her and she could help if he lost his balance again. The smoldering sensation of being tucked at his side slid over her body. He was holding on to her for a practical reason, but her emotions couldn't discern the difference. Feelings she'd stifled sprang to life and she rested her head against his shoulder. How could a relationship that felt so right in one way be such a painful disaster?

They walked toward their car, heads down. Susan's heart beat rapidly, her body too warm from their digging and leaning against Brady, her hands, feet and face cold from the winter air.

What if they were stopped? What was in that canvas bag? Wads of cash would make them look guilty. How could Brady explain where they'd gotten it?

"Hey, you!"

Susan froze, but Brady hugged her closer. "Don't stop. Keep walking," Brady said under his breath.

"Hey, you, you dropped something."

A voice she didn't recognize. The sound of footsteps approaching faster had Brady swearing under his breath. "Let me handle this."

Brady dropped his arm from her shoulders and turned. The loss of contact gave her a moment to regain her emotional composure. Susan pinned her eyes to the ground, letting loose strands of dark hair fall over her face. Her face had been on the news in connection with Justin's death, but the lighting here was poor. Was it enough to prevent her from being recognized?

"You dropped this," the man said, extending his hand, giving Brady a glove.

"Thanks. Must have slipped from my pocket. Have a good one," Brady said. He turned away, giving the man his shoulder.

"Wait, do I know you? You look familiar," the man said.

"I have one of those faces," Brady said. He took Susan's arm. "We've got to haul out of here."

They walked faster. The fewer people who recognized them, the more difficult they'd be to trace. Otherwise, they'd leave a trail for the men who wanted her dead to follow.

Once they were in the car, Brady handed Susan the canvas bag. His knee was throbbing and stiff from working in the dark for an hour. He needed a hot soak and a deep tissue massage. At the rate things were going, he wouldn't get either.

"Open it," he said.

Susan did so and gasped at the contents. "What is this?"

It was self-explanatory, but maybe Susan couldn't believe he had made these preparations. "Stuff I need to stay under the radar for a few months." Working in special operations required his silence about where he worked and the specifics of what he did. He sometimes overheard top secret mission information, sometimes worked in volatile parts of the world and sometimes had to complete tasks knowing little about the big picture.

It was part of the job description and one he'd accepted and been discreet about as needed.

He and Susan both needed to disappear for a while. Brady had no delusions that the people stalking Susan would give up. They wouldn't stop looking for her until Brady shut them down.

"You have a gun in here," she said.

"I know," he said.

"Please take it."

He reached across to her lap and took the gun. He checked the safety and set it next to him. It hadn't been serviced in some time, but it would have to do for now. He cursed his luck in losing his original gun in the water at the marina. Another mistake he'd made and one that could have dire consequences.

"Why do you have these things? Is it legal to have a fake ID and credit cards and this much cash?" Susan asked.

Legal, yes, in a sense. "I told you. I was assigned to difficult and complex missions overseas. If things went wrong and I had to return covertly to the United States while the dust settled, I needed supplies. I planned to stay in an area familiar to me, but keep myself untraceable."

Susan was turning the identification over in her hand. "This looks real."

"It is real. It was created using the same equipment the DMV uses." He'd gotten most of the contents of the pack from his superiors in the Air Force. The cash, that was his. The credit cards could be traced by the military, and if he had to disappear, Brady wanted to do so on his terms.

"If something had gone wrong and you had to hide

out under a different name, how long would you live that way?" Susan asked.

"Worst case scenario, indefinitely. Best case, a few weeks," Brady said. He was no longer in that line of work and lying wasn't necessary. His backup identity wasn't classified any longer. It pained him to think about it. His work had been a source of great pride and meaning in his life. What did he have now? A dead career, a weakened body and the personal life of a hermit.

Susan had gone still. "You're saying you could have disappeared without a word and I would have been left wondering where you were." Her voice was calm and cold, and anger tinged the edges of her words.

Disappearing for a period of time wasn't his ideal scenario. Losing contact with family and friends would have been difficult and Brady would have only taken that option as a last resort. "That's one way to look at it. If they couldn't safely get me out of it, the air force would have told you I was dead," he said.

Susan gritted her teeth. "Oh, well, that would have been much better."

It had occurred to him how unfair it was to her. It was a huge part of the reason he'd broken up with her. Did she see that he'd been trying to do right by her, to give her a chance for the life she wanted?

"I knew how difficult my job would be when I took it. It would be hard on my family, my friends and anyone who relied on me."

Susan scoffed. "What a load of crap."

Her anger incensed him. Was she calling him out for his dedication and devotion to his country? He prided himself on being loyal, true and courageous.

"What is a load of crap?" he asked. He sensed this was a fight that had been brewing for some time.

Susan threw the contents of the stash pack on the floor of the car. "You loved your job. You loved everything about it. It was a bonus that you had an excuse to be free to do as you pleased without commitment, without considering anyone else."

Now it was his turn to call crap. He had considered how his friends or family would feel if he disappeared and they were told he was dead. It had bothered him to think of what his mother, his father, his brothers and Susan would have to live through.

"You have no right to judge what I did or what choices I made. I made a sacrifice for my country and it wasn't an easy one. How can you say I'm selfish? That I only care about myself? What am I doing now? Only looking out for number one? No! I'm here. With you. Putting my life and my integrity on the line to keep you safe. If I'm such an inconsiderate jerk, why would I have bothered with you or with any of this?" Hot rage coursed through him. She didn't see it. She didn't see how much he'd cared then and how much he cared now.

Long seconds passed. Finally, Susan spoke. "You're right. I don't know what you were thinking and you made a tremendous sacrifice for our country. I should have seen it sooner. I should have known you were a man who put his career first. I should have seen it coming."

She was bothered by how he'd ended their relationship. How could he make it right? Rehashing the past wouldn't help either of them and they'd skated around it enough. Addressing the heat between them by kissing her hadn't helped. Brady had closed the door on the past and his mistakes. He didn't like to think about his injury or his last tour with the air force. Resentment and frustration reignited whenever he did. He didn't like to think about losing her as part of his life. He had to live with the choices he'd made. "We've moved past it. We have other problems to worry about." They needed to focus on finding out who was chasing them and why, and stop them.

"We do have other problems," she agreed. It sounded as if she had more to say, but she remained quiet.

Brady would have given a fortune for her thoughts. Was she dwelling on the failings of their relationship? Getting angrier about how he had treated her? Was she thinking about the relationship in the present? Was it arrogant to think he would occupy some of her thoughts even though she was grieving for another man? Or were her personal relationships a distant second to finding Justin's killer and staying safe? "Are we okay with the past? Okay with putting it behind us?"

Susan folded her arms over her chest. "Sure. It's over. We've both moved on."

Her tone gave her away. She wasn't okay with it and he wasn't sure how to fix it. He only knew how to keep going. In his life, in his career, when things hit the skids, he kept moving. Now, he needed to find a way to move in a direction that wasn't aimless.

Susan reached for the radio dial. "Maybe we should see if the fire at the marina made it to the news."

Brady had been avoiding the news for that reason. Listening to it might add to Susan's guilt and stress. "What good does it do for us to hear about it? We know what happened."

Susan adjusted the station. "We know what happened, but we don't know exactly who is responsible or why. Maybe we can learn something about the fire."

They listened to the radio for twenty minutes before the station switched to local news. The boat fire at Cherry Creek was third on the agenda after the weather and a report about an apartment fire that had destroyed twelve family homes, no casualties.

"Maybe I'll get blamed for that, too," Susan muttered.

"Another fire broke out tonight at the Cherry Creek State Park marina. The police have received an anonymous tip from a witness placing two suspects in connection with that fire at the scene. The police are looking for thirty-year-old Susan Prescott. The boat had belonged to her fiancé, Justin Ambrose, who went missing a week ago. The police suspect foul play, but no one has been officially charged in that murder. The police are narrowing their suspect list."

Susan snorted. "Narrowing it? It has one name on it. Mine."

"Thirty-two-year-old Brady Truman, Susan's exboyfriend and former air force pararescueman is wanted for questioning in connection with the blaze," the report continued.

Brady swore inwardly. The media had connected him and Susan as intimately involved. Dragging his connection to the air force would stir up more drama. The military would be quick to distance themselves from him. Would Justin's father speak out against Brady or act on the threat he'd made?

"The mayor had this to say about the suspected arson," the reporter said.

"Susan Prescott is a menace. I urge the police to complete their investigation and arrest Justin Ambrose's murderer before someone else is hurt." The sound bite ended and switched back to the reporter.

"Anyone with information is urged to call the police. A reward of twenty thousand dollars is being offered in exchange for information leading to an arrest."

The news moved to another story and Brady turned down the volume. "Anonymous tip? Right. Like the men who tried to kill us calling in that we were at the scene."

Susan appeared so tense he thought she might crack if he touched her.

"We're okay," he said.

"We are not okay," Susan said, whipping her head toward him. "We're wanted by the police. The entire state is looking for us. You heard the mayor. I'm a menace."

The mayor was a pompous windbag spouting garbage for his friend the lieutenant general, and Susan was being melodramatic. It wasn't everyone in the state looking for them. Just the police officers, whichever local citizens wanted to get involved and the men hunting them. It wasn't a good situation and it was getting worse by the minute. But these were the cards they'd been dealt. "We'll be fine. The mayor shouldn't be saying anything about an ongoing investigation."

Brady set a hand on her thigh and a current of heat ran between them. Susan didn't move his hand away. Was his touch comforting to her? When they'd been a couple, touching her had been second nature. Were they falling into old habits for sheer comfort? Or did touching mean more? Their physical connection was the one part of their relationship that hadn't been a problem. He didn't want to make it one.

Susan jammed her hand through her hair. "This is getting out of hand. Maybe we should turn ourselves in and answer their questions."

An adamant no sprang to mind. "How do you know the mayor's pressure won't force the police to make an arrest? I can't protect you while you're in custody. We don't know who the men are who are looking for you. What if they have connections within the police department?"

Susan's look of shock almost made him wish he hadn't spoken the words. But she couldn't be naïve about this. He'd learned in the military he was in the most danger when he'd underestimated his opponent.

"You'd know the truth if something happened to me," Susan said, covering his hand with hers.

"It wouldn't help you be undead. I'd have proof of nothing. I don't have an alternative theory of the case. I won't risk your life," Brady said.

She squeezed his hand. "I'm sorry I can't give you another theory."

"I'm not blaming you."

He didn't have to turn to feel Susan's stare. "You're blaming me for what happened to Reilly."

"Categorically untrue," Brady said.

Susan pulled her hand away. "You blame me for Justin's death."

Brady shook his head. "Again, untrue." Where was she getting this?

"Well, if you don't blame me, you should. I blame myself for this. For making terrible choices. All the signs point to me being involved. I hurt Reilly. I made you come to the crime scene and now the police want to question you." Her voice broke. "I shouldn't have been involved with Justin. We were wrong for each other. I knew it. He knew it."

Brady fumbled to process her words. Hadn't she been in love with Justin? They'd been engaged.

"If you didn't love him, why did you agree to marry him?"

Susan let out her breath in a rush. "On paper, we looked great together and when he asked, I didn't have a reason to say no. What was I supposed to do? Wait for you? You made it clear you didn't want to be with me. You didn't even want my friendship."

Again, bringing up the hospital. Which was bothering her more, that they'd broken up or that he'd been harsh with her when she'd visited in the hospital? "I explained to you—"

"No." Her hand sliced through the air. "You explained you had too much going on to deal with me. Friends aren't something you deal with. Friends are people who want to help you."

"I'm not good at asking for help," Brady said.

She let out a bark of bitter laughter. "At least you can admit it."

It wasn't easy to ask for assistance when Brady was used to being the person giving it. It made him feel weak and needy.

"Let me ask you something, Brady. What's your plan?" Susan asked.

"To get you to Connor's cabin, do some digging and make our next move carefully," he said.

"Not your plan for me. Your plan for you and your life. Before you were injured, you had a plan. Your plan was to be in the military and you were great at that. You had a plan you didn't want me part of. Tell me your plan now."

He'd never wanted her not to be part of his life. He just hadn't seen how he could give her the things she wanted and deserved.

"I'm planning to keep us safe." It was the best he could offer.

"Stop thinking short-term. Tell me where you'll be in six months."

Six months was an eternity. His plans from the past were moot. He had limits and obstacles now. "My long-term options are limited," Brady said, thinking about his knee. Frustration renewed in his chest.

"Were you irrevocably brain damaged by the event?" she asked.

Was he acting brain damaged? Loopy? "No," he said. Where was she going with this?

"Then your options aren't that limited. You're an intelligent man. You've spent your career in the military, but that's not all you are. You're smart. You can do other stuff."

The problem was that "other stuff" was vague and he had always wanted to serve in the military. He'd spent years chasing that goal and reaching it, and now he had to start fresh. What else did he want to do? What else would make him happy?

Susan. Susan had made him happy. Brady hated to admit it, but she had. When they'd been together, he'd had fun. He'd had a reason to come home. Now Susan wanted him to come up with career options to move past his work with the pararescuemen. What was he trained to do? His entire career had been spent in the military doing a job he loved. "The air force is all I know. It's all I've ever known. It's shaped my career since I was eighteen years old. I don't know what to do next." The words were difficult to speak. Brady liked being in control. He wasn't in control of his injury or healing. Finding another career wasn't easy and failure wasn't a result he embraced. "At least it gives me time to help you."

Susan pressed her lips together. She was deciding whether or not to continue the conversation. "Your injury doesn't define you. Everyone has challenges to overcome. I never thought I would see the day you would let circumstances dictate your fate."

She was making him sound weak, like a jellyfish tossed about by the sea. He didn't take kindly to that. "I am working within the confines of my restrictions."

"You're being emotionally paralyzed by a physical limit," she said.

Coming from anyone else, he would have dismissed the comment. From her, it hit him hard. Was he making excuses for sitting around, stewing and waiting for physical therapy to return to him the knee he'd once had? His doctors had told him it wasn't possible. Was he clinging to that hope anyway?

"I'm doing the best I can."

Susan shot him a disbelieving look. She'd hit the nail on the head and even he didn't believe his protests to the contrary.

But helping Susan had given him a purpose. She'd gotten him off the couch. Now, he needed to figure out what he could do next.

Chapter 7

They were an hour outside Denver when Brady decided to stop for supplies he hadn't gotten from Reilly's. Susan had fallen asleep in the passenger seat.

If they could get to Connor's cabin undetected, rest his leg and dry out the notebook, they could figure out their next move. If Brady wasn't in pain for a little bit, he could think clearly and lay out what they knew about Justin's death and the men following them. The more he knew, the better he could protect Susan.

The white-and-red light from the twenty-four-hour drugstore glared into the dark. At this early morning hour, the parking lot was near empty. Brady parked behind the drugstore and touched Susan's shoulders.

She woke, mumbling groggily. "What's wrong?"

"I'm getting supplies. Stay in the car with the doors locked. I'll leave the gun in case you need it."

Susan's eyes opened wide. "Why would I need a gun?"

He didn't like the idea of leaving Susan unarmed and without resources. "In case someone approaches you. It's unlikely, but I want you to be prepared." He pointed to the stash pack on the floor. "Don't forget about the cash. I only took what I think I'll need. If I don't come back in twenty minutes, take the car and get out of here. Find a pay phone, borrow a phone, whatever you have to do, and call Harris. He'll tell you what to do."

Susan's eyes narrowed in confusion. "Why wouldn't you come back?"

"Just in case. Contingency plan."

Susan unfastened her seat belt. "Stop. I won't leave you if you get into trouble. If you think something isn't right or someone is looking at you too long, get out of there."

"I'll do my best."

She wrinkled her nose. "Why don't I come with you?"

Brady hadn't had time to check out the security situation and he didn't want to risk revealing her face. He was accustomed to working under the radar. She wasn't. "Whoever is looking for us is looking for two people and they'll assume we're together. It'll invite less attention for me to go alone. We haven't been followed. You'll be okay in the car for a few minutes."

Susan's narrowed eyes turned into a full-on glare when he got out of the car. "I'll make it fast. Doors locked," he reminded her.

The cold abraded his face and Brady mentally thanked Reilly for buying heavy winter boots and warm, lined clothes. As a police detective, Reilly spent a lot of time outdoors. He didn't skimp on cold weather gear.

Shoving his hands into the pockets of his coat, Brady pulled up the hood on the sweatshirt he was wearing and hunched his shoulders. He altered his gait to a slow lope to disguise himself.

Stretching his legs, moving his knee and inhaling the cold air was good for him, clearing his tired brain, sharpening his thoughts and taking the edge off his desire for Susan. What they'd had couldn't be resurrected. Why the kiss? The easy answer: he craved her in his arms. The more complicated one: they had some unexplored emotional fallout from their breakup and neither of them had figured out how to behave around each other.

Brady looked over his shoulder. He didn't think anyone had followed them, but he didn't know whom he was up against. If they were former Special Forces, they would have training in covertly trailing someone. Lucky for him, he had the same training and knew what to look for. At least Susan was right on that count. He might be physically incapable of performing at a Special Forces level, but his mind was still sharp.

He entered the store through the double set of sliding-glass doors. Luckily, the store wasn't crowded at this time of night.

A mom with her two children were in line at the pharmacy counter, a frazzled pharmacy technician was on the phone and a bored-looking cashier waited for customers, inspecting her nails and snapping her gum in her mouth.

Brady scanned the aisle markers. They needed basic

toiletries, trail supplies, a burner phone, hair dye and scissors. He'd forgotten to nab a pair from Reilly's. Susan hair was too long and too memorable.

Brady grabbed a red handcart and strode to the hair-dye aisle. He should have asked Susan her opinion on color before coming into the store. If he left now, checked with her and came back, it was too suspicious. He'd select the dye on his own.

Brady kept his shoulders turned and his head down. The large mirrors along the rear wall of the store were meant to discourage theft, but they gave a good view of the aisles and the people in them.

He grabbed a bottle of men's hair dye, easiest since the store carried limited options. He picked the box that read "fast and easy."

For Susan, he snagged a box of black dye off the shelf and tossed it in the basket. Susan would look great with darker hair, too. Maybe it would suit her art-ist persona. She might like it, or was it wishful think-ing? He hated doing more to upset her, but his top priority was to keep her safe and he would do what-ever was needed to ensure she was.

He searched the aisles for unlined paper and pen-cils for her. The best he found was a child's drawing pad and number-two pencils. He picked them up and tossed them in his handcart.

He found a prepaid toss-away phone, spent another five minutes in the toiletries section and took a trip down the food aisle. Then Brady headed for the ca-shier.

He froze when two policemen entered.

Were they looking for him and Susan? How would they have known where they had gone? Haley's sedan was an older model and didn't have a built-in GPS. Had his trail been caught this quickly?

Brady scanned for another exit. If he ran for the front door, the cops would see him. He'd told Susan he would be back and he had every intention of keeping his word to her. Letting her down again was unacceptable.

Brady crept closer to the front counter. The cops were talking to the checkout clerk. Brady couldn't hear what they were saying. Were they questioning the clerk or alerting her they were searching for two suspects in an arson? Were they handing out his picture?

As if sensing he was being watched, one of the policemen turned. Brady ducked into the aisle. He took his time perusing the shelves, keeping his face turned away. Would the police officers go into the parking lot and see Susan? Had the police realized he and Susan had taken Haley's car? He'd meant for his car, left at the bus terminal, to serve as a decoy for the men following Susan. If the police were also looking for him and Susan, would they see through the ruse?

The cops wandered up the first aisle. Brady had to pay for his items and get out of the store unseen. Or ditch the items and stop elsewhere for supplies. Had the clerk been alerted to the APB about him and Susan? As word spread about the boat fire, finding safe places to gather supplies would become fewer and farther between.

How long had Brady been in the store? Five minutes? Ten? Susan didn't wear a watch. After a few more restless moments, she turned on the battery in the car to check the time. She'd wait a little longer and then check again.

If Brady didn't come out, she was going inside the store to get him.

Brady. His behavior had always been a mystery to her. In some ways, he was an honest, straight-shooting man. He gave his opinion when asked and she never worried what he said would be a lie.

Brady's dishonesty was about omission. Brady kept parts of his life closed off. Maybe it came from the work he did in the air force and that he had to be private about it. Or maybe it was because a CIA agent had raised him. But that Brady kept closed off from her drove her crazy. She could sense when he wasn't saying something and she never knew the question to ask to prompt him for more.

Even during the best part of their relationship, when she'd felt closer to Brady than any other person in the world, he'd held back. Though he was never much for telling her how he'd felt about her, his actions had told her that he'd wanted her in his life. She had been caught off-guard when he'd ended their relationship. She'd come to understand Brady by his actions.

His actions now were decidedly unclear. Though he had no reason to, he was staying with her. Staying so close he'd kissed her as if it was the most natural thing in the world. In many ways, she'd sensed it coming before he'd pulled her close. She'd tried and failed to fight her body's automatic response. She'd sunk into the kiss, giving herself over as if surrender was inevitable. Weak. It was weak that she'd reacted that way.

If she let him inside, Brady would break her heart.

In addition to his past behavior, he was struggling with his own demons.

By the time her brain, and heart, had engaged, he had stopped the kiss. Ended it before she'd had a chance to process it. They hadn't had—and wouldn't have—a discussion about the kiss. It had happened. It might happen again; it might not.

No, definitely not. She would be more vigilant. Kissing each other and confusing a complicated situation was a mistake. He didn't want her in his life in any real way and she wasn't getting caught in another one-sided relationship with Brady.

Susan reached across to the driver's side and turned the key in the ignition again to check the time. Instead of the clock, her eyes fixated on the two policemen entering the store.

Panic seized her. Were they coming for Brady? Had Brady been recognized and detained in the store? She took a deep breath to calm her racing heart. What should she do?

She could dash inside and look for him. But that might get them both captured. She needed to call Harris. He would know what to do.

Her hand was on the door handle, ready to search for a pay phone, when Brady exited the store a few moments later, plastic bags in hand. He wasn't running. His didn't appear alarmed. He seemed confident and in control. He looked muscular and strong moving toward her.

He got in the driver's side and Susan let out a cry of emotion she hadn't expected. "Why were the cops in the store?"

"I don't know, but we need to get out of here before anyone spots us," he said.

Her nerves tingled. "Are they looking for Haley's car?"

"I don't know. Maybe. I don't want to wait around to find out."

"I think you need to adjust your definition of 'fast.' If you had been in that store one more minute with the cops, I was calling Harris for help."

Brady started the car. "Here I am, safe and sound. Most men would prefer a hero's welcome. But I guess veiled hostility is acceptable."

Hostility? Is that what he heard in her voice? She didn't mean to sound angry with him. She'd been worried by the police officers' appearance. Susan owed Brady for what he'd done for her. She leaned over and kissed his cheek. "There's your hero's welcome. You are a hero and don't let anyone tell you different." She'd guess the person who told him most often he wasn't a hero was himself.

It was difficult to tell, but in the dark, it seemed like Brady blushed. Brady Truman blushing? Susan couldn't believe it. Brady pulled out of the parking spot and turned onto the road, keeping his speed steady. Susan watched in the passenger-side mirror, expecting to see red-and-blue headlights pursuing them.

"We're okay for now, but we need to limit our stops. If I had to guess, Justin's father is calling in more favors to make finding us the mayor and police department's number one priority."

Susan closed her eyes. The weight of what Brady said settled over her. The police were looking for them. Someone was hunting her. She had the anger of a lieutenant general in the air force bearing down on her. She scrubbed her hands over her face.

"I'm sorry, Susan. I know you never wanted any of this—Justin's death, me in your life, the problems at your job...." He let his voice trail away.

He had part of it right. Her life was falling apart and she couldn't do anything to stop it. She hated that. But him? She had mixed emotions about Brady. For too long, she had harbored bitterness and anger. She'd wanted to forget about Brady and the happy memories they had shared. She'd wanted to forget how he'd made her feel when they'd been together: wonderful, loved and cherished. She'd wanted to cling to her anger and use it to sever her emotional ties to him.

Now that Brady was in her life again, she was forced to confront her feelings. Her attraction to him lingered. Her unresolved emotions pinged at her, plucking at the anger and sadness she had tried to put to rest. But surviving this ordeal required her to let go of the past and their mistakes and trust Brady. He was her one ally. If only setting aside their past and concentrating on the present was as easy for her as it seemed to be for him.

They made the hour drive with the radio keeping them company. Slushy, snow-lined the roads made the inclined terrain slippery for Haley's sedan. The car skidded several times and Susan had to close her eyes and breathe to stay calm. Haley's car was equipped with studded tires and Brady was a good driver.

The snow was falling harder, but the rising sun made navigating the narrow roads easier. Crosses and flowers were laid several places on the side of the road, locations where travelers had died taking the turns too fast or skidding into a tree.

"We'll be okay," Brady said. "You can open your eyes."

Susan opened one eye and looked at him. Was that humor in his voice? "These roads are borderline treacherous. Maybe we should go somewhere else."

"I don't know of any other safe place," he said. "And we'll make it."

"We had a good time the last time we visited Winter Park," she said. She'd hoped the words would diffuse some of the awkwardness, but the moment she replayed the words, she remembered how they had spent most of their time together—alone and in each other's arms.

Brady's shoulders tightened. "Yes, we did." Each word spoken slowly as if he was being careful not to ignite a difficult conversation.

Was he remembering the trip the way she did? The gentle easiness of new love, the excitement of learning about someone else, every new discovery fresh and exhilarating. New relationships were easier than old ones. No baggage. No resentment.

"Do you think part of our problem was that we got too involved too quickly?" Susan asked. After what her mother had been through with her father, Susan had learned to be guarded and careful in relationships. But then she'd met Brady. Once she'd made up her mind, she'd handed her heart and trust over to him completely. She'd told herself Brady was different from other men. Different covered all manner of sins. In the end, he'd broken her heart. It hadn't mattered that Brady had been—and was—a good man. When it came to love, no one was safe.

"The timing was wrong, but not in the way you mean," Brady said.

Susan waited for him to elaborate. He didn't. "If we had met now, would things have ended differently?" With his injury, Brady would choose a career that would be less adventuresome than his previous had been. His life would change. Would he grow resentful? Or would he take to his new job and enjoy it, closing the Special Forces chapter of his life and moving on to new and exciting opportunities?

The car slid and Brady turned the wheel, catching the vehicle and maneuvering it into the center of the lane. He didn't answer her question and Susan didn't repeat herself. Brady was intentionally not answering.

Fine. She was used to his silences. It was his favorite emotional response. She could read between the lines. If they'd starting dating now, he'd expect it to end the same: with a breakup.

Brady swore. "Someone is tailgating us. What kind of idiot does that when the weather and road conditions are like this?"

Susan looked in the side-view mirror. The narrow road leading to Connor's cabin was two lanes, one each way, and a dotted passing line between them. A black SUV was riding close to their bumper. A skier anxious to get to their vacation house? "If you slow down, maybe he'll go around us."

The SUV behind them sped up and rammed their car. Brady struggled to keep their car on the road. The smaller sedan lurched and swerved.

"How did these guys find us?"

Susan's breath caught in her throat and a heavy feeling settled over her stomach. "I don't know. We ditched your phone. Does anyone else know about this cabin?"

"Harris does," Brady said and grit his teeth. "But he wouldn't betray us."

Their engine revved and Brady climbed the road faster to get away from the SUV. The car's wheels spun and slid, unable to find traction.

"Turn around and see if you can get a look at the driver or passengers," Brady said.

Susan twisted in her seat. The driver wore a ski mask pulled over his face. She didn't see anyone else in the car. "I don't recognize him or the vehicle. I can't see his face. And it's just one person this time." Another mercenary closing in on them?

The SUV hit their car again and the sedan skidded across the road. Brady twisted the wheel and hit the brakes, trying to gain control of the car. Their car spun, moving into the other lane and facing down the hill. The black SUV struck them head on and their car bowled backward, slamming into the guardrail behind them. The sound of metal on metal filled the car, but their car stopped moving.

"Thank God," Susan said, her heart beating so fast she felt sick.

The SUV wasn't finished. It reversed and hit the front of the car again with a sickening crunch and twisting of metal. The airbags deployed. Their car seesawed against the guardrail.

"We have to get out of the car," Brady said. The car rocked on the edge of the cliff.

Susan looked around. She could get her door open, but then what? The incline was steep and slippery. Could she reach the road? Was the SUV's driver waiting for them? Would another car drive past and scare him off? She didn't have time to ask questions. There was a groan of metal, a snapping sound and then their car slid backward down the hill.

Susan braced her feet on the floor, trying to keep her body from slamming around the car. Her seat belt and the airbags pinned her in her seat. Brady's arm came across her, trying to stabilize her.

Their car pounded into something with the crunching of metal and breaking of glass and stopped moving.

"Susan, are you okay?"

"I'm fine," she said, trying to feel for the car door handle on her right. They had to get out of the car before it went into another free fall. They were lucky to be alive and conscious.

She released her seat belt and pushed at the air bag, trying to see around it.

After struggling for a few moments, Brady pulled open her door and dragged her out of the car. They were standing thirty yards down the hill away from the main road, their car caught on two large trees. Was the driver of the SUV checking if they had survived? Could he see down the slope?

Brady opened the backseat and pulled out bags, throwing them over his shoulder. Susan slipped in the snow and Brady grabbed her wrist to keep her upright. After regaining her balance, Susan reached for the stash pack and the plastic bags from the twenty-four-hour drugstore.

"Are you hurt?" Brady asked.

She didn't feel hurt. Shaken up, not injured. "I'm okay. I think. What about you?"

"I'm fine. He'll be looking for us. We need to make tracks," Brady said.

They hitched their supplies high on their shoulders and started moving through the snow, down the steep terrain, their feet sliding beneath them. Had Brady hurt his knee in the crash? Would he tell her if he had?

"Are you sure you're not hurt?" she asked.

"I can walk and that's what's important," Brady said.

Then he was injured and hurting. She didn't see any wounds. Didn't mean his neck or back or legs weren't hurt. Had he hit his head?

"What *was* that? Or maybe the better question is who was that?" Susan asked.

"My best guess is another operative making a determined attempt to kill you."

He wasn't mincing words. "How did he know where we were?"

"I don't know yet how they're following us," Brady said.

The sound of a gunshot sounded. The driver of the SUV was firing at them.

"Move faster," Brady said.

"Where will we go?" Susan asked. Around them were trees and snow. No signs of cabins or other roads.

"We'll get away from the wreck and look for shelter and help. Connor's cabin isn't the only one out here." Brady had a prepaid phone in his hand. "No signal. We'll preserve battery life for now." He turned the phone off and put it in his jacket pocket.

Brady changed directions a few times, zigzagging through the trees. The snow was falling, some catching on tree branches, some covering their tracks as they walked. In a few hours, their path wouldn't be as easy to follow. Was the driver of the SUV scaling the cliff after them or calling for reinforcements?

They were two people, lost in the woods, in the snow, without directions or GPS devices. What chance did they stand against a group of highly trained Special Forces ops stalking them? Hysteria escalated her heart. "Brady, how will we survive this? We don't know where we are or what we're doing."

Brady stopped and faced her, taking her by the upper arms. "Susan. Look at me."

Susan met his gaze.

"They won't find us. You have to trust me. If you lose it, then they gain the advantage. Ninety percent of my success with the Special Forces was a mental game."

Susan nodded. She had to have faith that Brady would get them out of this. "I'm sorry. I'll be calm. Just tell me what to do." She took a deep breath and let it out slowly.

"We need to move in one direction and look for help or shelter."

They hiked through the trees and Susan didn't see anyone or any place to go for help. Exhaustion was beginning to catch up to her. Despite the cold, she was hot in her jacket, the effort of lifting her knees high to progress through the snowdrifts wearing her down. Cold water from melted snow soaked through her jeans.

They kept walking, staying close together. How long had they been walking? How far had they traveled? "How close are we to the road or to other cabins?" Susan asked.

"I don't know. I don't know this area."

Fear took hold of her thoughts again. "How do we know we're not walking in circles? Everything out here is starting to look the same."

"If we follow the downward slope of the hill, we won't walk in circles. We'll find help."

Susan kept her feet moving, fatigue fogging her head and hunger cramping her stomach. A wave of dizziness hit her. "Brady, when can we stop and take a break? My feet are soaking wet and I need to rest."

Brady turned. "Next spot I find, we'll stop. I want to be sure we weren't followed. Then I'll start a fire. We need to stay dry."

They continued onward. She held on to his bag for guidance, her eyes beginning to close.

Brady finally stopped near a rock formation. He dropped the bags he was carrying to the ground. He opened one of them and rifled inside. "Take off your shoes and socks and wrap your feet with this." He handed her a flannel shirt. "I need to get supplies. Wait underneath this overhang. It will block some of the snow and wind."

"Wait here? What if someone comes?" She didn't stand a chance against an ex-Special Forces operative.

Brady pulled the gun from his jacket. "Take this."

"I don't know why you seem to think I'm proficient with a gun. I've never shot a gun. I don't know what I'm doing." She heard the panic in her voice and felt her control slipping. "I don't know what I'm doing with any of this."

Brady sat next to her. "You need to trust me. I've survived in worse than this. Picture being actively shot at, wounded and without any supplies. This is easy.

Like a practice drill with help nearby. You can do this. You've faced everything that has come our way and survived. We'll survive this."

He sounded confident and it eased her fears. He had training in the wilderness. She had none. "I hate that I can't be more help."

"We're both doing everything we can. We'll get dry, get something to eat and then make plans, okay?"

He gently touched the side of her face, stroking her cheek with his thumb. Heat diffused across her face.

"Okay," she said, his faith in her bolstering her courage.

He dug through their bags and handed her a box of graham crackers. She tore into it.

"No one will find us and I'll be gone for ten minutes," Brady said, taking one of the crackers.

He also took the gun with him. She didn't want it. She was more likely to shoot herself than someone else. Her feet felt better out of her wet shoes and socks. As food settled into her stomach, Susan's mind cleared. She looked around. Were there wolves or coyotes out in the forest? Would they approach a human?

A crackling of branches penetrated the silence. Fear closed over her. Susan looked around. Was the noise a tree limb giving out under the weight of the snow or someone approaching? Her breath puffed into the cold air and Susan pressed tighter against the rock formation. She wished for better cover, for ground brush or clothes that blended into the stark white and bare brown around her.

After several minutes of scarcely moving for fear of making a sound, Susan stifled fear-fuelled thoughts. No one had found her and getting hysterical wasn't helpful. Instead, she refocused. She needed to do something to help. Susan took out the notebook and pencil Brady had bought. If she could draw, she might feel better and work free the memories that had buried themselves in her mind. She started drawing the living room on Justin's boat, pre-fire, trying to let her subconscious fill in the details she was missing. What had it looked like before Justin had died? Could she remember the events of the night?

Guilt and grief returned. Justin deserved better. He deserved justice, no matter what he may have been involved in, and for that to happen, she had to remember. The men who had set fire to the boat believed she had killed him. She didn't want to think it was possible. A small lingering doubt whispered. Her mother had killed her father. She had witnessed how far people could go to defend and protect themselves. Had she had a reason to protect herself from Justin? He had never threatened her. Had never made her feel unsafe. Had something changed between them that night causing her to commit the ultimate act of violence?

Another sound of footsteps crunching through the snow and Susan held her breath. Brady appeared, his arms filled with wood, leaves and twigs. Relief washed over her. "Thank God you're back."

Brady cleared an area of snow and set out the twigs. "Did you think I'd leave you alone out here?"

The thought had never crossed her mind. "I thought I heard something. I was worried."

Brady looked around. "I circled the area. I didn't see other human footprints. We're alone for now."

Human footprints? "You saw animal prints?"

Brady arranged the sticks over the twigs. "I'm not

an expert in tracking, but they likely belonged to a smaller animal. Maybe a beaver or a fox. We don't have to be concerned. We'll get this fire started and get as dry as we can." He paused and looked at her. "The snow will make it difficult for a fire. Not impossible though."

In his words was a hint of cockiness from the old Brady, the Brady who wasn't injured and who believed he could do anything. After several starts and misses and borrowing some paper from the sketch pad, Brady fanned small flames into larger ones. He slowly added more kindling. Once the fire was going strong, he laid Susan's shoes and socks close to it. "We'll let those dry."

He then opened their duffel and rearranged their supplies. "We'll rest for a while, and then keep moving. The falling snow will cover our tracks, but an experienced tracker will find us."

"Do you think it was an experienced tracker that forced us off the road?" Susan asked.

"At this point, we need to be paranoid. Are you cold?"

"I wasn't while we were walking."

He handed her clothes from the duffel. "Layer your clothes. As we walk, you can shed layers you don't need. If we're resting, you have to stay warm."

He laid leaves on the ground underneath the natural overhang formed by the rocks. "These will keep water from seeping from the ground into your clothes. Lie down and rest. I'll wake you when we need to get moving."

"What about you?" She had slept in the car. Brady had been awake all night.

"I'll rest, as well," he said.

Susan lay on the leaves and set her head on her hands.

Brady spread more leaves behind her. "I'll sleep with my back to you, is that okay?"

It would be warmer and if he was close enough, the rocks would shelter him from the elements. "Of course. We have to do what we can to stay alive."

Brady shifted on the ground. It was too easy to get comfortable and fall asleep. He had to keep one eye open and rest for a short time. They needed the daylight to walk over the rough terrain of the mountain.

Their fire could draw attention. Though no worn path existed to follow them, their tracks could be traced in the snow. His training as a pararescueman warned him about getting too relaxed. He had to remain alert. He beat back the exhaustion that crept over him.

Susan's warm body was inviting in a way that was cruel to a cold man who'd been without a woman for too long. Brady had the burden of knowing she needed someone to protect her and he was that someone. An injured someone, a man who had been medically discharged from the air force because of his inability to perform at an acceptable level. It didn't bode well for them.

To heap more concerns onto his overtired brain, Susan had planted ideas about the future in his mind. She'd flat-out dismissed his reasons for not working toward another career. For the first time in months, shame for wallowing in his misery pummeled him. He'd felt he deserved self-pity and self-anger about his situation. Seeing it through Susan eyes, he felt weak.

And weakness wasn't a trait Truman men embraced. The future didn't need to be as bleak as he'd painted it. Maybe he could find something to do with himself, something that brought him the same satisfaction being in the air force had. Maybe he could get himself together.

For the present, despite his physical challenges, he had to keep her safe. Concern for his brother was playing a secondary role to his worries for Susan. He'd gotten involved to help Reilly, but he was staying involved because of Susan.

Susan rolled over and faced him, the skin under her eyes dark with exhaustion. "How is your knee feeling?"

He considered lying. Maybe it would lift her confidence in him if she believed it wasn't aching. But Susan knew him well and she'd see through the lie. "It's not great. The crash didn't help."

"Can I do anything?" she asked.

He wished she could. "Try to get some rest. We can't stay here long. If I keep off it for a while, it will feel better." He hoped it would feel better, but had his doubts. Physical therapy had helped strengthen it, but he'd been rough on it the past few days. Without pain medication or rest, how long before his knee gave out under the strain he was putting on it?

"Do you think I killed Justin?" she asked.

He guessed the question never stopped playing on her mind. He'd addressed that question before. Why did she need to hear it again? "Unequivocally, no. You did not kill him."

"My mother killed my father," Susan said.

"You think it's genetic?" Brady asked.

"I think I have it in me. If not me, then who?" Susan asked.

"We'll find out," Brady said.

Susan didn't appear convinced. "Is the snow falling on you?"

He brushed the back of his hair. "A little."

She squirmed nearer to the rock formation. "Move in. We're supposed to be getting dry."

He slid his body close and arousal and heat arrowed to his groin. Slipping his arm around her waist, he reveled in the feel of being close to her. It was a place he'd never thought he would be again. A fire started low in his pelvis and he chastised himself for it. She was hurting, worried and grieving. Pouncing on her like an animal wouldn't make her feel better. He marshaled the response and forced his libido to slow.

He would keep his distance and find a way to let her go when this was over. It was best for her. He'd done it once and he'd find the strength to do it again.

Sleep had chased away the worst of Susan's exhaustion. What time was it? She shifted, trying not to wake Brady sleeping next to her. Her arm had started to ache from being pinned in the same position for too long. She moved it slowly.

The rhythmic rise and fall of Brady's chest and the peaceful expression on his face caught and held her attention. He'd needed rest. They both had. With the tension gone from his face, he looked more like he had when they'd dated—relaxed, happy.

Guilt weighing on her, Susan crawled out from next to Brady and went to the fire, checking her shoes and socks. They were much drier. She pulled them onto her feet.

When she turned, Brady was awake, watching her with sleepy eyes. "How'd you sleep?"

"Good." Better than she'd expected under the circumstances. "You?"

Brady sat and rotated his torso, stretching. "It's been a long time since I slept next to a woman."

The words sounded intimate. When they were physically close, the seconds seemed to be laced with sexual tension.

"We'll break camp and get moving," Brady said. "I want to make the most of daylight. If we're lucky, we'll find a road or cabin."

Brady doused their fire and threw snow on top of it. After he added rocks, it blended with the ground around it. "I shouldn't have slept for so long. We're losing daylight."

"We're both exhausted. We need sleep to think and we needed to dry out." What would happen if night came and they hadn't found shelter? They'd need to protect themselves from the weather and nocturnal predators.

Brady reached to his knee and rubbed it. Had the rest helped? It was her fault his injury was worse. He'd been jumping in water, running from assailants and involved in a car wreck because of her.

Brady turned on the cell phone. "Still no signal. We'll keep walking. We'll find something."

Brady had rearranged their supplies into one bag. He lifted it over his shoulder.

"I can carry something," Susan said.

"We'll switch when I get tired," Brady said.

He was too chivalrous to let her carry the bag. "You won't let me help, but you should."

"I said I would look out for you," Brady said.

He was a man of his word. She got that. He was missing something important, though. "When you were on a mission with the Special Forces, did you work alone?"

"Of course not. You know I didn't."

"Then why do you want to work alone now when I'm standing here, ready and willing to help?"

Chapter 8

Brady frowned at her. "You aren't a teammate. You aren't trained in survival techniques."

"That doesn't mean I can't be useful," Susan said. Sleep had revived her and she was prepared to help however she could. She understood the obstacles they were up against.

Brady walked farther ahead. "We need to keep moving."

Susan didn't follow him. She was fed up with him ending conversations before anything was resolved. "Stop. Running. Away. Every time I try to have a serious conversation with you about something of significance, you blow me off and walk away." And not just in the last week. Their relationship had been that way, too.

He opened his mouth as if to offer a retort and then snapped it shut. "Bad timing."

To him, no time was a good time to talk. "That's an excuse. I want to know what you're thinking and not about Justin's murder or the people looking for me. I want to know why you're helping me. What you've done for me goes beyond helping your brother." He could have ditched her after she couldn't remember anything on the boat and written her off as a lost cause.

A muscle flexed in Brady's jaw. He looked at the treetops and then met her gaze. "You want to know what I'm thinking? I'm thinking I'm standing here, in the middle of the woods with you. We're tired and we're worn and I want to get into bed and hold you and protect you from whatever piece of crap has decided he'll take the next shot at you. As I'm saying the words, I know it's ridiculous. When I kissed you at Reilly's, it ignited those thoughts. Those got-to-have-you thoughts. I can't shut them off. I'm not doing this for my brother, not just for him. I'm doing this for you. Because I still care about you."

He'd given her what she wanted: an honest admission. Now she had to say something, too.

Did she want to diffuse the tension or did she want to leap headfirst into this conversation when she knew where it may lead? "We've been through a lot and that kiss was..." Explosive? Mind-blowing? Charged with a million watts of sexual electricity?

Susan's heart froze and then broke into a gallop. Did she want to open that box? "We can't have a fresh start."

"Do we need one?" he asked.

She had wanted him to open up to her, and now that he had, she was the one fumbling for words. His eyes burned into hers, the intensity on his face quickening her heartbeat. Brady closed the distance between them and she set her hand on his chest to stop him from coming any closer.

She shouldn't have touched him. Her fingers dug into his jacket. She was torn between pulling him close to her and shoving him away. Her heart warred with her head. She'd wanted Brady from the moment she'd laid eyes on him. Knowing what she did now, was kissing him a mistake? "We've been down this road before."

"This one might look the same, but trust me, it's entirely different. Do you want me to kiss you?"

Plumes of fire infused her body. Want him? Did she want him to kiss her? Her body answered with a resounding yes. She couldn't say she didn't need him. The words wouldn't form on her lips. Her anger over their past sparred with her desire in the present. Desire won. Her fingers tightened on his jacket and instead of pushing him away, she pulled him closer.

This time, she was going in with eyes wide open. She knew Brady's limits. She knew hers. She'd never been an impetuous person, but now, more than ever, she wanted to make the most of every moment.

His mouth touched hers, his lips skimming lightly, tasting and testing her response. She closed her eyes and let the feelings roll over her. The second touch was harder, his lips pressing into hers. The third touch was ravenous. She opened her mouth beneath his and wrapped her hand around his neck, holding him to her.

Brady dropped their bag onto the ground and

wrapped her in his arms. She melted against him, the softness of her curves into the hardness of his body.

She could handle this. Susan had learned something from the emotional wreckage of their past. This time, she knew what she was getting into with Brady. It was lust. It wasn't love. It was now and not for the future. As long as she kept that in the forefront of her mind, he couldn't hurt her.

Brady stilled. Pulling away again? Her frustration halted when she opened her eyes and saw the worry on his face. He pressed a finger over his lips and pointed behind her. Desire fled and terror gripped her. They'd been followed. The man who'd run them off the road had caught their trail. They shouldn't have lingered longer than they'd needed to.

Susan looked to Brady, hoping her face conveyed her question: *What do we do?*

Brady grabbed the bag and patted the front of his jacket where she assumed he had the gun. He gestured for her to get behind him. Behind him? Taking a bullet for her wasn't a help. She didn't want him hurt. They needed to run.

A man in military fatigues emerged from behind the trees sixty feet away, carrying a high-powered rifle across his chest. Fear clenched around her body and Susan grabbed Brady's arm. "We have to run," she whispered.

The assailant wore a ski mask, disguising his identity. He was the same man from the SUV who had run them off the road.

"I'll buy us some time," Brady said. Brady withdrew his gun and leveled it at the man. He fired in his direction and the man disappeared behind a tree. Brady swore. "Now we run."

Brady took her hand and they ran. They weaved through the trees, sliding on the snow.

The sound of gunshots exploded around them, echoing through the trees. The man was returning fire. Brady abruptly changed direction. "At the top of that hill, we're going to slide down it and put distance between him and us." His words came in breathless puffs.

The gunman would catch up to them and kill them. They'd become his prey and the men chasing them had proven relentless. She and Brady couldn't outrun a bullet.

When they reached the summit of the hill, it was steeper than she'd imagined. What now?

"Protect your head," Brady said, not changing his plan like she'd expected.

Susan looked behind her at the man in the ski mask approaching and then at the slope below. "He'll shoot at us!"

"Go now!" Brady commanded.

Not an answer to her concern, but she didn't have a choice except to do as Brady instructed. She and Brady ran and slid down the hill, tumbling, slipping. She lost track of Brady. When she stopped moving, shouts and laughter filled her ears. She sat up, brushing snow from her clothes and out of her coat and off her hands. She looked around. Had the gunman followed them? Was he closing in on them?

Fifteen feet away through a thin copse of trees, ski slopes were filled with skiers flying down the hill.

She searched for Brady. He'd landed three yards

away, his body pressed against a tree and their bag clutched in his hand. He wasn't moving. Susan scrambled through the snow to his side. His eyes were closed. She shook him. "Brady, Brady, wake up. Are you okay?"

He moaned. "I twisted my knee."

Would he be able to walk? Could she carry him if he couldn't? "We're near a ski resort. We have to go a few more steps and then we'll disappear into the crowd."

Brady opened his eyes. "Were we followed?"

Susan glanced over her shoulder. The man with the gun was moving in their direction, but at a slower pace, keeping his footing, clasping his gun. "Yes. I can see him. Hurry." If he opened fire on them again, they'd be in trouble. They couldn't move as quickly injured. Would the thicker cluster of trees provide some cover? Would moving toward the skiers create more victims?

Susan helped Brady to his feet. She threw their duffel over her shoulder and they struggled through the trees. Every step was heavy as Brady leaned on her. Susan's chest heaved with fear and she gasped for breath, the cold stinging her lungs. Emerging on the other side, they stayed close to the tree line and moved down the slope.

She didn't see the man in the fatigues behind them. She and Brady looked out of place among the skiers in their gear. Would anyone notice them and approach? Would they be recognized? Their assailant would be more out of place in his fatigues, his weapon impossible to hide. Brady had stowed his gun in his jacket again before sliding down the hill.

They reached the bottom of the slope. Around them,

children laughed, skiers waited in line at the lift and instructors gave advice to new skiers. It was good to disappear in the crowd, but Susan wanted to scream warnings. Was the assailant crazy enough to shoot at them here? Children were around! Families!

Brady straightened and Susan caught his sharp intake of breath. He was in pain. "We don't want to call attention to ourselves. I need a place to rest. We'll try to blend for a couple of hours before getting a room. If the guy following us asks around, he might think we've moved on or hitched a ride out of here."

Her adrenaline slowed and Susan took a deep breath. Brady had a plan. They weren't lost in the woods. She didn't see their assailant following them. He wasn't crazy enough to open fire into a crowd. Small doses of relief unwound the anxiety in her muscles.

The public ladies' room was nearby. "I need to wash up. Meet me back here?"

Brady nodded. "I'll step away and call Harris. I'll keep my eye on the door and the slopes."

Susan felt his gaze burning into her until the bathroom door closed behind her.

Brady left Harris a voice-mail message that he was safe and then disconnected the call. The prepaid phone had limited minutes and battery life.

In the Special Forces, Brady had been taught to blend. Though he was dirty and needed a shower, he sat in the dining area, keeping his posture relaxed, giving the impression he was another ski bum taking a break from the ski slopes. He watched for the man in fatigues and, seeing no sign of him, wondered if he'd turned around. Causing a commotion in a public area would be bad if he didn't want to be found, and if the man was former Special Forces, he'd want to keep his cover.

Susan exited the bathroom. She'd cleaned the dirt from her jacket and her hair hung over her face. Paper towels and water could work wonders, although seeing Susan with some wilderness on her had been a turn-on. Susan was usually put together and he'd liked the earthy touch of dirt smudges on her cheeks.

She crossed the room to him and sat. "Any sign of him?"

"Not yet."

She looked over her shoulders. "At least it's warmer in here."

Without the wind and falling snow and with Susan at his side, Brady almost felt at ease. The throbbing in his knee had turned to an ache.

"We can wait for a bit, and then I'll get us a room. We'll rest and think of a plan."

A few hours later, Brady checked them into one of the resort's rooms using his ID and cash from the stash pack. He also purchased a ski lift ticket. Better to look like a skier than raise questions about why he was visiting the resort.

After spending time in the snow and cold without easy access to food and shelter, watching their backs for whoever was following them, being inside the warm, albeit small, resort room was a welcomed change. Brady was physically and mentally exhausted. His knee was sore and he needed to rest. He was no good to Susan when he could barely walk.

Brady rubbed his knee, hoping for the best, expecting the worst. He could have torn tendons or muscles. He could have strained it. Warnings from his physical therapist about overexerting his knee ran through his mind. He could be damaging it even more permanently. "If you want to take a shower, that's fine," he said. He wanted a hot soak for his knee, but he'd let Susan use the bathroom first.

Susan's eyes traced from his face to his knee. "How's your knee feeling?"

It was pointless to lie. "It's been better."

Concern lit her face. "Why don't you go first? Rest it in some hot water. Or is ice better? I can get ice to numb it."

Her willingness to help touched him. "Either might help. We can start with the heat. I'll dye my hair first. Never know when we'll have to move again."

Susan slipped her arm around his waist. His first instinct was to push her away and prove he could do it alone. He changed his mind and leaned on her. He wasn't fooling her. He was hurting, and indulging in some TLC from Susan would help. He removed his shirt and Susan helped him color his hair and then rinse it in the sink. Then she ran the hot water into the bath. After a small hesitation, he threw care to the wind and undressed. She'd seen it all before. This situation felt less charged with sexual energy, more drawn from care and kindness.

She helped him into the tub and knelt at the side. "How's the temperature?" she asked.

"Good," he said, letting his head fall back against the wall. "I'm sorry this happened. I hate letting you down." Letting her see him weak and hurting left him feeling exposed and vulnerable. If he'd tried to hide the pain, pretend he wasn't hurt and press on, he didn't know if he could trust his knee to hold up. He'd made the smarter—if not more difficult—choice.

"You haven't let me down," Susan said, picking up a washcloth and wrapped bar of soap from the ledge of the tub. "If anything, I've let you down."

Failure. He understood the emotion if not her reasons to feel that way. "You haven't let me down."

"I haven't remembered that night," Susan said.

Their problems went beyond that. Though it might help, it may not explain why someone, or a group of people, wanted Susan dead.

Susan peeled away the paper on the soap and rubbed it on the cloth.

Brady watched Susan wash his chest, his arms and his lower abdomen. He didn't apologize for his body's reaction. Her hands moved over him, soft and gentle in a way he hadn't experienced in months. When she reached his knee, she paused.

"Tell me if I do anything to hurt you," she said. "Is the heat helping?"

It was and she was. She was helping in ways water or ice wouldn't. "You're being very kind." He didn't know the words to express what he was feeling. Gratitude? Desire?

"After what you've done for me, I owe you. I'm behaving like a decent human being is all," she said.

He caught her wrist and her gaze swerved to his face. "You're being more than decent." He didn't want her to blow off the magnitude of the emotion between them. That was his weapon of choice. He had walked out on her. He had hurt her. And here she was, taking care of him. It meant something to him and he couldn't dismiss it.

She blushed and returned to cleaning him. "Sometimes, I have too much to say to you and I can't find the right words."

He understood. When he'd walked away from her, it had been one of the most painful decisions of his life. He hadn't wanted to give her a reason to hold on to him, not when she deserved so much more and yet he hadn't wanted to be brusque and hurt her. Finding the words had been difficult and he hadn't chosen well.

They lingered in the bathroom until the bath water had turned cold. Then he rinsed in the shower. Susan waited, holding out a towel for him. "Careful not to slip on the wet tiles."

She waited while he dried and helped him into one of the robes provided by the resort. He reveled in Susan indulging him.

He vacated the bathroom for Susan to use. Brady lit a fire in the gas fireplace and turned the thermostat to a comfortable seventy-five degrees. When Susan joined him in the room, she was also sporting a fuzzy white robe and her newly darkened hair hung around her shoulders.

"I like the color," Brady said, hoping she didn't hate it.

"Black is darker than I've worn it. Not too bad, though. I can rock the tortured artist look for a while."

She was being a good sport. Brady loved that she was making the best of a bad situation. "You know how great it feels to be in this room after what we went through?" Brady asked.

Susan made a sound of acknowledgment from her place on the plush chair in the corner of the room, her body slumped low in the chair.

"I felt this way when I'd return from a tour overseas and come to your place." He didn't know why he felt the need to mention it. To explain his actions? To earn her forgiveness for hurting her?

Susan's eyes opened wide. "You never told me that."

"I never told you a lot of things." Which was part of their problem. It wasn't enough to have a fiery connection with her in bed. He hadn't viewed it as important to talk about problems and share his thoughts. He'd never been good with words and he figured actions expressed how he felt. Perhaps she needed the words.

Crossing the room, he knelt at her feet and set his hands on her knees. "I'm sorry. I should have talked more." He rubbed her inner thigh with his thumbs and her eyes flickered with expectation.

She leaned forward, taking the lapels of his robe. "Where is this coming from?"

Thinking about his life, how he'd dealt with relationships and how they'd ended made him reevaluate.

"Walking in the wilderness gave me time to think." The wilderness, time in the therapist's chair and months of idle thoughts, thoughts too often centered on her. He'd been daydreaming about her and about making love with her. Taking her to bed played on his mind as a fantasy.

"I should have sent you into the wilderness sooner,"

she said, a hint of teasing in her voice. She ran her hand over his roughened jaw line and slid closer on the chair.

He was grateful to have this time with the woman he desired above all others. He let his hands move higher up her thighs.

"I'm getting it now. I am."

Her breathing accelerated and heat crackled between them. Brady rose and moved his hand to the back of her neck, bringing her mouth close to his.

Susan had seen glimpses of change in Brady, in his admissions and his brutal honesty. The dam of her restraint collapsed, scrubbing away more of her resentment and giving her new insight into Brady and their ravaged relationship. He was explaining in bits and pieces now more than she'd gotten before. Their relationship was changing. It wasn't recycling the old. It was forming something new, something different from what they'd had before. She wanted to explore this newly opened side of Brady.

Brady's mouth moved seductively over hers. The prospect of letting the inferno rage between them, peeling away their clothes, tossing them to the ground and tumbling into bed was tempting. Susan reached for the belt of his robe. She loosened it and let the fabric and robe part in the middle. Brady was naked beneath it. The room was warm, the fire blazed and a shockingly sensuous feeling undulated over her.

She ran her fingers over his shoulders, along his chest, down his rippling muscles. She'd never met a man whose body turned her on the way Brady's did.

The strength, the power and the control were a potent aphrodisiac.

He lifted her into his arms and she looped her hands around his neck. Raw need pulsed from him and her body responded, straining to get closer. He set her on the bed and she pushed back to make room for him.

His eyes blazed sex. What started as a kiss took on a life of its own. Combustible attraction ignited between them and she didn't try to harness it. Susan went with it, following the current of her desires. At the moment, she couldn't think of anything she'd rather do than make love with Brady. She had no expectations, only curiosity. Her anger had dissipated and new understanding was refreshing, freeing. She wasn't worried about a future or wondering where he was being shipped off to and when he would return.

Without those worries, being in his arms felt lighter and carefree.

Brady crawled into the bed and positioned himself over her. "I have thought about you so much over the last months." He undid her belt. "When you came to see me in the hospital, you nearly broke me."

"Broke you?" she asked, grasping for the thread of the conversation.

"If anyone could have gotten inside my head, it was you," Brady said. "That scared me. That still scares me."

Why? Didn't he want someone in his life who could help him? Someone to confide in? She shut down her questions. She wanted to stay in this moment and not lose herself in confusions from the past and queries of the future.

Brady parted her robe and took his time letting his gaze roll over her. He let out a whispered breath. "I've missed you."

She pressed her lips to his and flicked her tongue against his lower lip. He parted his lips and returned her kiss, slow and unhurried. The experience was thoroughly arousing.

Brady drew back, his nose brushing hers. "I don't want to hurt you again."

His comment struck close to the truth. He'd hurt her in the past, but she'd learned. Back then, she'd wanted roses and romance. Now, she wanted Brady. He was working through problems. She had major problems of her own. This wasn't about the future. It was about now.

She kissed him again, not giving him a chance to say anything else. She didn't want to explore the past.

Brady leaned over her, one hand braced on the bed, one hand stroking her bare thigh. She slipped her hungry arms around his neck and pulled his body onto hers. She welcomed the weight of him.

He shifted, positioning himself between her legs. Brady wrapped his arms around her, heating her against his big body. His skin was hot against hers and every last shred of cold fled.

Susan ran her fingers to his hips. He took her hand, stilling her movement. A dozen emotions flickered across his face. She inhaled a quivering breath.

"I want you naked," he said.

He removed his robe and she shrugged out of hers. She rolled over him, wanting to take control, to set the pace. Trailing her fingers over his body, her hands brushed the scarred flesh around his knee and Brady tensed.

"It's okay," she whispered.

He reached for the blanket to cover his injury and she stopped him. "It's beautiful. You're beautiful." She had seen his scars in the bath. They were part of who he was and he shouldn't be ashamed of his battle wounds.

She set her hand on his thigh and brought her mouth to her fingertips. She kissed the inside of his thigh. Brady's breath hissed from his lungs.

"How does this feel?" she asked.

His fingers forked into her hair. "Good. Amazing."

Instead of kissing higher to where his arousal strained, she moved her mouth to his knee. He jerked and Susan moaned. Kissing him felt good. Everywhere her lips touched his skin, scarred or not, was a fierce turn-on. She lowered the blanket away from him.

"Susan, stop."

No. She wouldn't. He was a beautiful, strong, potent man and she was showing him that his scars weren't ugly to her. She accepted him for who he was, not just the parts that were perfect and flawless. He was concerned about being strong, fast and at the top of his game. The reality was that he was flawed. She was flawed. Seeing and accepting those flaws was what deepened a relationship.

She traced her hands over his skin. "Does this feel okay? Tell me if anything I do hurts you."

His gaze was transfixed as he watched her, though wariness touched the corners of his eyes. "You don't have to make a point. You were kind enough in the bath."

Susan drew her body up, letting her breasts press into his chest. "This isn't about being kind. The only point I'm making is that you're hot. Every part of you. Every inch of your body makes me burn."

It was as if she'd flipped a switch in him. Wariness left his eyes and he flipped her onto her back in one fluid motion. He left her for a moment, pulled his wallet from the end table and then covered her body with his. He rubbed his arousal against her center and she arched, inviting him, wanting to draw him inside her.

There was a crinkle of foil and without warning, or any more foreplay, he came into her, hard and deep. She was ready, wanting. She tilted her hips and spread her legs farther, adjusting to the size of him. He rocked inside her, filling her. Each time he plunged he felt bigger, thicker, harder. This was what she'd needed. This was what she'd wanted. The sensations were strong, blocking out everything else except Brady and how he was making her feel. Susan slammed her hips against his thrusts, meeting every glide with equal fervor.

It felt so good she wanted to scream his name, nonsense, whatever came to mind. Brady captured her mouth with his and his tongue mimicked the actions of his lower half. Excitement escalated inside of her and she ran her fingers down his back, over the hard planes of his body.

Her muscles clenched around him and Brady buried his face in her neck. He moved faster and the tension in his muscles increased. She wrapped her legs around his waist and held on to him.

"Susan." Her name on his breath, hot and soft in her ear.

Her body tipped over the edge of pleasure, trembling in mind-blowing waves of release. He joined her in an intimate explosion.

Sated, Susan reveled in the weight of Brady's body pinning her to the mattress. Susan didn't want to move. She could have laid on the bed for hours, her body relaxed for the first time in days, and her mind at ease. Brady rolled to his side, their bodies joined, and he managed to tug the comforter around them, wrapping them in a cocoon of warmth.

A rush of emotions swelled in her chest. Tears sprang to her eyes and Susan closed them to keep Brady from seeing how much he had affected her. How much the experience had affected her.

They lay in the quiet, lost in their thoughts and the rightness of the moment settled over her. Brady's arms were around her, their legs intertwined. Her heart stirred and confusion careened through her. This had been about sex, yet she didn't feel detached.

Snuggling closer, she let out her breath and relaxed against Brady, tucking her arms between them. Some part of her broken heart had ached for this moment since the day he'd left. She succumbed to the sensations and memories and nestled deeper into his arms.

Susan's heart was pounding when she awoke. It took her a moment to place where they were. A ski resort near Arapaho National Forest, in one of its guest rooms. How long had they been asleep?

As her pulse slowed, Susan took stock. She was on

the run with her ex-boyfriend. They had formed some pseudo-friendship, bound by the circumstances. Then, she'd made love to him. More than having sex, it had been about showing Brady what he meant to her. Erasing some of his pain from his injury. If it had been about pure sex, those things wouldn't have mattered.

Susan expected to feel sated and the sexual tension to be zero. But that wasn't the case. She could almost feel him inside her, her body still oversensitized. New tides of arousal swept over her. She wanted him to say something, anything to her to prove his heart was open. To touch her again with the same poignant emotion and tenderness. To deliver another soul-shaking kiss.

Whatever she had believed about her emotional reaction prior to sleeping with Brady, she was clear now that she couldn't have sex with him again without feeling something. Desire. Passion. Wanting. Those dangerous emotions that crossed the line between sex and love.

Susan rubbed her face against his chest and walked her fingers to his face. "Are you awake?"

"Barely," he said. "What's the matter? You have an oh-so-serious tone."

"Did this feel different than before?" she asked. Did he also feel the newness of the act?

Brady shifted in the bed, facing the ceiling. "Just relax. Everything was great. You were great." He leaned over and kissed the top of her head.

"I'm not questioning how great it was," she said. Could she talk to him? Could they have a real, honest conversation?

"Tell me what's on your mind," Brady said.

"A lot," she said. Her feelings for Brady were knotting around inside her, choking her.

"I hope by a lot you mean you've remembered something," Brady said, sitting up in bed, pulling her against him.

Susan sat and tugged the sheet around her naked body. "Remembered something? About Justin?" Why did he want to talk about Justin now?

Brady watched her expectantly. "You mentioned you and Justin were having problems. Did you fight with him the night he died?"

Justin wasn't her preferred topic, but if Brady wanted to talk about him, she was open. "We weren't fighting that night exactly, but we had fought the night before."

"About what?" Brady asked.

Susan hadn't told anyone this. Not her lawyer or the police. She'd been afraid it would make her look guilty. Could she trust Brady? The answer was automatic. Yes. She could confide in him. It might be easier to tell someone, to release some of the guilt from her chest. "Something did happen between Justin and me the night before he was killed." She took a deep breath and struggled to find the right words. "I told him I wanted to end our engagement and we argued. The next day, he begged me to come to the boat and have dinner so we could talk."

Brady stared at her. Long moments passed before he spoke. "Why would you end the engagement?"

Because Justin wasn't the right man for her. Because she wanted passion and excitement in her life, and what she had with Justin was lacking. "I told you we'd been having problems getting along."

Brady narrowed his eyes. "Be more specific. Was he going out more and not coming home by a certain time? Was he taking phone calls in secret? Was he staying at work late to have dinner with colleagues?"

Justin's schedule was predictable and he hadn't received strange phone calls when she was around. A few times, they'd run into colleagues or clients and Justin hadn't seemed any tenser than usual. When he'd had plans with business associates, he hadn't stayed longer than anticipated or forgotten to call her.

"Not those kinds of problems. I can't think of anything out of the ordinary. I can't get my brain around what he could have done to cause this." Frustration rose up inside her.

His hand stroked her arm. "Don't get upset. I just wondered if you'd remembered anything else that could help us piece together that night."

The pieces of that night haunted her. Justin's face. The last time she had seen him. The yacht and the blood. So much blood. Her thoughts shuddered to a stop. Brady had picked a strange time to discuss this.

"Do you think I've known how he died all this time and kept it from you?" She turned, moving away from him and covered her body with the bedsheet.

Brady held up his hands. "Whoa, whoa. I do not think you're keeping anything. I just know that you share more, are more relaxed and open after we've slept together. At least that was how it worked in the past."

Humiliation and anger burned through her. "You slept with me to get information out of me?"

Guilt flickered on his face. It was all she needed to know. He was using sex to manipulate her. "That's great, Brady. Sorry to disappoint, but I still don't know anything more than I've told you."

"Don't get upset. It was an observation. I was hoping you'd remember something."

"And did this observation occur before you slept with me or after?"

Brady forked his fingers in his hair. "Before. But that isn't the reason I slept with you."

She didn't want to hear it. How could she have been so stupid? She had been trying to keep any and all emotion out of having sex with Brady. She preferred that to him using sex to manipulate her. Susan moved farther away. "Forget it. I should have expected something like this." She struggled to see over him. The red digits on the side table clock read two o'clock. "We've been asleep for hours."

"We needed it," he said.

What she needed now was to put some distance, both physical and emotional, between her and Brady. How could she have slept with him and expected it to mean nothing to her? She now knew what it meant to him. She was half in love with him and he was working an angle. "I need to get dressed." Focus on anything but Brady. She grabbed her robe and pulled it over her shoulders.

"Are you denying that you're more open after sex?" Brady asked.

Why couldn't he let it go? "It's not sex that makes me open. It's trusting someone. Feeling connected.

Based on what happened here, we have neither of those things." How had she believed he'd changed?

"I didn't sleep with you as a manipulation tactic. I did it because I wanted to," he said.

She wanted to believe him. Memories of her heartbreak stopped her. "Let's not unleash this monster. Let's focus on other things."

"I haven't been dishonest with you." Brady turned on the light by the side table.

She'd seen it before with Brady. The lie of omission. Maybe he'd slept with her because he'd wanted to, but he hadn't mentioned his other objective: to get her to open up about whatever secrets he believed she was keeping. "You didn't outright lie. But you didn't tell me the whole truth either."

"If I had told you I thought you'd remember if we slept together, you'd have shut down. I wouldn't have been helping. Besides, I figured we'd never sleep together so what was the point in mentioning it? Did you want me to stop in the middle to tell you?"

Valid points. Still, she wanted honesty from him before the fact, not after. "You could have told me." Brady's stony face left her disappointed. He had started to open up and now, on the heels of a confrontation, was shutting down. "I need to see if my clothes are dry." She'd left them hanging in the bathroom.

"We might as well check the notebook, too," Brady said, seemingly relieved by the change of subject. "I laid it in front of the fire. I'll see if the pages are dry enough to read."

Her drawing notebook? The answer dawned before

she could ask it. Justin's notebook. The one they had found on the boat. "I'd thought we lost it."

"Nope. It was soaked and unreadable, but I'm trying to fix that."

Brady got out of bed. He didn't bother dressing. "The cardboard of the front and back cover are damp, but the pages seem okay."

He handed her the book. The pages could be turned without tearing. Ink had seeped between the pages, making some of it illegible.

Anxious for a distraction from Brady's naked form and from the fact that she'd been a fool and made love to her ex-boyfriend, Susan looked at the notebook and willed something to jump out at her. The names, the columns of numbers, the dates. What did they mean? Were they connected to anything that had happened the night Justin had died? Another fifteen minutes and impatience got the best of her. "Nothing. There's nothing here. It doesn't make sense." With Brady next to her, concentration eluded her.

"Would you like me to look at it?" he asked. He'd put the hotel robe back on.

His eyes moved to her mouth. He was thinking about kissing her. Or maybe thinking about getting into bed and passing the time in each other's arms. Heat pooled in her stomach. She wouldn't let the attraction and chemistry override her good sense. "If you think it will help."

He paged through the notebook a few times. "I don't know if these mean anything out of context. Let's focus on our next steps. The person who ran us off the road knows we're here or at least suspects we are. We need to find a safe place with a computer. I want to do more research and I need to know what's developed with the case."

Brady pulled a pair of jeans from the duffel. He slid them on and left them unbuttoned, hanging low on his hips. He dug through the bag again and pulled out another pair of pants. Digging in the pockets, he drew out a metal key ring with a canary-yellow key chain. "The keys from the safe!"

Susan rose to her feet. Like the notebook, she'd assumed they'd been lost.

Brady held them up. "I'd forgotten about these."

Susan frowned and took the keys from Brady's hand. Four metal keys. She flipped through each key, pausing at the smallest on the ring. "This one is strange. It doesn't look like it belongs to a house or a car."

She looked at the key and then looked closer. Along the key was a small inscription. "It says, 'W.H., number eighteen.' I wonder what that means."

"W.H.," Brady said. "Who or what is W.H.?"

Susan wracked her brain thinking about Justin's life. How had he gotten involved with such dangerous people? He had been a good man. Fun. A good friend. He'd had a lot going for him. A great career with challenging work. Business trips. Corporate perks.

Inspiration dawned. "I got it. The Windsor Hotel. Justin had a conference there a few months ago."

Brady straightened, his eyes sharpening. "That could be it. Most hotels use key cards, though. A metal key is rare."

"The Windsor is a historic hotel. They might not have updated everything."

She could see the wheels turning in Brady's head. Maybe it was nothing, but it was a place to start.

"If the room keys are digitized, it could belong to a liquor locker, or a banquet room, or a maintenance closet. Employee locker room. A cabinet or file drawer. Those places could use a metal key," Brady said. "We need to take it to that hotel and search. Maybe Justin hid something. Papers. Evidence. An insurance policy in case other documents were destroyed. Something to leave a clue about what he was involved with."

It was a long shot. "How will we check? We can't walk into the Windsor Hotel, hold up the key and ask if someone is missing it," Susan said.

"We'll fly by the seat of our pants," Brady said. "I don't have the answers, but I know we need to dig more into what Justin was doing and what he could have been hiding." He buttoned his pants and she hated the mild disappointment that blanketed her. Brady had hidden something from her. She couldn't ignore that or pretend her feelings for him were enough to make it work. She'd done that before and he'd broken her heart.

Susan ignored the twinge in her heart. Her priority was finding Justin's killer and the key was a good place to start. She didn't want to get her hopes up. So much had gone wrong for her and Brady. "This key could be nothing."

Brady sent her a look that socked her hard in the gut. "Or if we find where it belongs, it could be the key to your freedom."

Chapter 9

Brady picked up the toss-away cell phone from the hotel dresser. "We don't have much battery left. I'll make this fast. Since we're leaving, we can make a couple of calls from our room if we need to." Brady would call Harris first and he'd rather do it from the prepaid. He didn't want to put his brother in the uncomfortable position of needing to lie if asked about Brady and Susan's location.

Brady dialed his oldest brother and after a brief greeting, launched into his questions. "We're planning to change locations. Do you have anything new?"

"I'm glad you called. A couple of things have come up. The cops got a hit on one of the men who attacked you in your cabin. His name was Finn Tremain. He was former Special Operations, combat control team, discharged from the air force ten years ago and working as a private contractor. They're still trying to track the other guy."

Private contractor was a nice way of saying Tremain was a mercenary. Plenty of guys with Special Forces went rogue, chasing money and excitement, selling their skills to the highest bidder. Unless Finn Tremain had known Justin personally, Brady pegged him as a hired gun. Brady had been right in guessing the men chasing them had exceptional skills. "I've never heard of the guy. Let me run the name by Susan." After checking with Susan, she confirmed she hadn't heard of him either.

"I looked into J.A.'s personal accounts. Nothing alarming and he didn't have a criminal history. He wasn't moving money through his personal accounts. The company he works for is resisting letting the police have a peek into its affairs."

Not shocking. Most firms didn't want the police auditing their accounts and bringing bad press to their work. "Anything else?" Brady asked.

"You won't like this. Reilly is trying to get confirmation from a friend on the force peripherally involved with the case. We heard a rumor that the police connected large sums of money moving in and out of an account in Susan's name."

Brady appreciated that Harris called it "an account in Susan's name" and not "Susan's account." Susan would never knowingly be party to money fraud. "If an account like that exists, then Justin or someone he was working with set it up." Someone was framing Susan for Justin's murder and as the pieces twisted into place, they were going to form a noose around Susan's neck.

"I knew it wasn't hers, but if the account exists,

proving she wasn't involved might be difficult. That's all I got at the moment. Stay safe. Stay alert. They're looking statewide and the mayor is turning up the heat. I need to get off the phone." Harris disconnected. Harris was working undercover. How much risk was he putting himself at to help Brady and Susan? If Reilly was involved now, too, his brothers were both going out on a limb for Susan. Reilly had something at stake, as well, but it would have been the easier choice to stay uninvolved.

His brothers' loyalty proved again the strength of their family bond.

Brady's thoughts turned to what Harris had told him. A statewide manhunt. Brady had worked in dangerous, hostile territories on missions almost doomed to fail. He had nerves of steel in the field. But in this instance, he had Susan to take care of and that rattled him, increased the stakes. He was worried about her and his ability to protect her. Was he strong enough to be the man she needed him to be?

Susan was watching him expectantly. "What did Harris say?"

Which piece of bad news to give her first? "The guy who broke into my cabin, Finn Tremain, was former Air Force Special Operations. Justin might have known him from his time in the air force."

"Justin never mentioned him and I know a good number of his friends from the military." Susan took a deep breath. "I guess anything is possible. I don't know every person he knew. Did Harris have anything else?"

"Nothing's turned up in Justin's accounts. A rumor

is floating that you have an account with large sums of money moving in and out of it."

Susan's mouth dropped open. "Like the large sums we saw in the notebook?"

"Could be," Brady said, hating where this investigation was leading. The more evidence they found, the more it should point to the real killer, not Susan. Someone was doing a thorough job setting her up to take the fall for murder.

"I don't have any accounts with large sums of money. I am not involved in payoffs or payouts or whatever you're implying."

On the heels of making love, she was touchy. "I'm not implying anything. I don't believe for a minute you would commit financial fraud or theft. However, Justin has a history of dishonesty, but proving it could be impossible. His father did a thorough cover-up of the incident while he was in the air force, I'm sure."

Susan scrubbed a hand across her forehead. "I can't believe this. I can't believe we're finding evidence to use against me instead of evidence to help me."

Brady would work tirelessly to find the truth. "For now, we're going to keep looking and be careful. Harris told me the manhunt for us has gone statewide. The mayor is making locating us a top priority."

The yellow taxicab pulled up to the ski resort. Brady was grateful they had the extra money from the stash pack. They'd need it to pay for the trip to the Windsor Hotel.

Brady threw their duffel into the cab and climbed in. Susan followed him, keeping a ski hat she had purchased from the resort gift shop pulled low over her eyes.

"We need to get somewhere off the meter," Brady said.

The cab driver glanced over his shoulder. "That will cost you double the regular fare."

Brady would pay the cab driver any amount to keep quiet about this trip. It was a long shot for the police to contact cab companies looking for him and Susan, but if they did, Brady didn't want a record of them leaving the resort and arriving at the Windsor Hotel. Once the police had her in custody, Justin's father would put pressure on the mayor and the police to keep her there. She'd never get a fair trial and the police wouldn't search for the real killer believing Susan was their murderer. Brady didn't trust that Susan would be safe in jail. Once she was trapped, the killers searching for her would find a way to get to her.

Brady shoved a wad of cash through the open plastic window between him and the driver. "Will that work?"

The cab driver grinned and Brady read greed in his eyes. "Will you pay more for getting there quickly?"

Brady flashed some more cash. "Yes. We need to get to Slider's Café." It was a small restaurant located within walking distance of the Windsor.

They pulled away from the resort. Would the cab driver put together who they were? It was a long drive to the Windsor Hotel and he'd have plenty of time to think.

Brady doubted the driver cared. He was breaking his company's rules by driving his cab without the meter running and he wouldn't want to be fired. Besides, how many people took time out of their day-to-day lives to hunt for suspects on the run? Not many.

He and Susan didn't make conversation. Brady didn't want to give the cab driver any information about them, even if accidental. If the cab driver was questioned and mentioned he'd left two people at Slider's Café, it wouldn't tie them to the Windsor directly, though it would give the police a ballpark of where he and Susan were.

They'd make it fast at the Windsor. With any luck, they would find what they needed. The key could belong to a lock somewhere in housekeeping, the bar, maintenance, the employee break room or cabinets in the office or foyer area. Brady hoped it led them to something, anything to use for Susan's defense. The evidence against her was mounting. At some point, the police would find them and they'd be arrested and questioned. How could he protect her if they were apart?

The sidewalk and streets were crowded when they arrived at Slider's Café. Brady gave the driver his generous tip and he and Susan got out of the car.

"Wait here until the cab disappears," Brady said.

They stood outside the café with their heads bent together. He read worry and fear in Susan's expression.

He touched her cheek lightly, wanting to reassure her. "We'll be okay. Every day that passes is a day closer to finding the truth. We're making progress."

Susan tapped her foot against the sidewalk. "I'm glad you feel confident about this. I feel like we're walking into a trap. Someone else could know about the key or have another copy. The police are looking for us. Special Forces military men are looking for us.

Justin's killer is still at large." She let the rest of her breath out in a whoosh and held her head in her hands.

Brady ached to reach for her and draw her into his arms, to offer some comfort. Wanting more than emotional comfort, he was aware of his body hardening at the image of her pressed against him. He'd made love with her less than twelve hours ago and he was ready for more.

Susan met his gaze and Brady looked away. Staring at her would get him into trouble.

"Why are you looking at me like that? You think this is a mistake? That I'm right and someone is waiting at the hotel for us?" Susan asked.

He hadn't been thinking anything of the sort, though better for her to believe his stare had to do with the case and not how desirable he found her. When it came to Susan, he endlessly wanted her and perpetually desired her. Could he protect her and her feelings? He'd been working to earn her trust, but his admission that he'd expected her to remember more after they'd made love had hurt her more than helped. Could he earn her trust? How many chances could one man expect? He'd had her once and he'd blown it. His feelings for her now were as strong as his feelings for her then, and it seemed he'd have to get used to letting go of the woman he loved. Love. A powerful word that could cripple even the strongest man when unreturned.

He tried to soothe her fears. "No one knows about the key. If there's another copy and someone else knew what Justin was hiding, then we're too late anyway." A depressing possibility. Without the key and whatever it led to, they had the notebook, which hadn't provided much information. If the information inside the notebook pointed to an account in Susan's name, it only added to the evidence against her.

Susan pulled her hat off and rubbed her scalp with her fingertips. Some wisps of hair fell around her face and her fingers, the contrast between her dark hair and light skin mesmerizing.

"This is so frustrating. We don't know who we can trust or who to look out for. We don't know who's trying to hurt us," Susan said. "How can we protect ourselves from people who we don't know?"

"The same way we have been. We'll keep a watch for anyone who's staring too intently. If our instincts tell us we have a problem, we'll run again," Brady said. "Reilly and Harris are doing their best to help us. We can trust them."

At the mention of his brothers, Susan's spirits seemed to lift. "What's your plan at the hotel?"

Brady had a vague plan. "We'll go into the hotel separately. You'll hide somewhere safe and I'll get us a room. We'll meet up and get to our room and see as few people as possible."

"What if someone recognizes me while I wait?" she asked.

"I'll leave you my gun," he said.

Susan clutched his arm, her nails digging into him. "Brady, we've been over this. I don't know how to shoot a gun. I don't think I could shoot someone because they recognize me."

Brady removed her fingers from his arm and squeezed her hand, his protective instinct roaring to not leave her alone, his training telling him it was better to separate to avoid recognition. If put to the test, Susan would prove stronger than she believed. "You won't need to shoot it. Use the gun to buy yourself time to get away and hide if someone approaches you. Most people will back away from a show of strength and aggression."

Susan unclenched her fists and then rubbed her hand over his arm. Flames of heat burned up his body. If he let his hand linger on hers, would she clasp it? Intertwine their fingers?

He'd never consciously defined the difference before, but having sex with her wasn't the same as intimacy and trust. In the past, he'd associated the two as the same. Now, he was aware that hand-holding might fall into forbidden territory. A strange notion since they'd made love in the past twenty-four hours. As experienced as he was with women, he was equally as inexperienced with relationships.

He nearly groaned aloud as two emotions struck him at once: first, lust winding around the image of Susan's naked body moving over his, the sensation of sliding inside her, and the soft feel of her hands on his skin and second, embarrassment with the distinct impression he was overanalyzing, thinking about making love and sex and trying to slap a label on what they had.

It didn't need a label. They were two people in a tough situation protecting each other, and who, in the heat of the moment, had done what came naturally. He hadn't handled the aftermath well. She'd been angry and hurt and he hadn't known how to fix it. What could he say if the truth made her believe he was manipulating her?

Two beat cops strut down the street, the crowd parting for them. Were they looking for him and Susan or just walking their patrol? Brady grabbed Susan and turned her shoulders so she faced him. He buried his head in the nape of her neck. "Cops."

Susan's breathing escalated. "Did they see us?"

Brady angled his head, keeping his face as covered as possible. "They see us, but I don't think they recognize us. Pretend we're lovers." They didn't have to pretend, but Susan got the message. Her arms went around him and he slid his hands to her lower back, holding her to him.

Brady shifted, moving her between his hips. He rocked against her slightly. He wasn't into public displays of affection, but this was for their cover. Lovers on the street embracing.

Susan pinched the back of his neck. "Stop that."

He didn't want to stop. He wanted to grind his body against hers. He wanted to take her to the hotel, forget about the case for a few hours and make slow, thrilling love to her again and again. Until he proved to her how much he wanted her and how his desire for her had nothing to do with getting information from her.

"Are they gone?" she asked a hitch on the end of her question.

Brady looked up to see the retreating backs of the policemen. "Yes." Disappointed, he released his hold on her.

She drew her body away, her expression guarded. Leaving her mouth close to his ear, her voice was low. "You keep the gun until we get to the hotel. Then I'll do what I have to do."

He admired her courage and he tamped down his libido. He needed to shut these feelings down for a few minutes and get control. "I want to keep you safe, Susan. I want justice for what you've been through."

"I want that, too. And while we're making wishes, I want justice for Justin and Reilly, too."

Chapter 10

The Windsor Hotel was four stories high, shaped like an X. The first floor was comprised of a lounge, a restaurant and several ballrooms and banquet rooms.

"What if the hotel has security cameras?" Susan asked.

"Most hotels do. But the quality of the recording might be poor and the angle of the camera might be bad. Keep your head down and don't look around. It decreases the chance of someone seeing you from an angle they'd recognize."

Susan would feel better if they stayed together, but it was safer for Brady to handle this part alone. Based on his work in the air force, he had more experience with covert situations. "Are you sure the front desk staff won't recognize you from the news?"

Brady shrugged. "I can't be sure if I'll be recognized or not. My hair color change might help. If they ask for ID, I'll give them the fake. My picture won't look exactly the same, but at least the name is different. Staying here will make it easier to search and it'll be convenient to have a base close to the search area." He leaned close to her. The intimacy was unexpected. She felt something cold at her back. Brady was slipping the gun into her pants and covering it with her jacket.

She shivered. "I don't need it."

"I hate for us to be separated. We've had too many close calls. I'm leaving you with some protection."

She wouldn't read into the words. He wasn't referring to their past or the future with him. For those, the only protection she had was herself.

They decided on an entrance plan. She would wait behind the hotel in the greenhouse attached to the hotel, staying as inconspicuous as possible. Brady would enter through the main lobby.

Susan took several, slow deep breaths. The more calmly she behaved, the better. She was walking through the greenhouse admiring the flowers. No big deal.

Brady walked away without looking back. Susan took a deep breath and tried to control her racing thoughts. How had she ended up here? Hiding in a sun-warmed greenhouse, a gun tucked in the back of her borrowed pants, on the run from the police, her ex-fiancé dead, her home torched, investigated as the prime suspect in a murder and an arson, sleeping with her former lover, and pretending she could handle the cards she'd been dealt.

Emotions from the past few weeks caught up with her and the urge to cry overwhelmed her. It wasn't any one emotion—fear, anxiety, grief, sadness, terror or desire—it was the mixture of them creating a volatile cocktail.

It wasn't her best-laid plan to sleep with Brady at the ski resort. She blamed the setting. The stress. Her scattered emotions and her exhausted mind. Pretending it meant nothing hadn't worked. Writing it off as sex without emotion, a roll in the sack and nothing more, was harder than she'd thought.

Which frustrated her. She hadn't asked Brady to get involved in this situation. She hadn't wanted to see him again. She hadn't been prepared for his intrusion into her life. Now that he was part of it, he'd taken center stage again.

Susan wiped at her eyes with the sleeve of her jacket. She had to stay calm and think.

"Susan?"

Susan jumped at the sound of Brady's voice. Relief rushed through her. She whirled to face him. "Did you get a room?"

He held up the key card to the room and disappointment struck her. A part of her had hoped the hotel would keep to its historic roots and use metal keys.

"Went off without a hitch. Several people checked in ahead of me and the clerk didn't change her routine for me. I'll take the stairs from the main lobby. You use the stairs on the far end of the hotel so we aren't seen together. Third floor, room three-oh-five. Meet me there?"

Separated again. "Okay, sure."

"Wait a sec. Why are you crying?" he asked, concern in his eyes. He rubbed his thumb under her eye to brush away a tear.

She wasn't crying anymore. It had been a small

breakdown and she had a handle on her emotions now. "It's been a rough week."

Brady frowned and glanced around them. "We'll talk in the room."

Susan walked into the hotel and took the stairs to the third floor. She lingered by the window at the end of the hallway, pretending to enjoy the view and not wanting to draw attention to herself.

At the sound of footsteps, she turned. Brady! She didn't run to him, though she wanted to. She waited until he went inside the hotel room, then walked to their door, counting off the rooms with every step.

Susan slipped into the hotel room. She closed the door and watched Brady opening and closing the dresser drawers. "What are you doing?" she asked. In light of the concern he'd shown in the greenhouse, would he draw her into a conversation about her feelings?

"I'm looking for an in-room safe or cabinet. Maybe the key belongs somewhere inside one of the rooms."

Susan helped him look, checking under the bathroom vanity. "The room safe is here." She knelt and disappointment fluttered through her. "It's digital. Doesn't use a key."

Brady swore under his breath. "Was worth checking."

Susan stood and took his gun out of her pants. She handed it to him. "I can't get rid of this fast enough."

He slid it back into his hip holster. "Heavy?"

In more ways than one. The burden of using it would have weighed on her. How did Brady do it? "What is it like to kill someone?"

He cast his gaze downward. "It's not something I

enjoy, but in situations where I've had to protect myself or others, I've made my peace with it. Taking a life is awful, but sometimes necessary."

Susan touched his shoulder. Was he feeling too vulnerable or could she find a way for him to open up to her? "When we were together, you never spoke about it. You never mentioned much about your job and it was weird that something so important to you wasn't discussed." It had bothered her that a big part of his life had been closed off from her. His emotions and the experiences had been something he wouldn't—or couldn't—share with her.

"I don't want to burden you or anyone else with it. The man I shot in my cabin, Finn Tremain, is the first person I've killed outside a warzone. The circumstances were different in the military. When I had to kill someone on the job, sometimes I couldn't talk about it. Some of my missions are classified and discussing it would put me or others in danger."

Couldn't talk about it, or was it an easy excuse?

"Do you regret what you had to do?"

He shook his head. "No. Every time I've pulled the trigger, it's because I didn't have a choice." An injured shadow passed over Brady's face. Would he shut down and stop talking? "War is terrible. Frightening. The places I've seen are some of the darkest pits of humanity in the world. I have to block out the classified missions, but some I wanted to forget as fast as possible, classified or not. Reliving them, thinking about the atrocities in those places sickens me inside. If I let it, that darkness would poison me."

He'd never confided in her this way. She wanted him to tell her more. To share the burden. "That must take a terrible toll on you," she said, drawing him out, needing him to confide in her and to let her inside.

He shrugged. "I have outlets. Running. Exercise. Therapy."

But running and some forms of exercise had been taken from him after his injury. And therapy? "You've missed a few therapy sessions by now." Because of her and this situation. How was he holding up? She hadn't seen fissures in his demeanor, though she'd shown some of her own. Was he keeping it inside?

Brady shifted on his feet. He was uncomfortable and she didn't want him to stop talking. What could she say to help him understand it was fine to talk about his problems? It wasn't an admission of weakness. Sharing a difficult situation didn't make him less of a man.

"I've missed a couple of sessions. I'll explain to her later." He spoke the words stiffly.

"How is your knee feeling?" she asked.

"It's okay."

This time, she wasn't accepting his dismissive response. "You never told me how you were injured. When I came to see you in the hospital, no one would tell me what had happened. I knew from your walk it was your leg." She paused, fearing she'd stepped too far. She tried to explain. "Reilly mentioned you were home and I had to see you."

"Why?" he asked.

Why, indeed. Reilly had warned her not to, but she hadn't been able to stay away. "Because I wanted to know you were okay." A lie. It was more than that. Her bitterness hadn't severed her feelings for Brady, not entirely.

"You could have asked Reilly how I was."

"I needed to see for myself."

Brady rubbed the back of his neck. "If you're telling me half-truths, I have no reason to be straight with you either."

Susan was holding back. Taking an emotional leap with Brady was dangerous. She could easily be hurt. After they'd had sex, she'd gotten a dose of pain and a reminder of how easily he could hurt her. But if she wanted him to open up to her, she owed him the truth in return. Circling each other and putting effort into protecting their feelings wasn't working. "I missed you. I wanted to see you." An admission that struck her hard.

"You missed someone you were furious with?" he asked, challenge in his eyes.

"I wasn't furious with you. I was hurt and angry." Not the same.

"I must have added to that anger when I kicked you out of my hospital room." He spoke the words carefully, watching her face.

She lifted her chin. Brady's rejection had stung. "How did you feel when I rejected your offer for help the first time?"

"I didn't like it. But you're stubborn when you want to be," Brady said.

"Ditto," she shot back.

Brady laughed. "I missed this. Honest Susan, who gives as much as she gets."

"Then if that's true, give me something. I've confided in you about the most difficult parts of my life. I've told you about my parents. I've told you everything I know about Justin's murder. Tell me how you injured your leg."

Brady's eyes widened and he rubbed his jaw line. "Why do you want to hear about that?"

It had changed his life, continued to affect him, and having a real relationship meant sharing the good and the bad. "We're friends," she said, forcing out the word. Friend was unthreatening. Friend was open and relaxed. She could have used the words *partner in crime* or *lover,* but those had emotional implications. She didn't want him to put up emotional boundaries again and shut down or shut her out.

Brady inclined his head and the corner of his mouth quirked up. "Okay, *friend,*" he said, heavy emphasis on the word friend. Did he find it ridiculous because they'd slept together? Or was he as unsure as she was?

Addressing sleeping together felt less important than making an honest, real connection. They could chalk up sex to attraction, desire or hormones. Sharing painful parts of his life with her was progress she longed to have with him.

Brady took a deep breath, his broad chest rising and falling. He sat on the edge of the bed, elbows on his knees, hands clasped together. Finally, he spoke. "My team and I were following some intel to extract friendly forces from behind enemy lines in…in the place where we were."

When she'd asked him about his work in the past, he'd given her vague, dismissive answers. He was censoring parts of the story, but he was letting her in, and he'd never done that before. It wasn't the how of the events that was important but rather the how of his feelings.

"Our informant was a woman. Young, early twenties. Her husband had mistreated her for years and she told us where she believed they were holding the men we'd been sent to rescue. Her husband found out, or maybe she misled us, and instead of surprising them, they surprised us.

"One of the men on the enemy's forces was young. Too young to be a solider. I hesitated when he charged at us with his gun in his hand. The fear in his eyes told me he didn't want to be there. He didn't want to shoot that gun and for a moment, I thought he would turn and run."

Brady went quiet and hung his head. When he lifted his gaze to her, deep pools of sadness met her eyes. "I hesitated too long. He got a shot off on me and hit me in the knee. The bullet shattered the bone. A teammate returned fire and killed him. My screw-up almost cost the lives of my team and the people I was sent to save. The whole thing was flamed up because of me."

She set her hand on his arm, letting him know she was listening.

"I was medic'd out several hours later. Thirty dead on their side, five injured on ours, including me. Why did I hesitate? I'd been trained to protect. To do whatever was necessary to rescue our captured men." Guilt and shame shook his voice.

Susan took his hands in hers. He might have made a mistake in his way of thinking, but concern and humanity underscored his actions. "You made a decision based on compassion for another human being. You've been in difficult situations before and you haven't frozen."

"In the past, maybe. Since then, I've second-guessed myself. I've questioned my instincts and my reactions. When someone came for you at my cabin, he got a shot off because I waited. When we were in the woods being chased, I hesitated to return fire."

"One mistake during a mission doesn't mean you should question every decision you've made since then," Susan said.

"One time is all it takes to cost lives. I've frozen. I've hesitated. I've lost my edge, Susan. I'm a danger to the people around me."

She hadn't noticed any hesitation on his part when he'd stepped in to protect her. To her, he was Brady, protector, strong and fierce.

"I've never felt unsafe with you. You're the man who makes me feel safest in the world."

Brady's eyes met and held her gaze. He drew himself up.

"Were the men you were sent to rescue saved?" Susan asked.

The corners of his mouth turned up. "Yes. Thank God."

Then the mission wasn't a failure. "You made a mistake. Will you beat yourself up over it forever?"

He tilted his head back and looked at the ceiling. "In the past, I've told myself I was to protect and save those who can't protect themselves. But I failed. Every time I think about my bum knee, every time my leg gives out, every time I hesitate and question my instincts, I'm reminded of that day and my failure. Could my team trust me ever again to do my job? I'll never get a chance to find out. Surgeries and physical therapy can't fix my knee. I made a mistake and it ruined my career."

Brady sat on the bed and Susan wrapped her arms around his waist and rested her head on his shoulder.

Brady held himself to a high standard. He worked hard and wanted to be successful at every task he undertook. One mistake had cost him so much. It didn't seem fair.

He relaxed in her arms. "Are you sorry you asked?"

Not in the slightest. "No, I'm not sorry. I wanted to know how you felt. I'm glad you told me." He'd let her into a place in his life where she hadn't been allowed before today. It felt good and right.

She set her hand on his injured knee. He stiffened, but didn't pull away. Susan didn't know how many minutes passed before Brady spoke again.

"I'm worried that I'll fail you and I'll let Reilly down, too. You say you feel safe with me, but is that because I'm the only option? My knee's been a problem and I can't trust it. How can you trust someone who can't trust himself? How can anyone put their faith in a man who isn't a man?"

The question was raw and brutal and it took her a moment to process it. "What do you mean 'not a man'? Your knee has nothing to do with being a man. And you are not the only option. You're just the best option."

Brady's eyes burned into hers, unguarded pain shining in them. "My work defined who I was. I was proud of my work and proud of what I did for our country. Now what good am I? Everyone in my family does important work to help others."

Is that what he'd been thinking? He'd been struggling with building a new career. He'd been in physical pain. She had never drawn the conclusion that those things meant he believed himself worthless. "You've been helping me."

He slammed his fist into his open palm. "Have I,

Susan? I've failed you, too. When I broke up with you, it drove you into Justin's arms. Look how that turned out. When you came to see me in the hospital, I was too much of a mess to talk to you when having a friend was probably what I needed."

Susan should have seen it sooner. Brady was a man of actions, not words. His actions were those of an emotionally wounded man, a man in need of friendship and consideration and patience. She'd been quick to shut him out for fear she'd be hurt instead of giving him time to heal. "You can't blame yourself for choices I made," Susan said. She'd gotten into a relationship with Justin on the rebound, despite her better judgment. She had chosen to visit Brady in the hospital and then taken great offense when he'd rejected her.

"I almost missed the guy who broke into my house to kill you. I couldn't identify the men on the pier who shot at us. I got us run off the road and almost killed. The list of my mistakes is long and severe," Brady said.

Susan didn't think those incidents were Brady's fault. His actions had shown strength, loyalty and courage. "If it wasn't for you, I would be dead. You haven't failed me. You've protected me. You've sacrificed so much to keep me safe."

Seriousness rasped his voice. "Protecting you means everything to me. I won't let anyone hurt you, including me. I want you to be happy."

Emotion clogged her throat. He cared about her. For all his pushing her away and pulling her close, he cared.

She banded her arms around him and hugged him, wishing she could take the confidence she had in him and pass it through to him. They sat together for several long minutes.

"Tell me why you were crying in the garden," Brady said.

She'd almost forgotten about it and was pleased he hadn't. "Everything was catching up to me. I feel lost. Scared."

His arm slipped around her waist. "Hey, me, too."

The admission struck her. Admitting he was afraid? For Brady, that had to be hard. "You don't act afraid."

"I wouldn't be human if I wasn't. I'm trying to be strong for you. Trying to think positive when we don't have much to be positive about."

A lot had gone wrong for her and for them, but it had brought Brady back into her life. Initially, that hadn't seemed like a good thing. But without him, where would she be? Imprisoned? Dead?

She had loved him a great deal. As much as she had tried to close the door to the past, those emotions hadn't been extinguished completely. Clearing away the clutter and misunderstandings of the past had opened her eyes to the truth. She had tried to move on, her unresolved feelings for Brady manifesting into bitterness and an automatic defensive response when he was close. If she had moved on and let go of him, she would have felt nothing: nothing when he'd been injured, nothing when he'd rejected her in the hospital and nothing when he'd shown up in her bedroom. Her resentment had concealed a painful truth: she still loved him. Loved him and couldn't trust him. Did he even trust himself?

If they survived this, Brady had a long road to recovery ahead of him, dealing with his injury and the changes in his life. Susan didn't want to think about that now. She wanted to prove to Brady that his injuries didn't matter to her and they wouldn't matter to others.

Susan traced her finger along his jaw. "Kiss me."

Without hesitation, Brady brought his lips to hers. The kiss was soft and unhurried.

Susan broke the kiss and pulled her shirt over her head, Brady's eyes on her. Wicked, hot pleasure danced along her skin.

He reached to touch her and she shook her head and stepped away, never breaking eye contact. The last time they'd made love, it had been frantic and hurried. This time, she wanted to take their time. She turned and unsnapped her bra, shimmying her shoulders so the straps fell. She looked over at him, keeping her back to him, and tossed the strip of fabric to him.

He reached to touch her and she shook her head. "No touching until I say."

He caught it and growled. "You are playing with fire."

"You're too much of a gentleman to violate my rule." She tossed him a smile to let him know she was teasing.

Brady gripped the bedspread. "Susan."

The begging in his voice. The expression on his face. He wanted her. A man as powerful as Brady needing her was a thrill. She bent over, hooking her panties with her thumbs and slid them to the floor. She tossed those over her shoulder, as well.

She pivoted and took two steps toward him. His eyes burned with wanting and sweat broke out on his forehead.

She shoved his shoulders, pushing him back on the bed.

His eyes flickered with provocation. "Now. Let me touch you now."

She shook her head. "Patience."

"I don't have any of that."

She laughed. She kissed his forehead, his nose and his cheeks. She nibbled his ear lobes, letting her hands rest on his chest and her thighs brush his.

"Susan, I only have so much control."

She brought her mouth to his ear. "You'll have me. I promise," she whispered. "And I'll have you."

She peeled his shirt away from his skin. Running her hands over the hard lines and planes of his body, she shivered with excitement. Anticipation hummed in the air.

She unbuttoned his pants and slid down the zipper. Reaching inside the dark fabric, she freed him with her hand. She knelt between his knees and watched his face as she took him into her mouth.

His breath came out in a hiss of air. His hands fisted the blankets. Then her name, loudly, clear on his lips.

She slid the length of him in and out, hallowing her cheeks, enjoying the sensation, the feeling. Toying with him, she watched emotions play across his face.

"Susan, I can't hold on much longer. Please let me inside you."

She was enjoying herself, but she wanted him thrusting inside her. Susan released him and rose to her feet. She climbed on his lap, straddling his hips. She cupped his face and kissed him long and hard. Their tongues danced and his hips brushed hers, his arousal pressing at her core, straining.

Her intentions to go slow fled. Brady fumbled to put on a condom.

She lifted her hips and impaled herself, taking him deep, reveling in the sensations of him filling her. She rode him hard, gripping his shoulders. His hands went to her waist lifting and lowering her. Every movement was more incredible than the one before it.

This time, she held nothing back. Her heart was open. No boundaries. No lies. No hiding and protecting themselves.

He pumped inside her harder and her fingers dug into his shoulders. She was on the brink of release. The sensations heightened impossibly high, fevered and frantic. She arched her back and he surged inside her. She fell over the summit, and rhythmic cries rocked her. Her completion signaled his own.

Their breathing was labored and they collapsed on the bed, panting and spent.

Susan turned her head, brushing her hair off her face. They basked in the aftermath of their lovemaking. With her ear to his chest, she could hear his heart racing.

"Amazing," she said. Susan rolled to his side and he gathered her against him, spooning her body into his. "Maybe we can repeat that later." She strung the words out for him to latch onto, wanting him to give her a promise of a future.

"I could go for that. Name the time and place and I'm yours."

For the first time, she felt that he was. Maybe not tomorrow, but at least for now.

Chapter 11

Susan roused from sleep when Brady shifted next to her, pulling her against him. They couldn't stay here forever. She should get up and start looking for the lock where the key fit. She should be reading Justin's notebook or looking for a computer to check the news or turning on the television news stations. Her future depended on resolving the past.

She told herself five more minutes wouldn't hurt. She closed her eyes. When she opened them, forty minutes had passed. This was what she remembered about life with Brady. He relaxed her. He made her feel at ease in a way others couldn't.

She tried to climb out of the bed without disturbing him.

"What's wrong?" he asked.

"We've been asleep for a couple of hours. I want to start looking for the lock."

"Give me a minute to check in with Harris. Then we can start looking around," Brady said.

He turned on the prepaid phone and dialed. Susan got dressed, listening to one side of the conversation. Mostly, Brady made sounds of acknowledgment.

Brady disconnected and looked at Susan. He had a haunted expression on his face. "A body washed ashore at the marina. It's been leaked and the media is going wild with speculation."

Susan froze and bile rose in her throat. "Justin?"

They'd found his body. Would it help if the ME found evidence to exonerate her? What evidence could they find on his body to prove Susan hadn't killed him? Or would the ME find more evidence to use against Susan? What if finding Justin's body proved she had been involved? Old fears and guilt rose making it hard to breathe.

"The identity of the body hasn't been released to the public, but Harris confirmed it was a male aged between twenty and forty. Harris didn't know if the body had any stab injuries or gunshot wounds. The body has been in the water awhile."

Thinking of Justin's body floating in the marina made her sick to her stomach and sad for his family. They had to be going through hell. She wasn't happy they had chosen to blame her, but with the body in the ME's lab, they could have closure. "This will clear Reilly. The ME will see that Reilly had nothing to do with killing Justin. It might point the finger at me."

Brady picked up his clothes from the floor. "You didn't kill Justin."

"The men hunting me think I did. Justin's father thinks I did."

"I don't."

He spoke the words with absolute conviction. Her heart swelled at his faith in her. Though she couldn't provide a strong defense, Brady didn't doubt her innocence. If only she had the same conviction about herself.

"We'll wait to hear what the ME learns. I don't know what being in water does to any forensic evidence on the body," Brady said.

Panic flared. "Again, it might point the finger at me."

"Harris didn't say that. He was getting his information from a friend on the force. The friend isn't directly involved with the case. He was sharing what he knew and Harris doesn't want you to get your hopes up about what this could mean."

Anxiety heaved inside her. "All that was stopping the police from arresting me for murder was lack of a body. They have a body. They'll speak to me as a person of interest in the fire at Justin's boat. They won't believe me if I tell them someone else started the fire. They'll put me in jail for his murder. We're no closer to learning anything about that night. We have accusations that someone wants me dead. How will that hold up in court with no other evidence in my defense?"

Brady tugged Susan against him, wrapping his strong arms around her. Without him, she might come apart at the seams. "I won't let that happen. We're getting answers. Would it help if you saw the body?"

She leaned away and looked at him. Was he serious? The look on his face said he was. "How would that help?"

"Might jog your memory about that night."

Frustration renewed inside her. "I can't remember anything. I've tried."

"We need to tell your side of the story."

"My side of the story hasn't changed. I've told you everything I know."

Brady pressed his lips together. "If it comes out that you and Justin broke up the night before, that'll look bad. We need a way to spin that or to find some evidence to prove you had no reason to kill him. What if the police say you went to the boat in a rage? Or that you and Justin had a fight that spun out of control?"

That was why she hadn't mentioned their breakup to the police. In retrospect, her omission might have been a mistake. Wouldn't the police find out and use it against her? Justin might have mentioned the breakup to someone who would come forward. Not telling made her seem guiltier, as if she had something to hide.

"I didn't kill Justin." Doubt and guilt slivered into her words. If she was innocent, why wasn't anyone finding evidence to support her? Why did she have suspicions about her involvement?

Brady had faith in her. He and his brothers could be powerful allies, except in this case; with the mayor wanting her arrest and ex–Special Forces trying to kill her, the odds were stacked against her.

"We're working on borrowed time now. We have to do something. We need to find the lock," she said.

Brady pulled on his shirt. "I saw the hotel fire evacuation plan posted behind the front desk. No room number eighteen is listed. We can exclude that."

"What if we're recognized while we're looking around the hotel? What if someone is fiddling with their smartphone and sees our picture on a news site?

Or remembers us from a news program earlier? If a body was found, that will bring the story back to the headlines and to the forefront of people's minds."

Brady finished dressing and put on his gun holster and gun. "We'll keep to ourselves. We can keep our heads together like we're in private conversation."

"You sound sure of yourself."

"I am sure. This is the only way we can make progress."

Brady reached into his pocket and handed her a hotel room key. "If we get separated, here's a key to the room. Come back here as the meeting point. If we have to run, if you think someone recognizes you, don't go to the stairs where you can be cornered. Go outside."

Fear rose in her chest. "Why would we get separated? What do I do once I'm outside?"

"Wait for me to find you. This is a contingency plan, that's all. There's no reason for us to get separated."

Brady took her hand in his. His skin was warm and she felt safe with him. As safe as she could be with thousands of cops, brutal mercenaries and an entire city looking for them.

Brady reached into his pocket and reassured himself the small metal key was inside. He jingled it. He and Susan would locate what that key opened. Without it, they had nothing except a coded, blurry notebook of numbers. The stakes were higher now that a body had washed up in the marina, and when Justin's father identified him, a warrant would be issued for Susan's arrest. Tim Ambrose would demand the mayor see it done.

Susan had to remember the night Justin died. For

her sake. Brady couldn't stand the idea of Susan in jail and unprotected.

They'd made love and the memory hadn't been shaken loose. He'd misjudged the key to Susan's innermost thoughts. She didn't trust him. No amount of sex would change that. He'd have to prove to her he was trustworthy with her heart.

They left their room and took the side stairwell to the main floor. "I saw some offices on the first floor. We can try those."

They made a right turn out of the stairwell. They stopped at the sales office, and with Susan standing in front of him blocking the view, Brady inserted the key in the doorknob. He twisted it left and right slowly and as quietly as possible. If someone was inside, he didn't want to alarm them. The lock didn't open. He shook his head and Susan's shoulders fell.

"You didn't think it was that easy, did you?" he asked.

Susan brushed her hair behind her ear. "I hoped we'd catch a break."

They continued walking. Next to the sales office was another locked door. Brady tried the key. No luck.

A maintenance room and two closets: nothing.

Susan rubbed her forehead. "The hotel has hundreds of locked doors. We have to narrow it down."

"We'll find it. Let's look around the lobby. Maybe it belongs to a cabinet? A decorative bookcase?"

The lobby was in the front of the hotel. They were within hearing distance of the front desk, but out of sight, when they heard their names.

"We don't have anyone by those names listed," the front desk clerk was saying.

"A cab driver dropped them off a few blocks from here. They are dangerous fugitives. They could have used an alias or checked into the hotel separately. Can you speak to the shift before yours and get a list of who checked in today?"

Brady could see a reflection in the windows. Two police officers were speaking to the front desk clerk.

"I'll check with the other clerk when she gets back from her break and I can leave a note for the front desk manager to call you. I don't know how much information I can give out about our guests."

"I'm a police officer. You can tell me whatever I need to know," the officer said.

The police were closing in, and he and Susan were no closer to finding the truth. Brady's fear for Susan and his determination to protect her mounted. Brady couldn't let her down again. Not when she'd shown so much faith in him. He couldn't become a failure in her eyes.

"I'll check with my manager. I don't want to get into trouble." The clerk sounded nervous and unsure.

The officer sighed loudly. "Do you mind if we look around on our own?"

"No problem. Our award-winning greenhouse is open to the public," the clerk said.

The entrance to the greenhouse was through the main hallway where he and Susan were standing. Brady looked for an escape route. They whirled and ran into the hallway from where they'd come. The women's bathroom was on the right, a single room with a toilet and sink. They darted inside and shut the heavy oak door.

Leaving the lights off, they waited in the dark.

Brady held Susan against him. His body reacted to being hip to hip with her, heat arrowing to his groin. Brady wanted her. Had always wanted her. Would always want her. On some primal level, that couldn't change.

Her hands went to his shoulders. "Do you think they're gone?"

"Wait a few more seconds," Brady said. The phone in his pocket rang and Brady rushed to silence it. He answered it in a whisper.

"Yeah?"

"Bad time?" Harris asked.

"Not great," Brady said. He didn't see a better time on the horizon.

"I heard from my contact at the police station. Justin's father and family went to the morgue to identify the body. The body was badly deformed from being in the water for so long and the ME's office is getting his dental records. On my request, a friend from CSI took a look at the evidence and report by the lead ME assigned to the case. She found some discrepancies in the general findings."

"Such as?" Brady asked.

"Some of the conclusions written into the initial report were subjective. Like the blood at the scene. She suspects a fight or a stabbing took place, but she wouldn't have concluded the boat was the homicide scene. It could have been a secondary location after Justin sustained injuries elsewhere. My friend is wondering what else in the report is fact versus opinion. CSI didn't test the blood from multiple locations. We could find someone else's DNA at the scene. It's a long shot, especially because we can't go back to the boat to collect more evidence, but some samples were taken. The killer's DNA could have been left at the scene."

Blowing holes in the case against Susan, or at least raising questions, was what they needed. "Harris, you are freaking brilliant."

"Not brilliant. I've made friends in useful places. But if you think that's brilliant, you'll love this."

"You found evidence that Susan isn't responsible?" Brady asked.

Susan's hand fisted around his shirt.

"Close. I had my friend retest the wineglasses from the scene for chemicals that aren't included as a part of routine tests. One of the glasses has residue of a sleeping drug inside. That could explain why Susan doesn't remember anything. She was drugged."

"By who?" Brady asked. And why?

Harris sighed. "Hard to say. Justin might have drugged her. Maybe someone had gotten onto the boat before they arrived and planned to frame Susan for Justin's murder. It's speculation at this point."

An alternative theory of the case that Susan could present to her lawyer. The sleeping drug in the wineglass was forensic evidence. The prosecutor could accuse Susan of drugging Justin, but would the police be required to search for more concrete evidence?

"Are you and Susan making nice?" Harris asked. "That's a rhetorical question. I know you are. Don't bother denying it. I hear it in your voice."

Brady wouldn't deny it. He and Susan were getting along better than he'd expected.

"My friend is looking into what she can do about requesting a second review of the evidence. All of the evidence," Harris said.

252   *Shielding the Suspect*

"You are a master. While working your own undercover op, you're pulling strings," Brady said.

Harris laughed. "Trumans don't take bull lying
down."

"Thanks, man, I owe you," Brady said.

"No, you don't. We're family," Harris said.

The phone beeped that its battery life was ending.
Brady and Harris disconnected the call.

Before Brady could relate what Harris had said,
Susan spoke. "I could hear him. This is great news.
Can he go to someone in charge of the investigation
with that information?"

"I'm sure he will. But it takes time. We want the
right information in the right hands at the right time.
If he turns over evidence or raises questions to the
wrong people, he could be silenced and brushed aside.
We know there are others looking for you. Until we
know who they are, we need to be extremely careful."
They'd received the first sliver of good news in days,
but Susan had more than the police searching for her.
Trained killers wanted her dead.

Voices drifted into the bathroom. "No sign of them.
We need a list of guest names. Did you call the ADA
and ask about a warrant?"

The police looking for them weren't giving up. Their
voices faded as they moved away from the bathroom.

Brady took Susan's arm. With a body in the morgue,
the police closing in and the men tracking them locating them after every escape, he could feel the noose
around their necks tightening. He might have to choose
the lesser of two evils: turn themselves in to the police
instead of risking their lives running. He didn't want
a shootout with the police and he didn't want the mil-

itary men hunting them to get lucky. "Susan, if this goes south, I need you to know that I never made love with you to get information from you. I wasn't trying to manipulate you. I would never play with your trust that way, not when I've been trying to win it back."

Susan gave him a sideways look. "Why are you—"

He had to finish his thought. "I don't want to leave things the way I did before, open and unsettled. If the cops find us…"

Susan shivered. "I won't blame you for what goes wrong. You've been doing everything you can."

Brady rolled his shoulders. "That's what worries me. Doing everything I can and yet the cops and the men hunting you are somehow faster and still find us."

"We'll find the truth," Susan said.

Brady knew how much was at stake and how many things could go wrong. The cops at the hotel could find them before they found out where the key belonged. With the pressure from Lieutenant General Tim Ambrose and his buddy, the mayor, Susan could be arrested and tried without a proper investigation. Without due diligence on the part of investigators, Justin's killer would go free. The men hunting Susan could find a way to get to her.

"I don't like where this is leading. We have a lot working against us. I can't defeat a team of trained ex-Special Forces soldiers while the cops are hunting us and the mayor is out for blood. I don't want to let you down. You'd be better off with Reilly. Or maybe taking our chances with the police." Shame and self-doubt filled him. He couldn't protect her and he couldn't give her the life she deserved.

Susan stepped away from him. "I can't believe

you're doing this again. Now of all times. You're pulling your ejector seat way too early."

"I'm trying to be reasonable and honest."

Susan blew out her breath. "No. No, I don't accept that as a response. You are the man I need to protect me. You're the man who makes me feel safest. You're the man who stepped up to stand by my side when everyone else fled. And now, you're saying I have it wrong? That somehow, despite how much you've done, you're giving up and walking away?"

He wasn't a quitter. "I'm not giving up. I'm giving you the best chance for happiness." Like he had when he'd walked away before.

Susan threw her hands in the air. "What do you mean the best chance for happiness? I can't have a chance for happiness with you in my life?"

"No, you can't. Why do you think I walked away before? Why do you think I stayed out of your life? I wanted you to have the happiness you deserve. I couldn't give you the life you wanted when I was in the military, and I sure can't give it to you now. Look at me! I'm a mess." Humiliating words to speak, but they needed to be said.

Long, tense moments passed.

"That's why you broke up with me? Because you didn't think you could make me happy?" she asked, anger hot in her voice. "You could have explained this before now."

Brady blinked at her. "Before when? While you were engaged to Justin? I'd lost you. It didn't matter how I was feeling. I thought you were happy and I stayed quiet. I didn't want to ruin anything for you.

Tell you after he died? You were his grieving lover. My feelings for you didn't rate."

Susan shook her head. "You will always rate with me. If you had told me…"

"Would it have changed anything? You were with someone else. You had moved on with your life. And then, just like now, I'm not capable of being in a relationship with anyone. I don't even know if I'm capable of being a friend."

"If you thought your job made you a bad boyfriend or husband, why didn't you ask me to wait until you changed jobs? Injury or not, you wouldn't have been Special Forces forever. Wouldn't it have been better to be together when we could rather than apart for good?" Susan asked.

It sounded good in theory. But how could he ask that of someone he loved? "Ask you to wait for what?" Brady asked. "I couldn't ask you to put your life on hold for me. What if I never came back from a mission? You could have thrown away the best years of your life waiting for me, only to be alone in the end."

She scoffed. "In other words, you decided that I shouldn't wait. You decided that it was better for me if you ended the relationship rather than be honest and let me make a decision. What about the thousands of men and women who have spouses in the military? Is it better for them to walk away? Should people with dangerous jobs be forbidden from being in a relationship?"

She didn't give him a chance to answer. "Of course not! That's ridiculous. But I'm going to make it easier for you this time. You don't get to decide for me what I want and what makes me happy." She snatched the key away from him. "I'll find where this key belongs. You don't get to dictate what is best for me. This time, I'm walking away first."

Brady wouldn't let her search alone. Not with policemen circling the hotel looking for her and ex-military stalking her. Brady followed her past the front desk. He couldn't argue with her in public and draw attention.

Brady noticed in his peripheral vision a flash of silver. A guest was handing a key—not a key card—to the front desk clerk. The clerk took the key, asked the man a question, smiled and turned away from the front desk. She opened the faux front of the cabinet behind the front counter to reveal a series of safe deposit boxes.

A few moments later, she slid a long plastic drawer to the man, who opened it and withdrew his items.

A safe deposit box. Justin had used a safe deposit box. To open it, he would need the key currently in Susan's possession and the master key, likely controlled by the hotel clerks.

Brady took Susan's arm and spun her, gesturing to the safe deposit box.

"Stop following me," she hissed.

"Not going to happen. Especially not now," Brady said. He pointed again to the front desk. Susan's gaze followed his hand.

A moment of confusion was followed by dawning realization. Excitement burned in Susan's eyes.

It had been months. What had the hotel done when Justin hadn't returned the key? Had they called a locksmith to pop open the lock? Thrown away the contents of the safe?

How could Brady check? If they kept records of usage and asked for ID, Brady wouldn't be able to get inside Justin's safe deposit box. The police had been at the front desk asking about them. Had the police showed their photo? Would the hotel staff be on heightened alert for him and Susan?

Brady didn't have time to come up with a plan B. The fire alarm in the hotel went off, strobe lights flashing and bells shrieking.

"Are you kidding me?" Susan muttered.

Brady looked around the lobby. No sign of flames or smoke. He didn't see the police officers who had been at the front desk looking for them. Their experiences this past week told him whoever was after Susan liked using fire. It seemed risky to set fire to a hotel, endangering the lives of dozens of people, to flush him and Susan out.

"Something is off. You can be mad at me and you can write me off later, but we need to stay together," he said.

Susan blew out her breath. "We'll stay together for now, but you're not calling all the shots."

"Agreed." Anything to keep her safe.

Could the alarm be a ploy to get them out of the hotel?

The hotel had three entrances: the front door leading to street, the back door leading to the greenhouse and a side door. Would the police have those doors monitored? Could the ex-Special Forces operatives hunting Susan be poised to attack?

"I don't trust this," Brady said.

Susan's eyes widened with fear. "I don't either."

People were streaming out the front door. Could Brady and Susan blend and get out of the hotel without the police or former Special Forces operatives spotting them?

Their best move was to get out of the hotel and flee as far as possible from the scene. "The cops who were asking about us at the front desk moved to the back of the hotel. I don't want to isolate ourselves from the crowd. Let's follow everyone else out. Stay close to me. We cannot get separated," Brady said. Especially not now. Susan wouldn't leave his sight.

Susan grabbed Brady's hand and squeezed it. A temporary truce. He was forgiven for now. The direness of the situation required it.

They walked into the line of people vacating the hotel. Outside, some hotel employees were on cell phones and others were directing people to the parking lot. If the fire was real, it would be a nightmare for the hotel employees to locate their guests. They could be in their rooms, they could be somewhere else in the hotel or they could be out for the day.

A siren screamed and emergency response horns blared. The fire department was taking the alarm seriously.

"Let's get on the street and get away from this," Brady said. He navigated through the crowd. If he and Susan were corralled in the same place where the police were, they'd be spotted. When more police officers arrived on the scene, they might recognize him and Susan. They needed to beat feet.

A hotel employee stepped in front of them. "Sir, ma'am, you need to follow the others and stay in the parking lot. We need to account for our guests. I'm sure you understand it's a precaution to ensure everyone's safe."

"Okay, sure," Brady said, not wanting to put him and Susan on center stage by making a scene and taking off.

When they were away from the employee, Brady lowered his face to Susan's ear. "As soon as we're out of sight, we'll look for an exit and bolt out of here."

"Where are we going?" Susan asked.

"Somewhere to lay low until we figure out what this fire is about." If the police searched the rooms, would they locate his and Susan's things? Did they have anything with them that could give them away? The notebook was in the room! Brady swore.

"We left the notebook in our room." It could be an important piece of evidence. Whatever Justin had left in the safe deposit box could also be critical. If the hotel fire wasn't controlled, they could lose vital information in building Susan's defense.

Susan swallowed. "Should we go back inside to get it?"

The hotel employees might have the doors covered. It might be better to take their chances rather than be captured by the police. "No. Leave it for now."

He and Susan stood with the crowd in the parking lot. One of the police officers who had been looking for them was standing near a hotel employee who was holding a clipboard and calling out room numbers.

The officer was smart. In his position, he could look at every hotel guest and find him and Susan.

Brady and Susan skirted to the edge of the crowd and ducked behind an SUV. "We'll weave through these cars. Don't look back. If someone shouts at you to stop, don't turn around, keep walking. We'll blend with the street traffic and disappear."

The evacuation of the hotel was drawing a crowd, making it easier for him and Susan to get away from the scene.

A fire truck pulled into the parking lot, and the crowd separated to allow it to pass. Brady took the opportunity to run.

"Hey, you! Stop!"

He and Susan didn't stop. Brady's knee burned as his feet slapped the pavement. A cop car pulled in front of them and a police officer sprang from the front seat and drew his weapon. Brady pivoted on his heel, looking for a place to escape. Another officer appeared behind them, out of breath, cheeks red and gun in hand.

"You shouldn't have made me run," he said. His uniform's nameplate read "Barker."

He took out his cuffs. "Hands behind your back," Barker said to Brady.

An SUV squealed to a stop at the curb, swerving to avoid running up on it. A man holding a semiautomatic weapon and wearing a ski mask and military fatigues got out of the driver's side. The cops turned their guns on him, surprise written across their faces.

Brady recognized the build and the posture as the man who had chased them in the woods outside the ski resort.

"Both of you," the man in fatigues said, pointing his gun at Susan and Brady, "get in the car. Get in the car now."

The police seemed unsure what to do, moving their

guns between the man in fatigues and Brady. "Sir, drop your weapon or we'll be forced to shoot."

The man in the ski mask was faster or cared less about the body count. He pulled the trigger on his weapon, taking out both officers. Susan shrieked in surprise, backing up against Brady, her hand over her mouth. Brady grasped her arms and moved her behind him. Who was this person who would open fire on police officers in public? This man must have a death wish.

"Hurry up! Get in the car!" the man in the ski mask demanded in a hoarse voice. "You," he said to Brady, "hands in the air or I will kill you."

Brady had no doubts of the gunman's willingness to shoot them. He'd just proven he would shoot anyone who disobeyed him or got in his way. Brady looked at the two officers on the ground. If Brady delayed or could stall, someone would come to their aid. Two officers down in the middle of the city was a big deal. Most people in the area were focused on the fire at the hotel, but someone had to see them. Cars passing by, foot traffic, anyone.

"You're making a mistake," Brady said. Someone would realize what was unfolding and follow them or make a phone call to emergency services.

"Shut your mouth and get in the car," the gunman said and aimed his gun at Brady.

Susan and Brady got into the back of the SUV, a metal grate between them and the front seat. The back door locks and windows would have been disabled.

The gunman threw two pairs of cuffs into the backseat, holding his gun on Brady and Susan. "Put them on."

Brady couldn't get to his weapon fast enough to take the gunman out. Not with a gun trained on Susan. This time, Brady's hesitation in reacting was intentional. He'd buy them time and get them out of this safely. Brady wasn't as skilled with psychological profiling as his brother, but he knew this man lacked impulse control. He'd hunted him and Susan in the woods like animals. He'd killed two police officers in cold blood. Had this gunman arranged the other attacks or was he another hired gun? Brady didn't believe he was taking direction from someone else. He'd never known a trained operative to react rashly and desperately in the face of trouble, and killing two police officers was the definition of rash and desperate.

This man, whoever he was, was violent, impulsive and reckless. In other words, he was the greatest danger they'd faced.

Brady slid the cuffs on his wrists and Susan did the same, locking them into place. With his hands in front of him, he would have some leverage.

The gunman watched from the open back door of the car, keeping the gun trained on Brady. Once the cuffs were on, the gunman reached to Brady's side and took his gun.

"We're about to go on the chase of your lives." The gunman laughed maniacally and slammed the door. Susan cringed.

As the gunman circled the car, Brady checked the door. He and Susan were locked in, as he'd suspected.

"How are we going to get out of this? Kick out a window?" Susan whispered.

"Stay calm. Do as I tell you. This guy is reacting on a hair trigger. Don't set him off," Brady said.

The gunman climbed into the running car and pulled away from the scene with the same perilously fast driving, slamming on the accelerator.

If the gunman had been hunting him and Susan, why not kill them at the scene? What did he gain from killing two cops and kidnapping him and Susan? The terror on Susan's face had Brady reaching for her hands to offer some reassurance.

Brady didn't have control of the situation, but letting fear enter the equation would tilt the favor more toward the gunman. He'd been trained to assess a situation and then respond to it. At the moment, he didn't know whom he was dealing with.

The gunman wove through traffic and Brady braced Susan as much as he could to prevent her from sliding around the backseat. The SUV continued away from the center of town and turned off-road onto a narrow dirt path, reminiscent of the place he'd rented from Connor: quiet, hidden and difficult to find help.

Panic flared in Susan's eyes. Brady worked overtime to keep his face and posture neutral and calm. She had to know he wasn't afraid. He would get her safely out of this somehow. She could count on him.

The gunman slammed the car to a stop in front of a run-down brick building. Parts of it were crumbling; the roof was collapsed in the back, sagging in the front and the entryway overgrown with ivy.

The gunman got out of the car and pulled open the back door. He was holding his gun in his right hand. "Get out of the car," he commanded.

Gone was hoarseness in his voice. Something in Brady's memory stirred. The voice had a familiar quality.

Susan's mouth fell open. "I don't... Justin?"

The gunman ripped off his mask and threw it to the ground. His eyes glittered with malevolence. "Hey there, Susan. Happy to see me?"

Chapter 12

Susan couldn't move. It was as if her muscles had seized up from shock. "Justin, you're alive. What are you doing?"

"I was waiting for you." He glanced at Brady, rage hot in his eyes. "Which is more than I can say for you."

Waiting for her? To do what? "I thought you were dead." She heard the confusion, fear and anger in her voice. It was nothing compared to the litany of questions and accusations firing in her brain. Confusion dwindled away and anger took full hold of her. Justin had allowed her, his family and the world to believe he was dead. He hadn't cared how much they'd been hurting or who else would suffer from his lies. He'd killed two police officers. But why?

"I wanted you to think I was dead. I wanted everyone to think I was dead. But you flamed up my plans and now you need to make amends for that," Justin said.

Terror ripped through her. Why hadn't Justin shot her on sight? The ex-Special Forces men who had attacked her and Brady believed Justin was dead. How was Justin involved with them? "How can I make amends?" She fought to keep her voice from cracking and failed. Brady's hand was at her back, reassuring her.

Brady. Horror and sadness consumed her. She had brought Brady into this mess. Justin couldn't hurt him; she wouldn't allow it. Brady had enough battle scars to last a lifetime. What could she say or do to protect the man she loved?

"Give me what you took from my boat," Justin said.

"We don't have anything from your boat," Susan said. How did he know they had taken something?

Justin let out a burst of sharp laughter. "Stop with the games. I saw you running away from my boat the night of the fire. When you left the ski resort and showed up at the Windsor, I knew you'd taken my keys. Tell me where they are. No one can know I'm alive."

Did the keys lead to evidence that Justin was alive or was he concerned about her and Brady telling someone? Susan was sure Justin was planning to kill them. "We don't have them. They're in our hotel room," Susan said. The safe deposit key burned a hole in her back pocket. Should she give it to him? Would he believe her lie?

"Did you get into my safe deposit box? Did you take the cash? The documents?" Justin's voice had taken on an edge of panic.

"No, we didn't," Susan said. Cash and documents, likely his nest egg for wherever he was planning to run and set up a new life with a new identity.

Justin sighed. "Give me your hotel key. I'll get them myself. Say goodbye to Justin Ambrose." He narrowed his gaze on her. "I had a new identity in that box for you, too, Susan. We would have started over and had a good life."

Susan reached into her front pocket with her cuffed hands and took the room key Brady had given her. She sensed him behind her, crouched and ready to spring. What was he waiting for? What would he do and how could she help? She handed the room key to Justin.

"Get out of the car," he said, grabbing her by the arm and dragging her out. Gravel and dirt bit into her as her body slammed against the ground.

Brady got out of the car slowly, silently. She recognized the dangerous look in his eyes. His face was passive, but his not eyes. He was enraged. What would he do? How could she help? Justin had taken his gun and their hands were cuffed.

Justin hit Brady across the face with his gun. Brady's head swung to the side, but he didn't fall. It seemed to anger Justin more. "Guess you were happy to see me out of the way. Didn't take you long to get her back into your bed."

Brady met Justin's eyes. His face was bleeding from where Justin had struck him. "You got what you needed. Leave us alone." The warning and threat that underscored the words was tangible.

Justin shrank away from Brady. Justin had always been intimidated by shows of strength. It was one of the reasons his father had been such a controlling presence in his life, one Justin resented but couldn't seem to throw off. Susan rolled and positioned herself to kick Justin if he came near.

Another car barreled down the dirt road behind them. Was it the police? Had help arrived? The car showed no signs of slowing or stopping. Adrenaline fired in her veins and Susan dove away. Brady leaped to cover her. The second car smashed into Justin's, sending it sailing forward.

Metal twisted and glass shattered. Two men got out of the second car, guns drawn. They were dressed in black with weapons strapped to their sides and backs.

"Isn't this convenient?" one of the men said to the other and then looked at Justin. "Looks like your dear old dad was right. You are alive. And you so kindly orchestrated this meeting so we can clean up in one fell swoop."

Anger and fear showed plain on Justin's face.

His dear old dad? Justin's father? He had been grieving for a son he'd known was alive? Demanding the mayor apply pressure to the police department to arrest her for murder when Justin wasn't dead? Why would he do that?

Was he hiding his involvement in Justin's disappearance or working with his son to cover it up?

Justin's father was a major player in the air force. What was his connection to the former Special Forces operatives who had tried to kill her and Brady? A lieutenant general in the air force would have access to the names of former Special Forces and Tim Ambrose had the money and gall to hire them for his personal use. Was it possible the lieutenant general was working against his son?

"How did you…?" Justin asked, his voice trailing away. He didn't struggle when one of the men took his gun.

"Find you?" The man with a jagged scar along his cheek nodded at Brady. "You always have been sloppy."

Brady positioned his body between Susan and the other men.

Susan looked between Justin, Brady and the two men, unsure what was unfolding. She couldn't read the situation and didn't want to make it worse by speaking.

"Everyone up and into the house. I don't want to make a mess and I don't want bodies found. Move it," the other man said, lifting his sunglasses onto the top of his head.

Sunglasses and Scarface pulled her to her feet and she, Justin and Brady walked at gunpoint toward the house.

The porch creaked beneath their feet and the splintered door opened with a kick from Scarface's boot. "Inside."

They trudged inside and Sunglasses pointed at Brady. "Sit by the fireplace. Don't move. Don't breathe." He held his gun on Brady, recognizing him, even unarmed, as the greatest threat.

Scarface gestured at Justin and Susan. "Sit. Wait." He took out his phone and dialed. He left the phone on speaker, the ringing loud against the silence of the cabin.

The phone was answered on the first ring. "You better have some good news." Susan recognized the voice as Justin's father.

"We have the best news. Found your lying, sack-of-garbage son. He did one good thing for us. He had both Susan and Truman with him," Scarface said.

"We'll deal with Truman first. He wants the same thing we do."

Susan looked at Brady. He was still, watching and waiting.

"Truman, my offer stands. I can make this go away for you and your brother. Your military record will stay in its near-pristine state and I'll explain to the mayor how your brother is innocent and have him cleared of any wrongdoing. Hell, I'll even have the mayor issue a public apology for the accusations leveled against him," Tim Ambrose said.

When had Brady spoken with Justin's father? Tim Ambrose was presenting a great offer. Brady wouldn't take it. Ambrose would ask for too much in return. Men like Tim Ambrose didn't do favors for free.

Brady's face was impossible to read. "What do I need to do to make that happen?"

Shock sliced through Susan. Brady was making a deal with Justin's father, the same man who had made arrangements to blame her for Justin's supposed murder. Was he going along with him to buy them time for help to arrive? Was help en route?

"Good thinking, soldier," Justin's father said, smugness tight in his voice. "You need a new job and I need you to walk away from this. If you work for me as my personal soldier, I'll take care of everything."

Work for Lieutenant General Ambrose as his personal soldier? Sounded like a deal with the devil to her. Susan watched Brady. He didn't look at her. He appeared to be considering the lieutenant general's words. It had hurt Brady deeply when he'd lost his job with the pararescuemen. He had been wandering, unsure of his next move, questioning his life and his worth.

Lieutenant General Ambrose had offered him a solution to that problem on a silver platter. Would Brady want to work as someone's mercenary? Susan didn't think so. After what Justin's father had done and given Brady's personal code of honor, she couldn't imagine Brady agreeing to work with him.

"You'll have my silence and I'll work for you in the same way these guys work for you? You promise to protect my brother and restore his job?" Brady asked.

"Yes," Tim Ambrose said, sounding victorious and pleased.

"Deal," Brady said.

The word came down on Susan like a hammer and a wave of dizziness hit her. It wasn't possible. Brady wouldn't betray her this way.

"I need a show of good faith," the lieutenant general said. "Something so I'm certain whose side you're on."

"Tell me what you had in mind," Brady said.

"Brady!" His name left her mouth in panic. Was he negotiating with them, hoping to get them out of this situation unscathed? She'd known him to be a man of honor. This was borderline impossible to believe. He'd told her he couldn't be the man she needed. He'd seemed convinced this story would have a terrible ending. Did he believe he didn't have other options?

"Kill Susan," the lieutenant general said.

"No!" Susan said. Brady wouldn't do that. He wouldn't turn on her. What Tim Ambrose was offering was a nice deal to save Reilly and give Brady the career he wanted, but he wouldn't take it at the cost of her life.

Brady had said he wanted her to be happy. He had

walked away from her thinking he couldn't make it so. He wouldn't hurt her now, purposefully.

Brady rose to his feet. "I'm sorry to see her go, but I want to clear Reilly. He's family. Susan's nothing to me. I never pretended otherwise. She got mixed up in this and here's a quick way out."

Hurt coursed through her. She had known she was outside his inner circle, one that only included his family, but this was extreme. His career wasn't more important than her life.

Brady took the gun offered to him by Scarface, then looked at his bound wrists and the gun. "This is a bit dramatic for shooting someone. I prefer to do things with less flair. It calls less attention." He looked at the gun again, adjusting it in his hands. He shrugged and lifted the gun. "To be clear, I kill Susan, Reilly is taken off administrative leave and his service record kept clean, and I get a job doing what I love?"

"You have my word," Tim Ambrose said.

Whatever that was worth. Susan couldn't believe what she was seeing and hearing.

"Susan?" Brady asked.

"Yes?" She waited for him to change his mind.

"I'm so sorry."

She squeezed her eyes closed and the sound of gunshots reverberated around the room. Something heavy slammed into her and she opened her eyes. Brady! He had thrown himself over Susan and was pressed against her, shooting from the ground at one of the lieutenant general's underlings, who'd taken cover behind an old couch.

Brady continued shooting and the man fell backward. Brady rolled to his feet, swinging the gun at

Justin. "Susan, get the phone. It's on the ground. Call for help."

Susan scrambled to stand. She found the phone in the hand of a dead Scarface. She called 911 and waited on the phone while the police dispatcher took her information.

"Tell me why you did this," Brady said to Justin. "What is the point of running away like a coward? What does your father have on you?"

Justin glared at Brady. "You wouldn't understand. I was going to have the life I dreamed of. With her. With plenty of money."

"With plenty of money that you stole," Brady said.

Would Justin admit the ledgers they'd found on Justin's yacht were records of stolen money? And the account in her name the place Justin was keeping it?

Justin seemed surprised. "I can't take total credit for that. My father helped. How do you think he pays for his personal soldiers?"

Brady kept his gun leveled at Justin, disgust on his face. "Your father figured out you were planning to run away with the money, so you faked your death, framed Susan and took off like a deserter. But you forgot the key to your precious safety deposit box."

Justin snorted. "You think you have it figured out. You don't know anything. I didn't leave it behind. I was interrupted. I had an escape plan in place for months. I would have taken her and the money with me away from this. If she hadn't ended our engagement and if my father's enforcers hadn't shown up to stop me, we could have had a good life. We would have disappeared and no one would have found us. Instead, she made the perfect scapegoat to give me time to get away without the police on my tail."

Brady's eyes narrowed. "Who else is after Susan? Tell me now."

Justin shrugged. "You'll have to ask the lieutenant general about that. He doesn't leave loose ends. He probably has more men on their way here. If we're smart, we'll get out of here before that happens."

Susan's heartbeat escalated. If Justin was telling the truth, could they stand up against a second wave of men? Tim Ambrose might send more this time. The police were on their way, but what would it take to stop former Special Forces operatives with a mission? They'd proven to be tenacious in their goal.

"I'm done running," Brady said. "If the lieutenant general is going to call in the cavalry, then so will we. The Truman family may not be as connected as your father, but we stand by one another. If he's worried about loose ends, I'd say you're his biggest one."

Keeping his gun on Justin, Brady pulled another phone from the pocket of the downed mercenary. He dialed a number and flipped the phone to speaker.

Reilly's voice came on the line. "It's good to hear your voice, brother. I already heard about Susan's call on my police scanner and am in my car. Harris is on his way, too," Reilly said. "No way were either of us staying put when you're in trouble. We'll be there as soon as we can."

Reilly Truman arrived on the scene before the police. He looked angry as he entered the rundown shack. He wasn't in his police uniform. He wore jeans slung low on his hips and a flannel shirt. He shot Justin a disgusted look. "What is this piece of crap pulling now?"

"Justin and his father embezzled money and Justin planned to take off with it," Brady said. "When his father found out, he sent his own group of enforcers after Justin to stop him. Justin decided to disappear and pin his disappearance on Susan. The lieutenant general was probably happy the police believed Susan was responsible. It prevented any further inquiry into Justin's disappearance and Justin and his father's criminal activities."

"The evidence at the scene was good. How'd he pull that off?" Reilly asked, narrowing his stare on Justin.

"My father has resources you couldn't dream of having," Justin said.

"The lieutenant general planned to clean up his own mess, even if that meant killing his son. No honor among thieves," Reilly said. His brow furrowed as he swung his attention to Brady and Susan. "Are either of you hurt?"

Brady shifted on his feet, rubbing his knee, keeping Justin at gunpoint. "I hurt my knee in a shootout and I'd like these cuffs off."

Reilly lifted a brow. "That statement should shock me more. Knowing you, it doesn't. A shootout sounds about right. Susan, are you okay?" He crossed the room to Justin and pulled him to his feet. He checked his pockets and withdrew the key to the handcuffs.

Susan held up her cuffed hands. "I'm fine, thanks to Brady."

"At this point, it's safe to say Justin and his father will be spending time in prison," Reilly said and then chuckled. "What I wouldn't do to get a look at the mayor's face when he learns his bosom buddy is neck-deep in criminal activity." He unlocked Susan's cuffs and then Brady's.

"Aren't you upset about how you were treated?" Susan said, guilt nibbling at her. It was turning out okay, but Reilly had been through a lot.

"Sure, but what can I do? It'll work out. With any luck, I'll get an apology and a vacation out of this," Reilly said.

The police arrived and Reilly met them outside, taking unofficial control of the scene and providing explanations. They brought Justin into custody and Reilly made sure everyone on the scene understood his brother and Susan were no longer persons of interest in Justin's disappearance or the boat fire at the marina. When Harris showed up, he was accompanied by several thuggish-looking men. Actually, Harris was looking thuggish himself, his blond hair set in spikes around his head and dark black eyeliner rimming his eyes. He came to Susan first and hugged her. "Please excuse my appearance. We're on an undercover op and I didn't stop to change."

Brady joined them, slapping his brother on the back. "We're expecting retribution from the lieutenant general."

Harris nodded. "That's the message I got. Sadly for him, I have some agents tracking him. Once he's in custody, we'll tear apart his life piece by piece and shut him down. He's looking at prison time and dishonorable discharge. I don't know which he'll hate more."

Susan shivered. "What about the men he's already sent after us?"

Brady took Susan's hands in his. She felt immediately better being close to him, her hands in his. "For a mercenary, the work is never personal. Once the paychecks stop, so do the services. We'll put the word out that Tim Ambrose is looking at prison time and won't be making any future payments for services rendered."

"Let me see what else I can find out," Harris said, taking out his phone and moving a few steps away.

It was the first time she had been alone with Brady since Justin had kidnapped them from the street outside the hotel.

"You thought I was going to shoot you," Brady said, running his hand across her cheek and through the ends of her hair.

She might have questioned Brady's words, but her heart had remained true. She had never completely believed Brady had turned on her. "I didn't want to believe it. You are a very convincing liar."

Brady wrapped his arms around her, putting some of his weight on her. "I've told you before, winning is ninety percent a mind game. I had to make them believe I was on their side."

"When you never were?" she asked, knowing the answer, but wanting the words.

"Of course not. I've been on your side from day one," Brady said. "I needed them to believe that I would kill you to get what I wanted. That I didn't care about you in the least. But I wanted you to be safe. I wanted you out of here without getting hurt."

"You hurt your knee. Again," Susan said.

Brady shrugged. "It's a hazard of the job."

"You know what else I noticed?" Susan asked.

Brady inclined his head. "What's that?"

"You didn't hesitate. When my life was at risk, you didn't freeze. Not for a moment."

"Darlin', are you saying I'm cured?" he asked.

"I'm saying you're darn close," Susan said.

"You might have noticed I didn't hesitate, but I noticed something, too," Brady said. "I never considered taking the job even if it put me back in action. I realized what I want with my life. I want you, all in one piece, with me, for good."

"For good? I like the sound of that," Susan said.

Brady brushed his hand over her shoulder, her arm and her backside. She swatted his hand away.

He grinned at her. "Just checking that it's all in one piece."

"All in one piece and all yours."

Epilogue

Three months later

"I'm appreciative of the work you've done here," Tom Watts said. "You and Susan have been a real asset to our program."

Brady and Susan had been volunteering with the Wounded Warrior Project, a program dedicated to helping severely injured servicemen and women transition from active duty to civilian life.

It had been healing for Brady, on many levels, to see men and women more injured than he was starting new lives, interesting lives, and not letting their injuries stop them from achieving their goals or having fulfilling careers.

"It's been good for me to work here," Brady said. The time he'd spent with other veterans had not only put his injuries in perspective, but had given him role models. "I've enjoyed every minute."

Tom folded his hands across his desk and leaned forward. "With that out of the way, I want to put you in touch with a friend who's looking for someone with your skills."

Brady lifted a brow. "My skills?"

Tom spun in his chair and grabbed a manila envelope from the shelves behind his desk. He handed it to Brady. "The FBI is looking for someone for their counterterrorism team. If you read the job description, you'll see you have everything they need. Their field office is cutting-edge technology. Working from behind a desk will be a change of pace for you from active duty, but I have a feeling it will be a good fit."

Brady took the folder and opened it slowly. He skimmed the papers. "Thank you, Tom. I'll talk it over with Susan and give your friend a call."

Tom smiled. "He's waiting to hear from you."

Ten minutes later, Brady was waiting outside the classroom where Susan was teaching art to some participants in the program. When he noticed her class cleaning up their supplies, he entered.

Susan looked up at him with a big smile on her face. She was sitting at her desk fiddling with the new camera Brady had bought her to replace the one Tim Ambrose's mercenaries had stolen and destroyed. The former lieutenant general had feared it contained evidence against him and Justin. "You're early."

"Just by a few minutes." Every moment together meant so much to him.

"Have you given any more thought to the surgery?"

Brady's doctors had recommended a new, experimental surgery that could restore function to his knee. It didn't guarantee he'd perform at the same level he had previously, but it gave him the slim hope it was possible. On the other hand, the surgery required months of rehabilitation and if unsuccessful, he would be no further along than he was now. It could make it worse. "I don't think it's right for me now."

Susan inclined her head. "But if everything went well, you could return to the Special Forces."

Maybe. But he didn't want that. Not anymore. The future he had with Susan was too precious to walk away from again. He had found happiness with her. "I don't want to return to the pararescueman."

Susan's mouth dropped open. "That's all you've ever wanted."

Brady took her hands. "No. You're what I want and this time, I'm not letting you get away."

"I love you. I have no intention of running," Susan said, stepping closer to him.

"I love you, too," Brady said. "Ready to go? We don't want to be late for dinner with our family."

Susan slipped her arm around his waist. "I love that your family includes my mom in their plans. I love that you're in my life. And most of all, I love you."

Brady kept Susan tucked against him as they walked to the car. His life wasn't what he'd expected. It was much, much better.

* * * * *

*If you love the Truman brothers,
don't miss PROTECTING HIS PRINCESS, coming
soon from Harlequin Romantic Suspense.*

COMING NEXT MONTH FROM

HARLEQUIN™

ROMANTIC suspense

Available October 1, 2013

#1771 KILLER'S PREY
Conard County: The Next Generation
by Rachel Lee

After a brutal attack, Nora Loftis returns to Conard County and the arms of Sheriff Jake Madison. But her assailant escapes, and he's coming for her. Can Jake protect her and heal her soul?

#1772 THE COLTON BRIDE
The Coltons of Wyoming • by Carla Cassidy

Heiress Catherine Colton broke rancher Gray Stark's heart, but when danger surrounds her, he steps up. A marriage of protection will keep her safe, but he finds his heart at risk.

#1773 TEXAS SECRETS, LOVERS' LIES
by Karen Whiddon

With her best friend missing, Zoe risks her life to find her, but she can't do it without Brock McCauley, the man she left at the altar five years before—and never stopped loving.

#1774 THE LONDON DECEPTION
House of Steele • by Addison Fox

When a sexy archaeologist teams up with a mysterious thief to unearth a cache of jewels in Egypt, the competition turns deadly and the only person either can trust is each other.

HRSCNM0913

REQUEST YOUR FREE BOOKS!
2 FREE NOVELS PLUS 2 FREE GIFTS!

ROMANTIC suspense

Sparked by danger, fueled by passion

YES! Please send me 2 FREE Harlequin® Romantic Suspense novels and my 2 FREE gifts (gifts are worth about $10). After receiving them, if I don't wish to receive any more books, I can return the shipping statement marked "cancel." If I don't cancel, I will receive 4 brand-new novels every month and be billed just $4.74 per book in the U.S. or $5.24 per book in Canada. That's a savings of at least 14% off the cover price! It's quite a bargain! Shipping and handling is just 50¢ per book in the U.S. and 75¢ per book in Canada.* I understand that accepting the 2 free books and gifts places me under no obligation to buy anything. I can always return a shipment and cancel at any time. Even if I never buy another book, the two free books and gifts are mine to keep forever.

240/340 HDN F45N

Name _____ (PLEASE PRINT) _____

Address _____ Apt. # _____

City _____ State/Prov. _____ Zip/Postal Code _____

Signature (if under 18, a parent or guardian must sign)

Mail to the **Harlequin®** Reader Service:
IN U.S.A.: P.O. Box 1867, Buffalo, NY 14240-1867
IN CANADA: P.O. Box 609, Fort Erie, Ontario L2A 5X3

Want to try two free books from another line?
Call 1-800-873-8635 or visit www.ReaderService.com.

* Terms and prices subject to change without notice. Prices do not include applicable taxes. Sales tax applicable in N.Y. Canadian residents will be charged applicable taxes. Offer not valid in Quebec. This offer is limited to one order per household. Not valid for current subscribers to Harlequin Romantic Suspense books. All orders subject to credit approval. Credit or debit balances in a customer's account(s) may be offset by any other outstanding balance owed by or to the customer. Please allow 4 to 6 weeks for delivery. Offer available while quantities last.

Your Privacy—The Harlequin® Reader Service is committed to protecting your privacy. Our Privacy Policy is available online at www.ReaderService.com or upon request from the Harlequin Reader Service.

We make a portion of our mailing list available to reputable third parties that offer products we believe may interest you. If you prefer that we not exchange your name with third parties, or if you wish to clarify or modify your communication preferences, please visit us at www.ReaderService.com/consumerchoice or write to us at Harlequin Reader Service Preference Service, P.O. Box 9062, Buffalo, NY 14269. Include your complete name and address.

HRS13R

To unearth a cache of jewels in Egypt, a sexy archaeologist teams up with a mysterious thief from her past.

Read on for a sneak peek of

THE LONDON DECEPTION

by Addison Fox, available October 2013 from Harlequin® Romantic Suspense.

Rowan wasn't surprised when Finn followed her into the elevator, but she hadn't counted on his rising anger or the delicious sensation of having his large form towering over her in the small space.

"I can explain."

"I sure as hell hope so."

"Rowan. Listen—"

"No." She waved a hand, unwilling to listen to some smooth explanation or some sort of misguided apology. "Whatever words you think you can cajole me with you might as well save them." The elevator doors slid open on her floor and she stomped off.

She was angry.

And irrationally hurt, which was the only possible reason tears pricked the back of her eyes as she struggled with her electronic key.

"Here. Let me." Finn reached over her shoulder and took the slim card from her shaking fingers. The lock switched to green and snicked open.

She crossed into the elegant suite and dropped her purse on the small couch that sat by the far wall, dashing at the moisture in her eyes before he could see the tears.

"Rowan. We need to talk."

"You think?"

"Come on. Please."

She turned at his words. "What can you possibly say that will make any of this okay?"

"I couldn't tell you."

"You chose not to tell me. There's a difference."

He was alive.

The young man who she'd thought died saving her was alive and well and living a life of prosperity and success in London.

"Do you know how I've wondered about you? For twelve long years I've wondered if you died that night. I've lived with the pain of knowing I put you in danger and got you killed."

"I'm fine. I'm here."

"And you never even thought to tell me. To contact me or give me some hint that you were okay. That you'd lived."

"It's not that easy."

"Well, it sure as hell isn't hard."

**Don't miss
THE LONDON DECEPTION
by Addison Fox,
available October 2013 from
Harlequin® Romantic Suspense.**

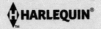

HARLEQUIN®
A *Romance* FOR EVERY MOOD™

Love the Harlequin book you just read?

Your opinion matters.

Review this book on your favorite book site, review site, blog or your own social media properties and share your opinion with other readers!